THE LAST COMMUNIST VIRGIN

THE LAST COMMUNIST VIRGIN

STORIES
BY WANG PING

COFFEE HOUSE PRESS
MINNEAPOLIS
2007

COFFEE HOUSE PRESS books are available to the trade through our primary distributor, Consortium Book Sales & Distribution, 1045 Westgate Drive, Saint Paul, MN 55114. For personal orders, catalogs, or other information, write to: Coffee House Press, 27 North Fourth Street, Suite 400, Minneapolis, MN 55401.

Coffee House Press is a nonprofit literary publishing house. Support from private foundations, corporate giving programs, government programs, and generous individuals helps make the publication of our books possible. We gratefully acknowledge their support in detail in the back of this book.

To you and our many readers around the world, we send our thanks for your continuing support.

LIBRARY OF CONGRESS CIP INFORMATION
Wang, Ping, 1957–
The last communist virgin : stories / by Wang Ping.
p. cm.
ISBN-13: 978-1-56689-195-0 (ALK. PAPER)
ISBN-10: 1-56689-195-7 (alk. paper)
1. China—Fiction. 2. Chinese—United States—Fiction.
3. Chinese Americans—Fiction. I. Title.
PS3573.AA4769L37 2007
813'.54—DC22
2006038522

FIRST EDITION | FIRST PRINTING
9 8 7 6 5 4 3 2 1
PRINTED IN CANADA

〜

I'd like to thank my editors from Coffee House Press and the entire staff for their hard work and dedication. My gratitude also extends to Lewis Warsh, Jesse Katzman, Larry Dunn, and Big K who read the stories and helped me with some detective work in NYC. And finally, my sincere thanks to the generous support from the Bush Foundation, Minnesota State Arts Board, The Loft, Freeman Foundation and Wallace Research Grants from Macalester.

"Where Poppies Blow" and "Crush" first appeared in *Hanging Loose,* "House of Anyting You Wish" first appeared in *The Fourth River.*

CONTENTS

Where the Poppies Blow

I turned the corner, and clouds of pink blossoms under the windows of New Paradise exploded in front of my eyes.

I had seen vegetables flower in my own garden—cucumbers, beans, sesame, mustard greens—shy and fleeting among thick leaves. But these flowers were completely different. They were so unabashedly pink and unbearably beautiful that I couldn't breathe. Pain gripped my gut. I wanted to run away as far as possible from the sweet scent of this "bourgeois poison," but my body refused to obey. I felt pulled closer, to bend over and dip my face in. In a trance, I started to count, one, two, three, ten, twenty, a hundred . . . my head reeled. I turned to my sister for help.

"Wh-what are they?" I stuttered.

She had already run up the steps and was jumping into the arms of the twin daughters of Admiral Yang, head of the East China Sea Navy Base. They spun in a circle, heads thrown back to the sky. I stared, waiting to be summoned up into their two-storied house, which had a garden, a maid, and a guard. Whenever my sister described the twins' bedrooms and the common rooms they shared with their parents, her eyes sparked with envy. My sister and I had nothing in common—our looks, manners, social skills—except for one thing: our wish to have a little bed of our own. Our bathroom window faced this luxury compound, where the top navy officers lived. We used to drag a chair to the bathroom and lean on the windowsill, gazing at the red brick houses hidden among blue pines and bamboo, and guarded by handsome soldiers. The compound had an official name, "Antibourgeois Village." My sister changed it into "New Paradise." She vowed to get herself invited as a guest into one of the ten houses.

Her charm was truly unsurpassable. Not only had she befriended General Yang's notorious twins and visited them daily, but she had also brought kids from our compound, Ocean Village, to their home as her guests. They had all come back looking dazed. Her connection with the "paradise" had established her leadership among the children in Ocean Village. They obeyed her like dogs so that they would be rewarded with an invitation to New Paradise. I had never asked her to take me, knowing I was too awkward and dumb to even hope for such a thing.

But this afternoon, after I finished my chores, my sister told me to comb my hair and change into a clean jacket. As we walked out the door, I asked her where we were going. "Over there," she said coolly, "as I promised. I'm a man of my word, remember?" She had been assigned to write a poem for the birthday of the Communist Party, and had totally forgotten about it until the night before. She came to me for help, promising me all sorts of rewards. I didn't budge until she mentioned New Paradise. I had been dying to see what it was like to have one's own room. So I wrote her a poem, and she came back the next day after school, telling me that it was too good. The teacher said she had copied it from some newspaper or magazine.

"I told the bitch she could punish me any way she wanted if she could prove it. Otherwise she'd better shut her stinky mouth and put some trust in the revolutionary mass," my sister said, eyeing me curiously. "You really did write it yourself, didn't you?"

I gave her a dirty look. She should have know better. Newspapers and magazines were nothing but stale bread for political morons. I read juicy "poisonous weeds," books of Chinese and Western classics. That was the secret we had been sharing. Whenever I got one through my network we'd take turns covering for each other while devouring the poison.

"Ask someone else to do your homework next time," I said.

"Gee, take it easy, sis. But you're right. I watched you working on the poem that night. Oh, you were fast!"

For a second, I wished that her teacher would assign a poem every week.

"Who's that?" One of the Yang twins shouted suddenly, pointing at me.

My sister mumbled something and got a big slap on the shoulder.

"Get out of here!" she cackled. "That dry shrimp can't be your older sister. No way! Not in a million years! You're playing a trick on us again. Not a brilliant one, I have to say, but hell, it's funny."

The Yang girls bent over laughing. My sister gave me a quick glance that made me think she wished I'd vanish completely from the planet.

"You two resemble each other like a cat and mouse," gasped the short twin.

My sister laughed, then stopped when the tall twin pulled a long face. The comment also fit the twins, who had no resemblance to each other: one was tall and bony like a bamboo stick, the other short and round like a barrel. The only trait they shared was their nastiness.

I shuffled my huge feet, wishing I could hide them in my pockets with my hands, wishing I had the guts to spit and leave. I turned my eyes to the pink clouds.

For you I'll stay, I said silently to the flowers. *Once I know who you are and how to get your seeds, I'm out of here.*

I climbed the steps and followed them into the living room. A giant rug covered the wooden floor. The twins walked right on it. My sister wiped her feet at the door and followed them across the room. I tried to avoid stepping on it. Such beautiful art should be hung on the wall, not stamped under dirty shoes. I tiptoed along the wall and sat in the chair facing the bay window. It gave me a full view of the flowers. My sister gestured at me to sit in the far corner, away from the window, but I pretended not to see her. The three of them were immediately engaged in a heated discussion of female body parts. So-and-so had grown breasts with the left one much bigger than the right. So-and-so had her first "bad luck" last month, which smelled like stinky tofu. I watched their tongues darting in and out between their thin lips, wondering if I would be their next target. My eyes moved from their clattering teeth to the sky. The sun was going down, fusing me into the horizon of pink, orange, blue . . .

I'll bring you to my garden, I vowed to the flowers.

Not an easy thing. First of all, every inch of our family garden was used for growing vegetables, which my grandma guarded like a falcon. As food became more scarce and expensive with the escalation of the faction wars among the Red Guards and factory workers, any produce from our garden became indispensable. Once we plowed our front yard into a garden, our neighbors also opened their own vegetable plots. But ours remained the best and most abundant. Some jealous neighbors began stealing squash and beans at night. Whenever my grandma found vegetables missing, she would curse at length in the compound yard, pacing back and forth, her arms akimbo. Vicious words rolled out of her mouth like songs: whoever ate the stolen veggies would have rotten intestines, giant hemorrhoids would pop and their assholes would fly out of their behinds . . . She could go on for hours without repeating herself, and the whole compound would become as quiet as a cemetery. Recently she had started numbering things in the garden with red ink. Every morning, as I took out the chamber pots and watered the veggies with the liquid fertilizer accumulated through the night, my grandma would walk around counting and cursing.

No, she would never allow me to have a chunk of the invaluable land to grow something useless. I knew, from my gardening experience, that the flowers outside the bay window were too beautiful to become food. As my grandma put it: beauty and evil go hand in hand. She was suspicious of any good-looking people, women especially, including my mother, her daughter-in-law. My ugly face didn't fare better either. She believed that my small eyes, big nose, and bad complexion were reflections of my inner evils—pride, stubborn-ness, disobedience. Yes, my grandma would yank my flowers out of the garden, roots and all, before the Red Guards and neighborhood urchins got them. My only solution was to start a secret garden in an abandoned area.

The next problem was where and how to get the plant. Did it grow seeds? If it did, would it sprout and grow into a bush? Or did it grow roots that would sprout like potatoes? Even if it could do all these things, how could I get to them? I doubted if my sister would ever bring me back here. Since I walked in the house, she had been acting as if she didn't know me.

Don't panic, I ordered myself, *just find out the name first.*

I pointed to the window, saying as loudly as I could, "What are they?"

Mouths dropped, opened wide, then shut tight. The twins looked at each other in disbelief. My sister turned her back toward me. I flung my arm at the window again.

"The flowers, what's their name?"

The Bamboo Stick turned to the Barrel. "The flowers, what's their name?" she imitated in falsetto. "Since when did we become gardeners?"

"Ohohoh," the Barrel perked up with excitement as she imi-tated a gardener's male voice, "Beautiful Princess, those are nothing but some humble roses at your service. Beware of the thorns. They may prick your tender, white fingers."

They cackled like hyenas. My sister hid her head between her knees.

"Ah, rose!" I murmured. Immediately all the words of love and romance associated with roses rushed to my mouth. I almost mut-tered the first line of a poem I had found in a coverless book of poetry: *My love is a red, red rose.*

"Where is it from? How does it grow? From seed, seedling, or root?" I asked.

The Bamboo Stick stopped laughing and turned to my sister. "Is she for real or is she just dumb?"

My sister grabbed my arm, her nails digging into the flesh. "Time to go home," she hissed.

"Oh, can't she stay a bit longer? She makes me laugh so," said the Barrel from the floor. "Let her stare all she wants. She can't steal the flowers with her eyes. Poor thing! Probably never saw a rose in her life."

But I did steal them. When I left, I summoned their spirit to come with me. Day and night, I was wrapped in a pink cloud of roses. Wherever I looked, I saw their small faces bursting into the sky. I saw them on my sister's lips, on the crowns of roosters crowing in the morning, on the cheeks of clucking hens after they laid eggs, in babies' cries, in the twilight, in the elaborate patterns of Grandma's embroidery. A day passed without punishment became a rosy day; an evening without nightmares—a rosy night. I also invented terms like rosy news, rosy girls, rosy sky, rosy fruit. Sometimes my silent naming slipped through my mouth and my grandma would give me a funny look.

"What's up with you these days? Walking around like you lost your soul."

I almost said out loud, "That's right, Grandma, I lost it among the roses in New Paradise."

Many evenings, I sneaked into the bathroom, climbed onto a stool to gaze into the darkness through the high window. Gradually my eyes pierced past the football field and made out the shadow of Admiral Yang's house on the hill. Among the chirping of crickets in the knee-high weeds, I heard the sweet whispering of the roses: *Come, sister, come and join us.* My heart twisted with pain. I had realized, after days of speculation, that there was no way I could have a rosebush in our family garden or anywhere else. *Why don't you just let your heart die?* I chanted one of my mother's favorite sayings to myself. I tried, but the rose kept me awake night after night.

One hot afternoon, I was out looking for a missing hen. It was her hatching period. I searched the weeds in the abandoned football field till I came across an opening two feet wide, where an old wall had been toppled by a bomb. Through the barbed wire, I saw the roof of General Yang's house, but the roses were blocked by two other buildings. I gazed until my head started smoking with heat. As I was about to leave, I noticed a red flower in the bomb crater. Its velvet, half-transparent petals opened fully to the scorching sun, exposing its yellow heart and its pregnant belly underneath. I laid down on my stomach to take a closer look. The flower, with its brilliant color and petals like baby palms, bore little resemblance to the rose. They smelled very different, too. But its passionate embrace of the sky touched me.

"A messenger from my roses," I murmured. From the way its base bulged, I knew it was growing seeds inside.

Lying on the edge of the crater, I made a decision—to grow the unknown flower as a substitute. No, as a spirit of the rose.

I stood up, a plan forming in my head. I would put off looking for the hen until I harvested the seeds. She would be my perfect excuse to go out every day to check on my new treasure. The flower needed protection from animal and human feet. I threw some weeds around it to tone down its brilliant color and went home. I told Grandma I couldn't find the hen, and I'd go out again the next day. The hen would be fine, just fine. She was smart, knew how to find a secret place to hatch her chicks, and her natural enemies like eagles and yellow weasels were scarce these days, scared away by bullets and bombs.

For the next week and a half, I walked to the barbed wire to check on my flower after lunch, when everyone in the compound, including those in Paradise, was taking a nap. On the seventeenth day, the bulb popped, exposing tiny black seeds. Lying on my stomach, I dug under the wire until my arms reached all the way to the plant. I wrapped a white handkerchief around the stem, then flicked the bulb with my forefinger gently. Tiny white seeds jumped out of the bulb and landed in the cone. I pulled the handkerchief through the wire, spread it on the ground. The seeds sparkled in the sun, each shaped like a kidney. With the slightest touch, they danced as if possessed by spirits. I tied the handkerchief into many knots. Next spring, I would sow them in the garden and transplant the sprouts to a safer place before my grandma pulled them out as weeds.

I hid the seeds under the bedding, right beneath my pillow, and checked its safety twice a day—after I returned from school, and before I fell asleep. That winter, I'd never slept so well. My dreams were filled with roses and their phantom sisters. The overcrowded bed reeking of urine was no longer a torment, but a paradise of beautiful colors and intoxicating fragrances.

With a stoic patience, I waited for spring. Food had never been as scarce and expensive as in 1969. Lots of people died during the faction battles, and peasants, especially the suburban farmers who grew vegetables for the town, were too frightened to work in the fields. They said it wasn't worth the money to be shot by stray bullets. By the end of March, my anxious grandma wanted to plant the vegetable and corn seeds so we would have something to eat by May. If the frost killed the seedlings, she said, she had enough for a second sowing. I tried all I could to delay her plan. I had to make sure that the frost was completely finished for the year so my seeds would grow safely in obscurity among the vegetable seedlings, with enough sunlight and fertilizer. But would they escape my grandma's falcon eyes?

On April 1, Grandma suffered from a severe asthma attack and had to be taken to the hospital in an ambulance. The next morning, my father returned home, grabbed some clothes, and ran off again. Grandma had pneumonia and would be in the hospital for a long time, three weeks at least. I shut myself in the bathroom so nobody would see my smile. Three weeks! That would give my seeds enough time to sprout and grow strong enough to be transplanted.

I made a clearing as big as I dared in the garden and covered the spot with straw to keep the ground warm at night. Every morning I checked for the first sprouting. It was too early, but I couldn't help myself. After the seventh day, when nothing had happened, I panicked. Were the seeds crushed under my bedding during the long winter? Were they damaged by the powder Grandma had sprinkled all over the bed to kill bugs? Should I have soaked them in warm water for a day or two before I sowed them? I tossed in bed, now much more spacious without Grandma. For the first time, I wished she were around so I could ask her for advice. Then I realized it would only arouse her suspicion. Besides, I doubted she knew anything about flowers, though she seemed to know every edible plant on earth. Anyway, the seeds had been sowed. They were getting the best care I could give. The only thing to do was to wait.

I sneaked out whenever I could to search for an ideal spot to transplant my phantom rose. They mustn't be too far away for me to visit them every day. And they must be invisible to any human eye except mine. People had developed an instinct to pull out any flowers in the wild, just like their instinct to see all living creatures as meat. My sister roasted practically everything with legs or wings that she could catch: crickets, grasshoppers, cicadas, sparrows . . . She grilled them until their skin turned dark brown, snatched off the heads, then popped them into her mouth. The best delicacy on earth, she announced to a gaping crowd, chewing with exaggerated noises. And how she was worshipped for her hunting skill! Sometimes, when she felt generous, she would divide her catch and stuff it into my mouth, its intestines dangling from the broken end. I would run to the bathroom to vomit, while she laughed like an Amazon warrior.

So I searched far and near around Ocean Village. Nothing was suitable. All the good spots had been turned into vegetable gardens guarded with barbed wire or bamboo fences. Beyond the fences was an old paper mill on the riverbank. The murky water spewed a foul smell from the effluence that was dumped directly into the river. On the west side of Ocean Village, a highway linked New Paradise to the headquarters of the East China Sea Navy Base. On the east was the middle school, which had been occupied alternately as the headquarters of different factions of the Red Guards. Many battles had taken place there. It was not a place for anything green and alive.

I felt desperate.

One morning, I was told to do our annual spring cleaning. I started with the windows in my parents' room, and worked all the way to the bathroom. From the windowsill, I could see New Paradise. Had the rosebush in front of Admiral Yang's house begun to bud? My eyes swept across the abandoned soccer field and stopped at a mud pit as big as Grandma's wooden bathtub, about two hundred meters away. The pit was apparently created by a bomb. When the faction wars had started, the field, with its trees and weeds, was the attacking party's favorite route to get close to the opposition at the middle-school headquarters. I had awakened many times at dawn hearing gunshots and grenade explosions back there, mixed with shrieking and howling for help that gradually faded into moans for mothers and help from heaven. The next day, after the sun rose high in the sky, we would peek through the windows and find everything quiet and undisturbed. If not for the traces of bullets on the brick walls and wooden frames, one could easily think that the terrible noises had just been nightmares. Twice, my sister led a small group of the most daring kids into the field, bringing back bullet shells, blood-stained shoes, and unexploded grenades that they threw back into the ditch after showing them off. The shells became hot trading materials. The second trip lasted a short time. Through the window, I watched them suddenly crawl back as fast as they could as if they were being chased by a ghost. My sister had often laughed at the way those chickenhearted kids fled—*pi gun niao liu*— ran with rolling farts and wet pants. This time, she herself was doing the same. I had never seen her shake, never seen her lose the ability to talk. Later, she revealed to me that they had found a hand in a pit, with worms crawling in and out between the rotten fingers.

"The worst part was the smell," she said. "I almost fainted on the spot, I swear."

I smiled as I recalled how cute she looked when she wrinkled her nose and rolled her eyes, swearing like an urchin. She could get away with anything with a face like that. I was standing on the ridge of the building. I inched forward, my hands and stomach pressing against the wall like a lizard. My sister and her followers often walked to the end of the ridge like this and jumped over the fence into the soccer field. This was the only way to get to the pit. It might be an ideal place for my flower.

The field had been sealed off since a bomb had toppled part of the wall. Realizing that the battlefield was too close to New Paradise, the navy headquarters made a deal with the leaders from both factions. Trees were sawed off and the field was fenced with barbed wire. No one was allowed to enter the place except for a tractor to cut the weeds in the summer. An eerie silence had hovered over the field and the middle school ever since.

I tried not to look down from the wall. Below me was a deep ditch that ran around our building and the field, which carried away rain and summer floods. It was also a natural fence between Ocean Village and New Paradise. When I reached the end of the ridge, I noticed that the ditch became narrow, and the ground raised higher. It made jumping over the wire possible, though one still needed guts and great athletic skill. I wasn't as daring as my sister, but I was the high-jump and long-jump champion of my school. I turned around, bent my knees, and leapt. The moment my feet touched the ground, my heart surged with exhilaration. Was this why my sister loved her reckless adventures and why kids worshipped her?

I ran toward the pit as fast as I could and jumped in. It reached to my chest, and was actually bigger than Grandma's bathtub. I sat down and looked up. Ocean Village was as quiet as a gigantic grave, unusual for a Sunday morning. Perhaps everyone was busy preparing lunch? Then it dawned on me that I was looking at the back of the building with the high bathroom windows that kids needed a chair to reach. I had found a safe spot for my flower. I looked up at the sky. It was clear of clouds and flying creatures. The last bird I saw was being roasted over a bonfire, its body plastered with yellow mud mixed with salt. "It'll taste like a heavenly peach from the Western Goddess's garden," my sister promised her followers, instructing them to turn the bird this and that way for a thorough roasting. She had stolen that phrase from the book I lent her—*Journey to the West*.

I was patient: things would come back—the grass, the flowers, the birds, just as my seeds would push through the soil and their cloudy blossoms would fill up the bottom of this pit. I looked down, measuring its depth and width. There was no tree around. The summer sun would shine directly into the pit for at least six hours on sunny days. My flower would need this. I had seen how she guzzled up the light.

Now all I had to do was wait. On the eleventh day, when I felt that spring had definitely arrived and frost would not return till next year, I peeled off the straw. As I lifted the last bundle, I noticed a small patch of green as big as a coin. My heart raced as I knelt down toward the sprouts. How tiny they were, and how fragile, leaning against each other for support! I had mixed the seeds with very fine soil, hoping to spread them evenly. But they still came out in a crowd. I stroked them with my fingertips, pressed my cheek against the seedlings. I stayed in the garden until I heard mother calling me to make breakfast. I was in a delicious daze that day.

Within a week, the seedling bed was covered by patches of velvet green. The sprouts lingered in their infant stage for a few days, then suddenly grew like crazy, leaves shooting out of the stems like baby hands. Soon, the strong ones towered over the rest. I thinned the weak plants as much as my heart could bear. I had no choice. Only the strongest could survive the poor soil and harsh environment of their future home. I knew I must transplant them as soon as possible. That morning, during breakfast, I asked if Grandma had fully recovered and when she was coming home. My father gave me a tearful look, touched at what a filial girl I had finally become. He was planning to go to the hospital that afternoon to consult the doctor. Hopefully she would be released in a day or two. My mother glared at me. She had enjoyed having my father's full attention. The last thing she wanted was her mother-in-law returning with revitalized energy to boss her around. She didn't know that I, too, wanted

Grandma to be away as long as possible, even though her absence had doubled my chores.

I felt ill at ease at school that morning. A voice kept telling me that I should do something about the seedlings immediately. At lunchtime, I hurried to the garden. Everything was intact. The plants seemed to have grown taller during my four-hour absence. I remembered father's assurance that it would be another day or two before he would bring Grandma home. Tomorrow at noon, I promised myself and the plants. One more day would give them a better chance at survival.

In the afternoon, however, I couldn't do any work, my heart seized by an unspeakable fear. When school was finally over, I ran home. As soon as I unlocked the fence gate, I knew my grandma had been back. The garden had been tidied and weeded thoroughly. Uprooted weeds were piled neatly in the corner to decompose. Drops of water sparkled on the leaves. I tiptoed to the farthest end of the garden where I had sowed my seeds. My heart froze inside my chest. The small seedling bed had disappeared. Some mustard greens stood limp in the newly plowed spot where my velvet green plants had stood three hours before. For a second, I thought I must have walked into the wrong garden. I looked around, recognizing the old seedlings of mustard greens, cucumber, string bean, cauliflower, eggplant. It was my family garden all right. But where were my flowers? I threw myself on the ground, my face buried in the soil. I cried and sobbed, cursing my grandma, cursing myself.

Finally I lifted my face from the muddy puddle. Under a sagging vegetable, a tip of a green leaf stuck out beneath a lump of soil like a hand reaching for help. I turned over the lump. There they were, the seedlings of my phantom rose, crushed, yet still alive. It was shocking to see the roots, so thick and white. Could they have grown out of seeds tinier than sand? I turned every lump nearby, and rescued about thirteen seedlings, all damaged to different degrees. I hid them all under the wide leaf of a cauliflower. They should be safe till the next morning. Grandma never came out at night. She couldn't see a thing in the dark. Tomorrow morning, before the sun rose, I would move the plants to the soccer field.

I cleaned my mud-caked face with my sleeves and walked home. Grandma sat in a bamboo chair at the door. We stared at each other, eyes heavy with each other's secret. She finally spoke, a smirk on her face. "I see you've made some changes to the garden."

I passed without a word. "Just wait and see, just wait and see," I cried out to her in silence. I heard my father's angry voice, "What's up with that girl? This morning she couldn't wait to have her grandma back. Now she doesn't say a word, not even a fart!"

Grandma answered in a cool voice. "Son, your daughter is no longer a small girl."

I stayed awake that night, listening to Grandma's familiar snore, her stinking feet tucked right next to my shoulder. Did she know the secret plants were flowers? Probably. Otherwise she would not have destroyed them so mercilessly. What worried me most was her silence. Often it meant she had more schemes up her sleeves. I had to do something.

I tiptoed into the bathroom and bolted the door. It was just past midnight. No one would wake up to use the bathroom at this hour. I had sneaked the seedlings into the apartment before I went to bed and hid them on the bathroom windowsill so that I could transplant them the first thing in the morning. The idea came to me when I was locking up the chicken coop. What a smart move! I'd surely have awakened my father on my way out to the garden. He was an alert sleeper.

As I moved forward along the wall, carrying a spade and a bottle of water in my shoulder bag and a basket with the lumps of seedlings, I felt I had been transformed into a lizard by the full moon. If there had been a mosquito or a fly in front of me, I might have darted my tongue and rolled it into my mouth with delight. It suddenly occurred to me that I was becoming more daring than my sister. No one from the village would believe that an awkward, shy girl like me would climb a wall like this.

In the dead silence, I dug up the bottom of the pit as much as I could with my spade, planted the seedlings, and watered them. The thirteen plants I had rescued from my grandma's malice covered only one-fifth of the pit. They seemed fragile in the pale moonlight, drooping leaves and broken skin along the stems. I poked at the thin soil under my feet. Grandma would call it raw earth, because it had not been plowed or touched by human hands, no vegetable or weeds had grown, died, then decomposed there. Would they survive? I climbed out of the pit. I should bring in the rich, dark earth from the garden, what Grandma called *shu tu*—cooked soil—as soon as possible.

I managed to sneak into the field every day, mostly around midnight, sometimes before dawn. The transplant seemed to have stunned the seedlings. Eleven of them quickly turned yellow and faded away. The last two remained in their withered state for several days, then suddenly new leaves shot out from the top, and their stems grew thicker, taller, covered by hairy needles that reminded me of the thorns of the rose. Although I felt exhausted from lack of sleep, my eyes sparkled and my cheeks glowed with a rosy hue like my sister's. I did my daily chores and school work quickly so that I could go to bed at eight, an hour earlier than usual. No one noticed the change except Grandma, though she said nothing about it. Her scrutinizing eyes followed me like searchlights.

One morning, when I returned from my routine trip and unbolted the bathroom door, Grandma was waiting right outside, her eyes shiny with excitement at catching me red-handed. I froze at the door. She pushed me aside, entered the bathroom to search for evidence of my evil activities.

"What have you been doing behind this locked door?" she whispered.

"Nothing, just trying to shit." Not a bad excuse. I was known for my chronic constipation.

"For an hour? How come you didn't answer the door when I knocked?"

"I did. Couldn't you hear?" I replied in defiance, suddenly realizing that I had nothing to fear, since I had no evidence in my hands. The spade and water bottle were outside on the windowsill. She couldn't see them unless she stood on a chair. But with her stumpy feet, she would need help. If she was stupid enough to ask me for help, I would make sure that she had an accident. A slip or a wobble of the chair would do.

For two days I didn't visit my plants. My heart ached with longing and anxiety. Did they need water? Did the buds grow bigger? Fortunately, the summer started; so did the three-hour nap. Grandma had a weakness for afternoon naps. She slept soundly for two straight hours. Nothing could wake her up, not even thunder. I began to visit the field at noon, when all of Ocean Village was in a deep slumber.

Not quite everyone. In the daylight, I could see things in our thirty-four apartments through the bathroom windows, since every door, from the bathroom to the master bedroom, was wide open for air circulation and view. The apartments in our compound were designed for simplicity and openness: the front door opened into the largest room, which was used as the living room and master bedroom, then came the middle room for the kids and dining area, then the back room for the kitchen and toilet—a straight line like a railroad. My grandma loved it. When the doors were open, she could see everything going on in the apartment with one glance. But it made it impossible for us to sneak out of the house, since we had to go through our parents' bedroom. My sister often jumped from the window in our room. It was my luck that she had never thought of jumping from the bathroom window.

Soon I learned who kept the neatest house, who snored the loudest, and who had the ugliest expression in their sleep. One day, I passed by my friend Shi Hua's unit. The first thing I noticed was the closed bathroom door. I looked down and almost fell off the wall. Hua's father, a round-faced, good-natured officer with a pot-belly who every kid in the compound called Fat Uncle Shi, was sitting naked on a chair, facing his tiny wife. She was squatting over the toilet hole, her skinny behind sticking out from her white shirt. Fat Uncle Shi was playing with something brown and rubbery between his legs. It looked pathetically tiny under his towering stomach. What was he doing? Every officer was supposed to work in the headquarters or on a ship, like my father, although I knew they also took their naps over their desks. Hua had told me her father was on sick leave for his liver disease. Well, if he were really sick, why was he watching his wife going to bathroom instead of resting in bed? Slowly, he reached out to take Mrs. Shi's bony hand and placed it around that wretched thing of his. Her body became tense for a few minutes, then urine spurted out—quite a noisy splash for such a little woman. To my astonishment, what seemed so limp and small a minute before suddenly grew like a puffing fish, and soon Mrs. Shi's hand could no longer grasp it. He pulled her up to his lap. She closed her arms around his neck, her body sprawling like a sparrow with wings wide open upon his round stomach. They rocked and moaned. The chair underneath squeaked painfully under their weight. Suddenly she arched backwards, eyes and mouth wide open, her face looking painful and funny at the same time. I dashed away, baffled by what I'd just seen, wondering how I could face my friend and her good-natured father again.

A week later, my embarrassment was thoroughly counteracted by another scene I saw through the window of Unit 13, the neatest, most decorative apartment in the whole compound. Mr. Chief, head of the operation department, lived there with his Beijing opera actress wife and their two daughters. He had recently been promoted to the most important department of the navy base, after a long, cruel battle with his opponent Mr. Fu, who lived across from his unit. Mr. Fu ended the war by falling under his desk with a stroke and died in the hospital after three week's coma, leaving behind a half-deranged wife and a seven-year-old boy. For a whole month adults talked about nothing else at the table but this tragedy. My mother said she had known that Mr. Fu would end up dead and

Mr. Chief would win without lifting a finger. It was all written on their faces. It was true that Mr. Chief was handsome and elegant, his gray uniform pressed neatly against his thin, straight, fair-skinned body like a general's uniform, whereas Mr. Fu rushed in and out of the compound with bloodshot eyes, chapped lips, and sunburnt cheeks. He looked more like a fisherman than a navy officer. In a jealous tone, my mother added that as soon as there was a vacancy in Antibourgeois Village, Mr. Chief and his family would move into it. Since his promotion, he had a telephone installed in his apartment, a young soldier bringing food supplies and other rare things daily to their home, and a jeep taking him between the compound and the base. How lucky for that bitchy wife of his! What had she done in her previous life to deserve such a good life?

Now Mr. Chief's bitchy wife sat on a red velvet chair in the master bedroom, her legs wide open. Her skin looked creamy white through the lace of her black bra and underwear. I had never seen anything like that, so slim and tight against the skin, yet so pretty. Even my mother, who considered herself the best dressed in the compound, had nothing like this. Her floral cotton underwear and bras, the best brand from Shanghai, looked coarse and shapeless in comparison to Mrs. Chief's three-piece: the top just big enough to cup her breasts, supported by two straps, the middle a petite triangle barely covering her private parts, and the long lace that came up to her thighs like black snakes, suspended by two straps that hooked to her waist. I stared, wishing I could brag to my sister about what I had seen. I bet her eyes would have popped wide open.

Mrs. Chief sat facing the bathroom window, but I wasn't worried at all. She was very nearsighted, and too vain to wear glasses. Mr. Chief came to the kitchen sink and filled up a wooden basin painted with mandarin ducks. Ice cubes floated on the surface. Where did he get those treasures in the hot weather? Only people who lived in New Paradise had refrigerators. His bent head looked too heavy for his thin neck, and his pale limbs outside his tank and shorts looked too skinny. Why did Mother keep praising him as the most handsome man, and call my broad-shouldered father a country bumpkin?

Mr. Chief took the ice water to the master bedroom and placed it between his wife's legs. One by one he unhooked her lace stockings, peeled them off her slender white legs. He lifted her feet gently, put them in the basin, then massaged them from heel to toe. She moaned with her eyes closed. If my mother had witnessed this scene, she would have exploded with sour juice. Even I felt something as I watched Mr. Chief, the most promising officer in the compound, rub his wife's pink sole with such tenderness. Suddenly she kicked the basin aside, grabbed her husband by the hair and pulled him up to her bosom, rubbing his face between her full breasts while clasping his limp body with her thighs. Mr. Chief trembled like an injured boy. He knelt between his wife's legs, his feet kicking feebly against the floor. Mrs. Chief reached her hand down and grabbed his crotch.

"You good-for-nothing!" she shouted in her falsetto, pushing him on the floor, tears flooding down her white cheeks. "Am I supposed to live like a widow for the rest of my life?"

Mr. Chief, the young rising star of the East China Sea Fleet, rose slowly from the floor, embraced his wife's feet to his chest, then, to my greatest astonishment, sucked her toes one by one, starting from the pinkie toe. I stepped backwards, almost fell off the wall, but I grabbed the open window. The noise startled Mr. Chief. He quickly turned around, but I darted away as fast as I could.

Such a strange world, I said to myself, sitting face-to-face with my flowers at the bottom of the pit. The buds had already bulged to the size of lima beans, but even they couldn't bring me peace and concentration. My brain bubbled like half-cooked rice with a burnt bottom. Why did adults look and act one way in the public, another way behind doors? Were my parents like that, too? The thought sent a chill down my spine. I stood up and ran back to the building.

I tried to be cool, tried not to look into any more windows. But the desire to tell someone what I saw was driving me crazy. My flowers kept me concentrated and sane, kept my mouth sealed.

They bloomed on July fourteenth. I had a premonition when I woke up. As soon as Grandma's head touched her pillow, I grabbed a bottle, rushed into the bathroom, bolted the door, and climbed out. I traveled fast, my skill of walking on the wall ridge having much improved over the months. I didn't stop at any window, anxious to get to the pit. I passed Unit 13 quickly, would have passed Unit 14 the same way if I hadn't been stopped by a boy's voice, "Hey, you!"

My first instinct was to hide. But my curiosity took over. It was only little boy's whisper. I looked. It took me a few seconds to see. Honeydew, the deceased Mr. Fu's son, squatted over the toilet with a book open in his hand. He wasn't really going to the bathroom; he had his pants on. He was there just to read. My heart opened to him immediately. We shared the same secret: reading banned books in the toilet. From the illustration, I recognized *I Want to Read,* a favorite book of mine long ago. Honeydew got this nickname from my sister because of his perfectly round head, unusually large for his seven-year-old underdeveloped body. He rolled his round eyes, cupped his mouth with his free hand, and whispered,

"Come in and play with me."

I wished I could, but I had my flowers, and I was scared of his mom. "Sorry. Got to go."

"Where are you going?"

"Over there." I pointed to the distance, where New Paradise stood in the thick shade of trees.

"Take me, please." He threw down his book, hands together to his chest.

I shook my head. "I'll bring you a present, I promise." Before he said another word, I disappeared from the window. My heart trembled with some pain, but I forced myself not to look back. There was no way I could take him along. No way!

They were waiting for me in the pit, two stars with fully opened petals, one scarlet red, the other deep pink, the same color as the roses I had seen in New Paradise. "Phantom sisters of the rose, sun and moon," I murmured, rubbing my nose gently against the velvet petals. The flower hearts quivered with golden pollen, as if my words brought them great pleasure. Their fragrance was thick and dark, and made me sleepy. I laid down in the pit, my face in the shadow of the twin stars. New Paradise shined and shivered in rainbow colors on top of the hill, bathing Ocean Village in a brilliant light. Anything seemed possible, even hope, even happiness. I closed my eyes to the cloudless sky, letting the sunlight seep through my trembling eyelids.

Finally I got up. Time to go. I pinched a petal from the red flower and sealed it in the bottle. My present for Honeydew. A promise was a promise, though tearing the petal was like tearing my heart. Boys were not supposed to like flowers, but I knew Honeydew would. I didn't know him well. His mother rarely let him out of the apartment except for school. My brother once brought him home after school. They were in the same second-grade class. I helped them fold cranes and monkeys on a boat. When his mother came to fetch him, he lingered, taking time to gather his books, putting on his shoes. He seemed to have something to tell me. I slipped a crane in his hand before he was dragged out of the door.

As I got close to Unit 14, it occurred to me that he might be gone. Should I call out to him? What if his mother came? She was paranoid about everything, her doors always tightly locked, curtains drawn. Then I realized she might not be home. Didn't Honeydew invite me in? And the window was open, so was the front door. Was she sick, hospitalized? Who was looking after the boy?

I peeked into the window with caution, just in case. For an instant, I thought I had passed Unit 14 and stopped at the window of Unit 13 because I saw Mr. Chief's ghostly pale face. He was kneeling on the floor, sweat pouring down his squeezed-shut eyes. He was jerking back and forth in a violent motion, as if riding a horse. I'd never seen anyone going to the bathroom like this. And why was he doing it in Honeydew's place? I wanted to take a good look when Mr. Chief opened his eyes suddenly, all white, staring at me like two daggers. I scurried away as fast as my shaking legs allowed.

When I got home and squeezed into bed, steaming with sweat and body heat, I was trembling as if I had just been pulled out of an ice hole. My eyes were wide open. I was afraid if I closed them, Mr. Chief would crawl into my dream with his crazy white eyes. I didn't know what had happened, but what I saw couldn't be good.

I woke up hearing my sister scream: "Everybody get up. Honeydew is dead, hung in the bathroom. Hurry up! Go look!"

Grandma gasped as she trotted out on her tiny feet. My sister followed, but I grabbed her arms. "Stay home," I pleaded.

"What's wrong? Are you afraid of a dead body? Don't be such a chicken!"

She pulled away and ran after Grandma. I followed them. I was afraid of what I was going to see, but I was more terrified of being alone.

A big crowd had gathered in the yard. Everyone stared at the center. My sister pushed with shouts and elbows. As the adults moved their legs to let her in, I saw a tiny body on the ground, one leg curled up behind his ass, the other stretching out shoeless, a snaky rope wrapped around his neck, its tail extending all the way to my grandma's bound feet. I had a glimpse of his lips, swollen, blue like ink.

His mother was howling over his body, her arms tightly gripped by two officers.

"My son, my baby son, who killed you? Tell your mom who killed you. I'll tear out his heart and eat his liver."

One of the officers said something. She thrashed in their grasp, screaming, "No, my son did not hang himself! He was murdered. Murdered!"

An ambulance arrived. Two soldiers jumped out with a stretcher. Mrs. Fu screamed and writhed to free herself, to stop the soldiers from taking away her son. But she was pinned to the ground, face in the mud. As soon as the ambulance left, the soldiers let her go. She sprang up and threw herself upon the door of Unit 13.

"Come out, you snake, you murderer. I know you're there. You cut the weeds, then dug up the roots, right? Here's one more left. Come out, kill me so you can wipe out the whole lot."

The crowd watched in silence. No one dared make a comment. The mad woman was fighting against the most powerful man in the navy base, alone. But what did she have to lose after the death of her husband and son? Fate was a strange thing. If her husband hadn't died so suddenly, if he had won the battle, she would have been the most powerful woman in the district. Instead, she was throwing herself on her enemy's door begging for death.

I took a step forward. I wanted to tell her what I had seen. But she seemed to have gone completely crazy. Should I tell the officer who was ordering the soldiers to drag her away? Should I tell the crowd what I had seen? Should I tell my parents? Would anyone believe me? I looked up at the front window of Unit 13. A pair of eyes stared straight at me through the glass. All black, no white, two holes in a bone-white scalp.

I turned to run, and fell to the ground.

I didn't get up for weeks. When I opened my eyes, I was in bed surrounded by my family. Everyone seemed excited to see me. Everyone started talking at the same time. Grandma said I owed my life to her. "You burned like an oven. If I hadn't cooled you with cold wet towels day and night, you'd have been dead, girl." Mother mentioned how she had killed two chickens to make broth and spoon-fed me three times a day. Sister bragged that she had kept me alive by reading "poisonous weeds."

"See the blisters?" She pointed to her lips. "All from reading."

I closed my eyes and returned to the dreams: bitter waves tossing me up and down, giant sand dunes that buried me alive, ropes and belts from ceilings chasing after my neck, and the white eyes that followed me wherever I ran . . .

My last dream was filled with thunderstorms and hurricanes. Rain poured down amid whirling winds, sweeping everything away. I woke up in a puddle, my shirt, shorts, the blanket and bedding all soaked. I thought I had wet the bed, then realized it was just my own sweat. I was the only one lying in bed, and the sunlight was shining into my eyes through the window. I jumped in panic, but fell back. I was late for the morning chores, for the first time in my life. How come nobody woke me up?

My family was sitting around the table sipping porridge. A bowl was being cooled in my place. On top of the white gruel was an egg fried perfectly golden and splashed with a touch of soy sauce. Who made breakfast this morning?

Grandma looked up from her bowl and said, "Feeling better? Sit down and eat the egg. It'll be a nice day today."

My mother said, "Go comb your hair first."

My hair was matted as if someone had poured glue all over my head. Chunks of hair fell out as I brushed. My clothes hung loose over my body. I had shrunk during my long sleep.

I sat down, divided the egg into five pieces and gave each to Father, Mother, Grandma, Sister, and Brother.

"Good girl," my parents said.

"Eat it yourself. You need it," said Grandma, returning the egg to my bowl.

My sister smacked her oily lips and told me that the two factions had a bloody battle again last night, both sides armed with machine guns, grenades, and cannons. Many people had died. Even the houses in New Paradise got some windows shattered. But there'd be tons of shells out in the soccer field.

"Want to collect some later?" she whispered in my ear.

At noon I entered the bathroom while my family laid down for a nap. I looked around. No rope hanging from the ceiling like a snake. I climbed to the window and stuck out my head. The field was toasting in the midsummer sun. Not a trace of storm or battle except for the craters left by grenades.

I crawled through the window and stood on the ridge against the wall. The mere thought that I had to pass Unit 13 and 14 made me dizzy again, but I had to know what happened to my phantom roses. I walked the ridge with my back against the wall. A much harder job, but at least I didn't have to look into any units.

Both flowers were gone. Leaves had withered on the stems and petals were scattered around the roots. Two bulb-shaped heads remained on the top, bulging, pregnant with seeds inside. They reminded me of Honeydew. One of the capsules had apparently been scraped by a stray bullet. White liquid had filled the scar and hung like a dried teardrop. The wind started blowing. The bulbs trembled as if they were weeping, as if the whole earth were weeping. Suddenly, my eyes flooded. I looked up at the sky, the same void, the same silence. Nothing seemed to have changed, yet I was no longer the same.

I snipped the heads and put them in the bottle, together with the withered petal I had planned to give Honeydew. I wasn't sure why I was doing this. But I knew I would never return to the pit again.

I walked back facing the wall. The windows of Units 13 and 14 were closed. Mrs. Fu had been permanently placed in the psychiatric wing of the navy hospital—a place that no one came out of alive. My sister had imparted this information casually as if it were some old news. It was old news compared to the bomb she threw at us right after: Mr. Chief had moved to New Paradise with his family. Mother's face pinched with bitterness. She opened her mouth and was about to give her sermon on Chief's talent and his wife's undeserved luck when Grandma cut in, pointing her chopstick at her son.

"I'd rather die than enter that kind of paradise."

As I approached Unit 14, the window suddenly opened with a bang. I jumped, but looked in anyway. Nothing had been removed. The book *I Want to Read* remained open on the shelf, still at the same page Honeydew had been reading so long ago. The curtain stirred slightly as if a little hand were trying to lift it. My heart tightened.

"Who is it?" I shouted.

Honeydew's round face flashed by and vanished into the curtain folds. "Ah, it's you," I murmured, placing the bottle gently on the windowsill. "Here's your present."

Five minutes later, I squeezed into the bed with my family and fell into a deep sleep.

By the end of the summer, blossoms popped up and covered the entire soccer field. They were the same kind of flower I had planted in the bomb crater, only much more startlingly red and beautiful, as if they had absorbed all the spirits in the blood-soaked battleground and were releasing them into the air. It happened quickly. One night, the field had nothing but weeds, and the next morning, a scarlet ocean with a scent so heavy it lulled people from Ocean Village and New Paradise into odd behaviors. My sister took a group of kids into the maze to search for shells and didn't return after dinner. Father went to the fields and found them sleeping among the flowers. When night fell, noises that resembled cats in heat came from the field, and shadows frolicked like dancing ghosts. Then one day, my sister announced that the twins and other girls from New Paradise were caught in the field doing bad things with boys. Among them were Mrs. Chief and her husband's bodyguard.

Mr. Chief ordered a dozen combines and plowed the flowers under. That summer I turned thirteen.

CRUSH

What caused the ache was never clear, but it all started with "The Little Mermaid," the story I told to my sister and our upstairs neighbors on the night of the last and bloodiest faction war on the island.

It wasn't supposed to happen like that. I mean the war that killed hundreds of young people during the fourth year of the Cultural Revolution. After countless bloody battles, the two largest factions—the workers and the Red Guards—had finally agreed to negotiate steps toward fusing into a revolutionary committee. During those fifteen months, markets and shops reopened one after another, workers returned to factories and students to school for half days. Things seemed to be slowly getting back to normal.

But one morning, we woke up once again to a red sea of slogans drowning the concrete buildings of the middle school that had been used for headquarters by both factions since the Cultural Revolution began. One banner looked exceptionally sinister and frightening. FIGHT FOR OUR GREAT LEADER CHAIRMAN MAO TO OUR LAST DROP OF FRESH BLOOD! The big dark red characters had congealed and wrinkled the gigantic scarlet fabric. Grandma took a look at it and said it was written with human blood. She rushed us back to the apartment and ordered us to cover windows with paper strips, a measure proven to be effective to prevent glass from shattering. Everyone else in the navy compound followed suit. Before we finished, however, the war came.

That night, I was awakened by explosions. At first I thought Chairman Mao had issued another great teaching and the whole country was celebrating with firecrackers and parades. I was looking for my clothes in the dark when Father rushed in and pulled us off the bed. "Stay low and keep quiet," he whispered as he dismantled our bed and laid the mattress on the floor. Bullets flew in all directions. Windows shattered upstairs. We dropped down on our stomachs. Someone banged on the door.

"Stay where you are," Father said and crawled out. Soon he returned with two people and sat them down against the wall. He unrolled a bamboo mat on the cement floor.

"Just make do for tonight. Tomorrow I'll get something more comfortable," he said and dashed out again.

I recognized our upstairs neighbors, Dong Zhuo and her big brother Dong Sheng. I saw her every day, but the older brother was a stranger. He worked in a Shanghai radio factory and came to visit his parents once a year. My sister poked at me as she gasped at my ear, "Look, it's Dong Sheng. Isn't he handsome like a prince!"

In the dim moonlight, I stared openly at the sixteen-year-old young man, who was said to be the best-looking person in our compound. I couldn't see much except for his gleaming pale cheekbones and his long neck. Unlike his siblings who stretched out on the mattress, he sat and pressed his back against the wall, his hands jerking with each explosion.

"Pretty bad out there, eh?" my sister said as loud as she dared, her voice trembling with excitement. To have the "prince" sleep in the same room with her! It was better than having a pancake fall from the sky straight into her lap.

"Terrible. Our windows are all shattered. My brother almost got hit by a bullet, just an inch from his ear. I can show you the hole in the wall." Dong Zhuo answered for her brother. The explosions seemed to have turned Dong Sheng deaf.

"Wow, that's really scary!" my sister said. I gave her a nudge. Almost every day for the past few years bullets had been flying and grenades exploding around us. Our shattered windows were pieced together with layers of paper strips, our walls and doors covered with holes. Even the Dong siblings felt the exaggerated sympathy in her voice. For a while no one spoke. My sister grew restless, desperate to make an impression on the prince. If she missed this chance, she might never get another. The Dong family kept to themselves, especially when Dong Sheng came home for vacation. My sister had tried all kinds of tricks to break through, but had only managed to befriend the mother and sister.

"His visit is too short," she would whine each time she failed. "If he could just stay another week, it'd be a totally different story."

The gunshots stopped. My sister broke the eerie silence. "Let's sing a song." She had a sweet voice, and knew many forbidden songs as well as hundreds of revolutionary ones. I knew she was also dying to show off her sparkling eyes and rosy cheeks, to perform her five consecutive backwards somersaults, and stand on her hands for fifteen minutes.

"Don't be ridiculous," Grandma intervened. "If you want to die, go ahead. But I still want to live a few more years."

"We have to do something. I can't sleep. I can't stand this total darkness," she whined. "Grandma, tell us some stories."

"Nah, you've heard them a hundred times. They're silly, those stories about stupid sons-in-law and horny old men. Not suitable for our guests."

Even my grandma seemed to be in awe of Dong Sheng. She had never felt ashamed of telling her dirty old men stories.

My sister nudged close to me. "How about you, sis? Tell us a story, PLEASE!"

I was speechless. She had never called me sister. And she was giving me the chance to show my skill, the only thing I could do well. My sister could chat and sing for hours with utter grace, yet as soon as she began a story, she stuttered. I touched her arm to acknowledge my gratitude, and started searching madly in my brain for something to impress our guests.

"What about *The Merry Widow's Fan?*" she said. "The crazy love triangle. When the mistress couldn't get her lover to divorce his wife, she cut off the wife's private part and mailed it to the husband, and the enraged man retaliated by cutting off his mistress's nose. Isn't that wild?"

I sweated. My stupid sister was giving away our top secret. Before I shushed her, she babbled on. "Or the stories from the Bible you found in the garbage. That virgin who gave birth to Jesus, who can walk on the surface of the water and raise the dead."

"Isn't that all superstition and poison? I thought we'd burnt that up long ago," Dong Sheng said sternly.

The bullets and cannons started exploding again outside. People were charging across the football field in the back of our building toward the middle school headquarters. Something hot rose from my stomach, the same burning sensation that went down my chest when I drank boiling water or swallowed a piece of scorching bean curd. I sat up.

"I have a story, 'The Little Mermaid.' It's about a beautiful human fish who gives up all she has in order to win love from a prince."

Without waiting for approval, I started describing the beautiful sea palace, the six princesses loved dearly by their father and grandma, their impatient wait to reach fifteen when they could swim to the surface of the water to look at the other world—the world of humans who walk on their legs. I described in great detail the exquisite beauty of the youngest mermaid, her rescue of her beloved prince, and how she traded her voice for a pair of legs. A few hundred yards away, bullets whistled like fireworks, and people screamed in agony as grenades exploded. But none of us seemed to notice it. Even Dong Sheng stopped jerking at the sounds of explosions.

I'd always been a good storyteller. But that night the words rolled out of my mouth effortlessly. My feet felt the sharp pain of walking on knives with each step just as the Little Mermaid did, and my heart contracted with anguish as she danced with her bleeding feet at the wedding of the prince and the royal maiden, knowing that when the dawn broke, she would turn into a speck of foam on the ocean waves. The battle in our backyard seemed to have faded into the distance; my voice bounced from one face to another. Now the Little Mermaid sat alone on the deck, watching the skyline in the east turn pink. Her five sisters emerged from the water, their hair all gone, traded for the knife with which the Little Mermaid could save herself by killing the prince. Behind them was their grandma, her hair gray from sorrow. I paused to create suspense, to stop my voice from choking, when my grandma broke the silence.

"I say she's a silly girl, that Little Mermaid. Why the hell did she want to leave her father's palace to become some dumb man's slave? Let's not mention the way she had her body split in half, her tongue cut out, her feet bleeding. Worse than footbinding. I'm not even going to say how she neglected her duty to her family, the sorrow she caused."

"It's called *love,* Grandma!" My sister stared at her in contempt.

"Pooh, love. Can it feed you? Can it keep you warm? I've lived sixty-five years without it, and I'm doing just fine. No severed limbs or tongues, no broken heart, like that silly fish girl."

"That's because you've never met a prince. You're too old, anyway."

"I was young and pretty once," she snapped. "Besides, prince or no prince, it's useless if you can't speak up for yourself."

There was a painful silence inside and outside the house. The attackers seemed to have broken into the headquarters.

"Did she kill him?"

Everyone in the room was startled by Dong Sheng's voice. I shook my head.

"I don't know. The last few pages were torn from the book."

I had no idea why I lied. The book, hidden in the hole of the mattress beneath me, didn't have a single missing page.

Everybody accepted my explanation and went to bed. Dong Sheng seemed to have some questions for me, but checked himself. Soon I drifted into a dream, floating with waves until I reached the shore. I lay upon the sand; my body, starting from my feet, was melting into white foam. The prince knelt over me. He had finally realized I was the one he had always loved and wanted to marry, but it was too late. His tears dropped like pearls on my dissolving face.

I opened my eyes and saw Dong Sheng kneeling next to the mattress, his face a few inches from mine, his breath sweet and hot, his eyes wide open, yet he did not seem to notice that I had awakened. He lingered over my face for a few more minutes, and then bent closer. My heart thumped in my throat. Was he going to kiss me? He climbed on top of me, his finger tracing my nose and lips with tenderness. I dared not make a sound; my sister, grandma, and brother were sleeping next to me on the same mattress, and on the other side was Dong Zhuo. He remained motionless for such a long time that I began to panic. Suddenly he got up, returned to his mattress, lay down with his back toward me, and didn't move again.

I stayed wide awake until the dawn broke and got up for the morning chores. The only explanation for what happened was that Dong Sheng had been sleepwalking. But why me? Because I was the storyteller? He stroked my lips exactly the way the prince fondled the Little Mermaid while calling her "my dumb child." Was he acting like a prince in his dream? He must have known how people in our compound admired him. Had he mistaken me for the Little Mermaid? But nothing about me matched her, except that my mother and grandma also called me "dumb," with the double meaning of stupid and silent. Why didn't he choose my sister? She resembled the mermaid in every way, except for one thing—she talked too much, unlike the unfortunate girl who sacrificed her tongue for love. Should I feel lucky or take it as a bad omen? After all, in the story, the Little Mermaid was abandoned and lost her body and soul forever.

I walked in and out of the apartment in a trance, doing my morning routines. I let out chickens, lit the coal stove, made rice porridge and steamed bread for breakfast, then went to the market. When I returned with a basket of food, Dong Sheng and his sister were gone. They would not return tonight, my sister said. The workers, armed with the weapons from the navy, had seized the Red

Guards' headquarters last night. Many people had died, mostly students, but the battle was over, thank heavens. All morning, the loud-speaker broadcasted the announcement that the workers had officially taken over the school, that all the students and teachers must return to school to receive reeducation from the working class. I listened to her chatting, wondering if she had any inkling of what had happened last night between Dong Sheng and me. Then I heard her say that Dong Sheng was leaving for Shanghai in two days. His father got him the ticket that morning. Too bad, eh? But the good news was that Dong Sheng's mother had invited her to play chess with her son. My sister was the chess champion of the compound.

"I'll let him win no matter what," she cooed.

Grandma trotted in on her bound feet, holding Brownie, a young rooster, by its feet. "Chicken Yang is here. I want you to run out and get the rooster fixed. Hurry up. There's already a big line. He hasn't shown up for two weeks."

I took Brownie and walked away with an aching heart. What my sister had just told me made more sense than what had taken place last night. How then could I explain everything? I knew I hadn't been hallucinating. I could still feel his weight, still smell his breath, and my lips still tingled from his light touch.

Brownie struggled to get free, flapping his wings, lifting his head in vain. I was holding him upside-down by his legs, which Grandma had tied together with a straw rope. I turned him over and cradled him under my arm. I had brought him up from a wet chick pecking his way out of a shell into a brown-feathered, fourteen-month-old rooster. After he jumped the first hen, he'd been fed with special food. Once a week, Father drew his blood with a needle and injected it into Mother's buttocks. Mother had started acting strange after the Red Guards paraded her throughout the town on a truck, half of her hair shaved off to make "yin-yang head," like the rest of the counterrevolutionary demons on the same truck. Her moods swung between extreme happiness and depression. Her need to pinch and whip us became more frequent and unpredictable.

Everyone believed that the blood from a spring rooster was the best tonic. Father decided to give it a try.

The blood transfusion didn't change her much except to give her more physical strength when she chased us with a broomstick. Brownie, however, was a wreck from the loss of his blood. His feathers became dull and tangled. His pale crown sagged like Grandma's breasts. Father had abandoned him a week ago, and started drawing blood from Big White, our stud rooster, until two new roosters were ready to give blood. The wasted roosters were then fixed and they'd grow plump and tender and ready to be eaten. I looked at Brownie with sadness. His life was so short and joyless. Did he have a soul? If he did, where would it go when we ate his body?

The line moved. A rooster was screaming as Chicken Yang stabbed him with a knife. In front of me, everyone held one or two haggard birds upside down in their hands. The rooster blood transfusion was this year's trend. They all seemed to know the secret that a fixed rooster tasted better. Chicken Yang took something white out of the screaming creature and popped it into his mouth. He pulled a few feathers, stuffed them into the wound, untied the rope, and returned the rooster to its owner, who handed him a bag of chicken feathers. Yang poured it all into his gigantic sack.

Unlike other peddlers who sold noodles and bean curd, Chicken Yang rarely took cash for his merchandise—his malt candy or castration service. For fixing one rooster, he took a bag of feathers. He also accepted glass bottles, toothpaste tubes, cigarette wrappers, books, and scrap iron. Whenever his drum rattled in the yard and his chant "Chicken feathers, goose down" boomed across the compound, kids would run to him, singing, "Duck feathers, goose down, and Chicken Yang's pubic hair." He would pretend to chase us, and we would run away screaming and come back for more.

When we were tired of the game, we brought the feathers we had collected secretly and traded them for his malt candy, something strictly forbidden by our parents. They said his candy was made from his saliva, and he lured children away for some dirty business.

"Look at his meaty nose and lips, and the bald scalp, all from eating too many rooster testicles," my grandma said, trying to scare us. "All the male power in his body, with no outlet, living alone in a remote village."

But the more grown-ups forbade us, the faster we ran to him. His cackling laughter, his round trembling stomach and oily face, and what he did to roosters, all terrified and fascinated us at the same time. And how his malt candy made our mouths water as he lifted the greasy cloth off the tray, chipping pieces of his golden treasure with a chisel and laying them gently in our little palms. The sticky sweet candy stuck to our teeth, giving us horrible cavities and toothaches, but we didn't care.

"Hey, little girl, you want me to fix your rooster or not?" Chicken Yang's cackle startled me. I looked up. I was the last customer under the weeping willow where he had set his stand. The people behind me must have gone home for lunch or gone ahead of me while I was in a daze. I handed him Brownie. Yang tied his legs to a long chopstick, then plucked some feathers under the wing until his pale skin was exposed. He poked at the smooth spot, and then stabbed a thin knife into it. Brownie let out a hoarse screech, but was unable to move. Slowly he withdrew the knife, turned it around and stuck the other end that was shaped like a spoon into the cut. With a few stirs, he spooned out something that resembled a partridge egg. Not a drop of blood. Chicken Yang examined the egg with a grunt and popped it into his mouth. I stared with disgust.

"What are you eating?" I heard myself asking.

"Oh, rooster egg, little girl. Makes me big and strong." He flexed the muscles on his arms. "Good eggs are hard to find these days. The roosters are all wasted, like this one." He kicked at Brownie lying in the dust. "Hey, little girl, when are you going to bring me Big White? I'll give you a whole tray of my candy."

I shook my head and handed him a bag of feathers. It was from Black Widow. Mother had killed her to make broth after she stopped laying eggs. Since then, Big White had lost interest in food and sex. Of the eight hens, Black Widow had been his favorite consort. Whenever he caught a worm or found a grain of rice, he would call her over and dance around her as if crazed. Chicken Yang took out a handful of the shiny feathers and nodded in satisfaction. When he poured them into his sack, I asked, "What do girls eat to get big and strong, hen eggs?"

He burst out laughing. "No, no, no, little girl. Hen eggs won't do the trick. It's the other stuff." He looked me up and down. "How old are you, little girl?"

"Fifteen." I said, adding a year to my age.

"No good, no good." He shook his head as he rubbed his chin, scrutinizing me with his meaty eyes. "Hey, little girl, why don't you come with me. Chicken Yang knows how to fix you big." He bent over and cupped my flat chest with his giant hand. The heat from his palm scorched through my clothing and skin. "You haven't seen your ghost yet, have you?" He looked at me with pity. I froze in his grip. He loosened his hand. "Go home, little girl. Eat lots of chickens and eggs. Grow some meat on your bones first. Next time, bring Big White and I'll teach you some tricks." He chiseled a piece of candy from his tray and slipped it into my hand.

Every one was napping when I got home. My lunch, a bowl of rice with some stringy vegetable stems and brown sauce, stood humbly next to a pile of dirty dishes. Grandma spoke from her bed. "Did Chicken Yang eat up your soul or what? I thought you'd never come back. Finish your lunch and clean up. Your mother wants you to wash the windows today. Why don't you start with the kitchen?"

I ate, washed the dishes, and cleaned the kitchen window. Then I sat down on the windowsill and opened my braids. My hair hung all the way to my thighs. Whenever Mother saw me brush it, she would curse loudly. Now that she was asleep, I could take my time. How foolish of me to believe that Dong Sheng liked me, I told myself, leaning over the window so that my hair would fall outside. Even Chicken Yang didn't want me. When would I ever grow up?

When would I see my ghost, like my sister? She was younger, yet her blood had already flowed. When she first saw the red, she ran to me in tears, thinking she was dying of some horrible disease. We sewed layers of cloth to her underwear to absorb the blood, until one day mother saw the thickly padded shorts and threw a pair of rubber panties at her. Soon my sympathy turned into jealousy as I watched her waddling to show off what was going on between her legs, and her whispering to friends about her monthly visit by the "old ghost." I tried everything: jumping up and down, carrying heavy things, placing toilet paper in my underwear, but my ghost refused to show up.

On my fourteenth birthday, I punched a hole in an egg I found in the chicken coop and was about to suck it when my sister wad-dled over. From the way she walked, I knew she had been haunted by her ghost again. She threatened to tell on me unless I gave her the egg. I hurled it on the ground and yelled, "It's my birthday, damn it. I'm already fourteen, fourteen, do you hear?"

She gave me the same pitying look Chicken Yang had and pulled out her rubber panties. "Would you like to borrow them?" she offered. "Two of my friends wore them for only a week and the red poured out like crazy. I swear."

Outside the window, tall grass in the soccer field trembled in the breeze. I looked down at my belly, which was flatter than my chest. The only places that stuck out on my body were my joints and my big nose. My sister's breasts bulged just like the Little Mermaid's. So did the curve along her waist. I looked down at Big White in the coop under the window and rubbed the candy I had wrapped with cigarette paper. Should I go with Chicken Yang?

"You have the most beautiful hair on earth, my Little Mermaid."

I turned to the direction of the voice but dared not look. It was Dong Sheng, but how could it be true? It was impossible to be in the same dream twice. The voice came again. "Please tell me what happened to her. Did she kill the prince or did she let herself per-ish forever? Please tell me so I can sleep tonight."

How pale he looked! As if he had been tossed around in a storm all night, had just been rescued and brought to the shore. Perhaps what happened last night wasn't a dream. I looked into his dark velvet eyes.

"I thought you were playing chess with my sister."

He waved his hand. "Oh, I beat her in five minutes. Too easy. Well, what happened to the Little Mermaid?"

I shook my head. Too easy. Was the Little Mermaid also too easy? Was that why she lost her prince?

"Come on," he pleaded. "I know you have the whole story. What can I do to make you tell?"

I almost said, "I want you to love me. I want you to make me a woman."

Dong Sheng's mother shouted from upstairs to summon him. back to the chess game. He stamped his feet and stood up with a sigh. "I'll come back, you stubborn mermaid. I hope you won't make me wait too long. I'm leaving the day after tomorrow. By the way, your hair shines like a meteor shower in the night sky."

I sat on the windowsill until Grandma came into the kitchen and yelled at me to get down and start making supper. I washed and chopped vegetables, then sautéed them in the wok, my heart sizzling with a happiness I had never experienced. He likes me, and he will come back for me and for the story, I chanted silently to myself. If I were to die now, I'd have nothing to regret.

Dong Sheng never came back, even though his ship was delayed for a week by a typhoon. I was glad he didn't. That same afternoon, chopping vegetables in a daze, I had forgotten to wrap my head with a towel. At dinner, mother found hair in every dish I had made. She threw down her chopsticks, grabbed a pair of scissors, and cut my braids. My sister took pity on me and tried to trim my short hair into some kind of shape. It only made it worse. My hair stood up on my scalp like an angry porcupine. Grandma said it looked as if it had been bitten by a mad bitch. She also kept telling me *le ji sheng bei*—extreme happiness brings tragedy. I wondered if she had been eavesdropping on Dong Sheng and me that afternoon.

We encountered each other again the day Dong Sheng left for Shanghai. I was delivering Big White to our neighbor, Mr. Liu, who wanted our rooster to mate with his hens. Though Big White hadn't recovered from the death of Black Widow and the weekly blood transfusion, Mother agreed to the request from the charming and powerful Mr. Liu.

The Dong family was walking ahead of me, each carrying a parcel or a basket filled with food. Dong's mother was holding a black hen by its feet, upside down. My sister walked next to Dong Sheng, chatting like a magpie. She had spent every minute of her spare time upstairs for the past week. I tiptoed behind them, praying that no one would look back.

Suddenly Big White jumped out of my arms and charged at Mrs. Dong, pecking at her hand, wings wide open. He was trying to rescue the black hen from Mrs. Dong's hand. Mrs. Dong ran in circles screaming for help, yet refused to let go of the hen. Dong Sheng turned at the sound of the turmoil. Without thinking, he kicked the rooster with his steel-toed navy boot.

Big White staggered a few steps before he fell. I picked him up, put my hand on his chest, which was streaked with blood. He was still breathing. I looked up. Our eyes met. Dong Sheng quickly turned his head. I wasn't sure if he had recognized me with my dog-bitten hair. My sister watched with her mouth wide open. She knew what the rooster meant to me. If the culprit had been someone else, she'd have screamed and thrown herself upon him. Love had tamed her.

To my surprise, Mother only knuckled me a few times on the head and told me to keep an eye on the rooster. If it got better, she'd have Chicken Yang fix him. If not, she'd kill it early in the morning. It'd be at least good for a pot of soup. That night I stayed up at the coop watching Big White breathe on my lap. He'd never get better again. What for? To make a better meal? I took out my handkerchief and made a knot around his neck. "Forgive me, Big White," I said, and pulled. He opened his eyes wide for a second, then stopped breathing. He would be inedible by the time I reported his death the next morning. Mother would punish me, but Big White had been my best friend since he hatched before my eyes two years ago, and this was the least I could do for him—to keep his body whole, and perhaps his soul.

I buried Big White and put his feathers in a clean bag, together with Anderson's fairy tales. I was ready to go away with Chicken Yang, let him take me wherever he wanted. But three weeks passed by. His peddler's drum never rattled again in our compound. One day at lunch, my sister announced that Chicken Yang was dead. Someone believed he was shot by a stray bullet; others claimed he had done something bad to a village girl and was stoned to death by an angry mob.

"Too bad," she said, smacking her pretty pink lips. "No more malt candy."

HOUSE OF ANYTHING YOU WISH

I came here to lose. But the wheel won't let me.

Once again I pile all of my chips on three. People gasp. What are the odds for winning eight straight-ups in a row?

Fools! Don't they know wheels do not hold memory? That math and luck never go together? With roulette, every spin is new. Probability is as whimsical as life. Who would believe three is not even my lucky number?

You'd sneer at me, Mei. Superstitious, you'd say. But how can I not think that way? On March third, you walked out on me with our three-year-old son. Three years ago, you enrolled in Queens College to study English and computer science, and things began to go downhill.

Nonsense, you'd say. It has nothing to do with school.

But it does. How else could I explain your change of heart? I'm still the same Tiger Fan you loved seventeen years ago. Your mother threatened to disown you for going out with a guard soldier from the countryside. Your father pointed his gun at us when he caught me in your room. But nothing could stop you from loving me. You left your mansion without looking back and took the train with me all the way to the Pearl River. On the bank, we looked through the mist at Hong Kong on the other side. If we swam across, we'd be free. It would have taken only four hours. You shook your head, said you sank like a rock in water. But I knew you couldn't bear bringing your family down further. Once you crossed over, you'd be an enemy of China. Even if your father denounced you, his military career would be over. At the border town, you slid a Swiss watch into the registrar's sleeve and got our marriage certificate stamped. You sealed the red paper into a plastic bag and zipped it into my pocket, together with sixty U.S. dollars. How you got the money is still a mystery to me. If you make it, Tiger, you cried, hugging my neck, if we meet again, we'll never part, dead or alive.

Seventeen years later, you laid quietly on your side of the bed in our Chinatown home. So quiet I couldn't hear you breathe.

"Do you remember, Mei," I asked in the dark, "do you remember?"

"I was young, a foolish sixteen-year-old," you finally mumbled.

I don't believe it. How can you forget? The scars are there, on your belly, chest, limbs, scars you burnt through the skin to keep me in your heart. Twelve years you waited, though no mail or phone could reach you from Hong Kong. Your family forced you to move on. Tiger Fan is long dead, your father announced. He's married another woman and has children, your mother said. They brought you a troop of bachelors with great prospects for the future. But you faked insanity and checked yourself into a mental hospital.

And you couldn't possibly forget the day we met at JFK! The tears we shed without shame, the joy over our first condo on Bayard Street, our first car, my store on Broadway, your green card . . .

Remember the birth of Jia?

But your ears shut down as soon as I started telling you how I almost drowned in the Pearl River, starved on the streets of Hong Kong, my spirit shattered from working sixteen hours a day, seven days a week in restaurants and antique stores until I saved enough for New York. Useless to point out how I burnt my bridges applying for a green card as a political refugee so that you could come legally, as my wife.

"Sorry, I no longer speak Chinese." This is all I could get out of you after I spilled my guts.

The wheel shudders, stops at three. The dealer clears the chips from the losers, then stacks them up next to my bets. Thirty-five to one. How much have I won? Do I even care? Such dead silence around the table—all eyes wish me dead. I wish myself dead. I came to forget, but everything in this room—its Chinese name, Chinese customers, Chinese managers, and the damn Ping's Noodle in the corner—stirs up memories. Even the dealer looks like your twin sister. How her almond eyes glow like embers!

Those ember eyes of yours, Mei. They used to melt me with each blink. Now they spew hate and hunger. How did that happen? What made you start speaking English at home? First with our son, then with me, even when I laughed, mocked and begged you to stop. I can humor every whim of yours, but not this, not at home. After twelve hours of twisting my tongue to please tourists in my store, I need to feel like a person again. Is it too much to ask? Aren't we still Chinese?

"We're New Yorkers now," you said. "Let's speak like New Yorkers, our first step to success. Look around, Tiger. Do any of your friends live in this ghetto? No! I'm not saying we should live in SoHo like Master Yao and his artist friends. But even Yingying and Bunny Song live somewhere else, although they can barely afford a meal in a cheap restaurant!"

I'm successful, too, just like everyone else, I almost shouted. I built my antique store from scratch in the heart of Chinatown. Do you know that every square inch of land here is worth more than gold, and our condo on Bayard Street is just as valuable as the loft in SoHo? Do you know Master Yao spent more time in my little store on Broadway than in his own grand studio? But the smirk on your lips stopped me cold. Since when did you pick up that white man's look? I wish I could smack it off your face, once and for all.

"Dump that bitch, fast," my friends say. "She's your ill star, bringing you nothing but misfortune since you met her. She's not even pretty, jaw too square, cheeks too high, signs of a man-killer. You're still young, only thirty-five. With your looks and money, you can pick the most beautiful girls from Chinatown or Flushing."

It's true that women flock to my bed like moths to a light. Singles, divorcees, married women with husbands on the mainland, all beautiful and young, eager to please. They scream and writhe in my bed. They call me a true tiger and make me feel like a man. But as soon as they're out my door, I get sick to my stomach. I don't know what they're after, my money or my American passport. Probably both.

Ah, here comes another spin. My tablemates move their bets around as the ball leaps and rolls over the slot. Some pinch their chips between their fingers, waiting for me to make a move. I count out thirty-five chips and place them carefully on thirty-three.

Yesterday was your birthday. I made six dishes—three vegetarian and three seafood, your favorites—and a chocolate cake for our son Jia. I thought the little banquet might cheer you up. You often get depressed on your birthday. I dialed the number for your apartment in Sunset Park. It still blows me up whenever I think that you rented this tiny one-bedroom behind my back when we were still living together. Say whatever you want, but I just don't believe that a normal person can find happiness in a rat hole. For a long time, you wouldn't give me your phone number or address. Need to be alone for a while to clear your mind, you said. Clear my ass. Haven't you figured out you can't live without me? Don't you know it isn't that hard to find out where someone lives? Still so naïve, after all these years.

I listened to the ring with a clear conscience. It was your birthday, for heaven's sake. I was inviting my wife to her birthday dinner. I wanted to hear you laugh, tell you that thirty-three was an auspicious number, like cuddling lovers, the symbol of "double happiness" on the door of the newly-wed. The phone rang and rang. Finally you picked it up, but you sounded nervous, anxious to hang up. Then I heard him, reading a story to my son behind a closed door. It was deep, muffled, a voice that didn't need to shout to claim authority, a white man's voice.

"Come back home, Mei. NOW!" I screamed.

You waited till I lost my steam, then said, "Tiger, I just want a normal life. I want Jia to grow up good, not a hoodlum."

You hung up and unplugged the phone.

I dumped the dinner into the garbage can.

You think I'm a tong, bitch! But how can I blame you? All the movies and TV shows you watch, the rumors behind doors, the bullets flying around the dark streets. Yes, there are tongs everywhere. But that's only half of the truth. You never gave me a chance to tell *my* story.

The day I opened my shop, they drifted in the door like ghosts. Through their sunglasses, they looked at me without a word. I knew what they wanted. But instead of giving them the envelope with cash, I shouted, "Welcome to my store. Please have some candy and peanuts."

They couldn't believe their ears. You should see how their mouths dropped open like dead fish. The next day they came back and smashed a few plates and vases. They picked the biggest and shiniest ones, not knowing everything on display was imitation. The real stuff was locked in the safe. I opened the cash register.

"Look, it's empty. I haven't made a penny yet. If you loiter around my store every day, how can I get any customers? If I can't do business, how can I make money to pay you guys?"

They looked at me as if I were nuts. I bet nobody had ever talked to them like that. Two days later, they came and placed a little black box on my counter. I opened it. It was an ear, dried and shriveled like an autumn leaf. I looked at it, looked at the two young thugs, who had no idea what tough meat tasted like.

"O.K.," I said. "Tell your boss to meet me tonight, nine sharp, in the back room of Seafood Palace on Center Street."

I took out my gun for Russian roulette. It was the first thing I'd bought after I made my pledge to Uncle Sam. It had taken me six years and forty thousand bucks to become an alien in this Yankee town. A perfect gift for the celebration. I'd played it in Beijing and Hong Kong. Not my choice at first. But it was the only way I could fend off the soldiers and thugs. The only way to show them I could play, and play hard, despite my pale skin and my girly face. I'm good, real good. Know when to stop. It'd be the first time I'd use it on American soil, and I hoped it'd be the last.

I got there at eight-thirty, ordered an eighteen-dish banquet, poured two glasses of white grain spirit, and waited. The boss arrived, a scrawny little guy, guarded by his seven brothers. I stood up, showed him my full glass, bottomed it, then pushed his glass over. He stared in disbelief. His bodyguards lifted their shirts, showing off the knives that dangled on their belts. I laughed, pulled out my gun, put a bullet in, twirled the cylinder, and put it against my temple. I pulled the trigger.

They all went pale.

I placed my blue beauty next to his glass, still untouched.

He stared at it like a zombie.

I slid a red envelope to the scrawny shrimp. It was swollen with fifty twenty-dollar bills. "Believe it or not, you're the first people who stepped in my store. According to the custom of my trade, you get a present from me, as a lucky omen. Tomorrow I'll receive my regular clients. One of them is the head of the police station on Elizabeth Street, known as Hawk. I'm sure you're well acquainted with him. But I bet you don't know he's a fanatic antique collector. If you have a chance to visit his home, you'll see his collection. Perhaps you guys should drop by my store also, have a chat with him. He's not as ferocious as he looks, if you get to know him."

If you had seen the way they ran, Mei, you'd know they'd never show their pimpled faces in my store again. I sat down, alone, ate the eighteen-course dinner, drank the whole bottle of liquor. It's a shame to waste food, under any circumstance.

I wish you would believe that I run my business clean in Chinatown.

The wheel is slowing down. The dealer gives me a look, clears her throat. She seems to wait for me to change my mind before she calls out "No more bets." Thirty-three is just a column. It pays only two to one, far less exciting than straight-ups or splits. But what do I care? I didn't come here to win in the first place. Besides, once I make up my mind, I stand firm. I'm pigheaded like you. We have twin spirits.

The first night of our reunion, you wouldn't let me keep the light on. I thought you were just being shy. As I buried my face between your breasts, I felt the scars. I switched on the light. Your torso was covered, some perfectly round, like cigarette burns, some with perforated edges like a poppy pod.

"Who did that to you?" I screamed in horror. "Tell me who did it. I swear I'll get them, one by one."

"Shh," you hushed, sealing my lips with your slender fingers. "I did it to myself, just to prove I was mad, a real *huachi* who lost her mind for love, no longer fit for marriage."

I bawled into your belly. How could I ever pay back such love in this life?

"Tiger, Tiger, look at me." You cradled my face and cooed like a pigeon at my ear. "It wasn't painful, not at all, not compared to the pain of longing for you, for not knowing where you were, how you were doing. I knew you were alive, no matter what they told me. I knew you were alive because I was still hanging on. Tiger, my sweetheart and lover, look at me, look at my belly. What do you see? It's your face, your profile, if you link the dots together. Here's the forehead, the nose, the lips, and chin. Here, here, feel them." You grabbed my finger to trace the scars that formed a constellation.

And I remembered the first time I met you, outside your father's mansion. You were reading on the front steps, the breeze blowing the fuzzy hair of your nape this way and that, like the waves of a golden harvest. I felt dizzy, weightless, a buoy in space. I have been floating in your universe ever since.

But it all disappeared when you exploded without a warning. No, not true. There were signs. First the change from Mei to May, then the abandonment of Chinese, your hatred for Chinatown, and the constant nagging about me being a gangster. I shouldn't have laughed it off. I should have paid more attention.

I tried everything I could to clear my name. But you just yelled, despair in your eyes, "How could you survive in this town otherwise?

Those damn tourists stare at me like a whore. They even have the nerve to ask why I don't wear the sexy gown that splits at my thighs."

"All right," I said finally. "Give me a year to sell out. We'll move wherever you want, SoHo, Flushing, Brooklyn, White Plains, even New Jersey."

I thought you'd jump with joy.

"Doesn't matter where you live," you screamed. "*You* are Chinatown."

Bitch!

But you're right. I am Chinatown. I live there, buy and sell stuff robbed from tombs hundreds, thousands of years old. I wear my watermelon hat and silk robe, just like a Chinaman in a movie, to amuse tourists. I even smell like Chinatown—the stink of fish, garlic, and soy sauce. Is it a crime? I do whatever it takes to support my family. But are you grateful? Jia wouldn't even say hello when he came home from school. He chatted only with you, in English. The other day, I told him to speak Chinese like a good son, like a human being. Guess what he said after making a horrific face?

"Can you talk like a grown-up?"

I spanked him, for the first time. He's only five, already he acts like a little devil. What will he be like when he reaches fifteen, twenty-five? I might as well strangle him right now, to save trouble for the future.

I guess it pushed you over the edge.

Fine. We live in America. Spanking is not hip. I speak Chinglish. My clothes smell of rice and old graves. But do you have to get a white devil into your bed and have my son call him "father?"

I pulled out my gun. The cold metal soothed my throbbing temple.

The ball drops. I won again. Two to one. No big deal. But the message is clear. I'm not yet finished, not yet.

I'm tired of being out. I want to be in the game, before it's too late, you said.

Translated: you're bored as a merchant's wife in Chinatown. You want to be pampered by some white man.

With your China eyes and yellow skin? With your permanently accented English? Your job behind a receptionist desk in the Seagram Building and your rat-infested one-bedroom apartment in Brooklyn? You forget this is America, not Beijing. General's daughter or not, white men don't give a shit about your past.

I want to be in, too. Why do you think I swam through the night to cross the river? Why I cut off my ties with China and applied for citizenship as a refugee? Do you know how I felt when I stood on the harbor of Hong Kong, gazing at the mainland's shadow poking through the mist? For sixteen years I haven't returned home. Sixteen years. I want to see my mother one more time before she goes. She's blind, ready to join her husband, the father I've never met. Her coffin is made and varnished, her name chiseled on the stone. But she can't go without me, her only son, at her bedside, to guide her soul into heaven with my cry.

"What are you afraid of?" Mom asks whenever I call. "You're a foreigner now, a rich foreigner. Nobody can touch you."

"Yes, nothing to be afraid of." You tell me the same thing, when you see the pinched look on my face, knowing I'm homesick. "Now that you have an American passport, the old man won't dare harm you."

I laugh. What do you know about your father's other side? He can toast to his enemies at a banquet and have them eliminated before they have a chance to burp the gas out of their stomachs. He was so furious when he found out I married his only daughter that he instantly put me on the list of top spy suspects. He won't give a shit that I'm a "foreigner" with an American passport. As soon as my name appears on the computer screen at customs, he'll have me dragged to his cell. My only hope is to wait till he retires or dies.

Not a totally bad end, perhaps? At least he treats me as if I were still Chinese, not a "foreign devil." Even my own mother calls me a "foreigner." Being my mother, she doesn't say the word *devil,* but I can hear it in the awkward silence, the way she bites her tongue to stop it from slipping out of her mouth. Foreign devil, foreign ghost. Once you cross that bridge, once you turn your back to your mother, you become a ghost, a ghost without a grave, without a country.

"Nonsense," you said when I tried to tell you my morbid thoughts, your voice loud and shrill as if you were trying to scare away ghosts. "America is your home now. You belong here. We all do, dead or alive."

I looked past your shoulder, at the antique vase on the nightstand. It captured the scene of a slender maiden chasing a butterfly in the garden and a young man peeking at her from the wall, his eyes full of lust. It's the kind of vase that would have sold quickly, if not for the crack at the bottom. So I drilled a hole and turned it into a lamp. Tourists love Chinese antiques. Americans. Europeans. They come into my store. "I'm looking for a vase or plate with Chinese faces like you and her." They point their fat, hairy fingers at me, at my young assistant from Shanghai. When they get what they want, they pat me on my shoulder. *"Hsie hsie,* China Fan." Their thanks come out like "shit shit."

I gaze into their eyes: blue, hazel, brown, gray. Will they ever look at me and say: Perhaps he's an American too, just like us?

Do you know, Mei, that you're a walking Chinatown yourself?

But no matter. Nothing stops you. The stubborn dreamer.

Somewhere far away, slot machines sing in many voices: a Christmas bell, an alarm, a combat song. They remind me of those sleepless nights in Beijing, under my cotton quilt, my ear pressed against the old plastic radio for the static sound from the Voice of America. Turn to the dealer, now. Do not weep. Must not weep.

She returns my glare with a smile and turns the wheel.

Let's play then, Mei, you from your rat hole in Sunset Park, me from this Chinese casino room in Atlantic City. *Ruyilou*—House of Anything You Wish. See how I pile everything on the big red one? It stands tall, quivering, a pickax hacking into the belly of the game.

THE LAST COMMUNIST VIRGIN

I was waiting on a German couple and their three grumpy children when Victor, the head waiter, handed me a lunch menu.

"Some girl called and left this message. Wouldn't say her name," he said, and disappeared into the kitchen.

I read what Victor had scrawled on the flimsy take-out pamphlet: *Exboyfriend back from San Francisco. Need his place back! Now!* My mind went blank. She was doing it again, Jeanne Shin, playing the cat and mouse game with me. We were supposed to be friends, both of us born and raised in Shanghai, taking the same classes since we met at Hunter College. She treated me like a sister when she was in a good mood, sharing her candy, gum, and cookies with me. I never liked sweets, but I took them with gratitude because those were the treasures her mother had mailed from Shanghai. Once, she handed me a bag full of clothes, new and used. "Just so you don't look so obviously like someone who just jumped off the ship," she said. Then, for no reason at all, she'd turn into a tigress and tear me apart.

When I was evicted from my previous apartment in Queens, Jeanne Shin gave me the key to the Harlem apartment, her exboyfriend's sublet, and told me I could have it for at least a year. But it had been only twenty-eight days since I moved in. How could she expect me to find a place on the same day? I had only a few hours between my day job and evening class. What if I couldn't find anything? Where would I sleep?

The chatty German asked me if I was all right. I nodded and handed back his credit card. After they left, I started stacking their dirty plates on my arms, fighting the sickness in my stomach. A few minutes later, Mrs. Shen, the owner of the restaurant, called me over and pounded a piece of paper on the counter.

"Who's going to pay for this?" she asked.

It was the credit card bill from the German family, unsigned.

"I guess I will," I said.

"Next time, your squid will be fried," she said.

My squid had been fried three times since I came to New York, all because of money. I couldn't count, add, or subtract numbers for the bills fast enough. Customers complained bitterly to the manager when they caught me charging them more. When the manager caught me charging less, I had to pay the difference. I often ended up losing my entire tip at the end of a day, and then got fired.

This time it was the worst. Fifty-six bucks. Two days of work for nothing. I was lucky that the Germans were frugal and ordered only three dishes for the family of five. If it were an American family, it could easily have been over one hundred dollars. The hairy chatterbox seemed so kind, but he didn't even leave me a tip. What a cheapskate!

After the lunch rush, Victor put his arm around my shoulders.

"You look like a sick ghost, girl," he said.

I told him my problem.

"You lucky," said Victor with a wrinkled smile. "We've got a room for you. My roommate just left for China. His father has lung cancer that has spread to the brain. He won't be back for a while, I think. He's also looking for a wife there. His room is ninety-nine dollars a month. What do you think? If you want it, I can help you move after the dinner shift."

I thought I had hit rock bottom living in Jeanne Shin's Harlem sublet—the ninth place I had moved into since I arrived in New York eight months ago. The clogged bathtub and toilet, the stink in the kitchen, and the roaches that seemed to fatten on the poison I put out along the walls and stove. When I moved into Victor's basement in Jackson Heights, however, I realized how lucky I had been. The whole place was infested with mold. Rings of dark, fuzzy things grew on the ceiling and walls like clusters of mushrooms, and rat droppings were everywhere. My three roommates, Victor and two chefs from the same restaurant, always cooked up a storm no matter how late they got home. They drank, smoked, ate, and sang till daybreak. By the time they went to bed, it was time for me to get up for my morning classes.

For the sake of the cheap rent, I tried to hang on. I had come to New York with twenty-six dollars. I worked in three restaurants in three boroughs to pay rent and tuition, and took early morning and evening classes to keep my status as a full-time student. I was tired and hungry and lonely. But if I could tough out the first year in New York, things would turn a corner.

But my body refused to tough it out. My face was soon infected by the fungi and became a water-damaged map with scaling rings and moldy spots. Hives puffed up like blueberry pancakes. And migraines attacked me like vultures. One morning in my third week there, I opened my eyes to a thick layer of droppings the size of olive pits over a map of tiny footprints on my quilt. The scum-toed rodents must have carried my roommates' leftovers to my bed and had an all-night party there.

That was it!

I hopped on the subway to Flushing and bought a Chinese newspaper. It advertised hundreds of rooms and apartments in Queens, Manhattan, and Brooklyn, all in a range from $150 to $250 a month. I had moved ten times and lived in every borough except for Staten Island to know what those prices meant: one tiny room in the basement, and bathroom and kitchen shared with three or four tenants.

Then one ad caught my eye: *A clean, young female roommate wanted in a luxurious apartment in Rego Park. Nonsmoking. Rent negotiable. Interview with Mrs. Kao after 10:00 p.m.*

I had heard of Rego Park. It was an enclave of new and established immigrants from Korea and Taiwan. Real estate had boomed in the last few years when the new arrivals purchased condos, buildings, and businesses with cash.

The phone I shared with my roommates sat on the kitchen table. I didn't want them to know I was looking for another place. So I gathered my quarters and found a payphone on a quiet street.

Ten hours later, I stood outside Little Sakura on Twenty-third Street, at Fifth Avenue. A closed sign hung on the door. The place was tiny, like its name, but elegantly furnished. My mouth watered as the rich soy smell wafted through the window. I had come directly from school. I could have bought something from the campus cafeteria, but I had to save every penny. No one at home would believe I had never bought myself a Coca-Cola or a bag of chips, the famous American drink and snack. A gaunt, middle-aged woman was counting money behind the cash register. In the corner, a couple was finishing their meal. I tapped on the window and waved my newspaper. She buzzed me in. Before I had time to close the door, she barked,

"Miss Wan? I'm Mrs. Kao. KAY-OH, not cow, or gow."

She went back to her money. I stood at the threshold, not knowing what to do.

"I'm here for the interview," I muttered.

"I know, for Genji's apartment." She flung out her hand. I extended mine quickly, but she only pointed to the man behind the glass counter.

Genji waved and smiled, a gold tooth gleaming like a crescent moon on his fleshy face. Before I had a chance to study my would-be-landlord, Mrs. Kao's questions came.

"Where are you from? How do you make a living? What school are you attending? Family here with you? Father, mother still alive? Healthy? How badly do they want to come to America? How many siblings? Are they applying for visas to come here? Any bad habits? Smoke? Drink? Snore? Gamble? Drugs? Boyfriend? Clean? Pick up dishes after yourself? Make your bed?"

Sweat started pouring from my face. It was worse than being interrogated by the Red Guards and the U.S. consulate in Shanghai. They asked hard questions, but at least not so personal, and not as fast as if firing a machine gun at me like Mrs. Kao. I wanted to run, but Genji waved at me as if he had something to say. He was wrapping rice balls with a plastic sheet, his fingers swift and graceful.

I took a deep breath. I wouldn't panic till I had a chance to see the apartment. It had to be super-good, otherwise what was the point of such an intense security check?

The couple stood up from their table. Mrs. Kao jumped to open the door.

"Sayonara," she chanted cheerfully, a different person from a minute ago, as if she had just dropped her mask.

"Sayonara," they beamed, cheeks flushed from sake. "We'll come back when we visit the city again."

"What are you waiting for," Mrs. Kao scolded me as soon as she locked the door. "Help close up so we can get out of here."

My mouth dropped as Genji opened the bedroom door. It was a big space with giant windows, a mahogany king-sized bed in the center, flanked by Ming style nightstands. Soft light from the lamp shades brought out the luscious colors and texture of the antique vases. Above the headboard hung a woodprint of a slender geisha reading on a tatami mat, one pink nipple slipping from her blue kimono.

"Bedroom," barked Mrs. Kao.

Could she tell I couldn't really afford this apartment?

With just one glance, Jeanne Shin would say. Your bony body, your rotting pumpkin face, your imitation Gap jeans and T-shirt from China's black market, your uncombed hair, your garlic stink, your awkwardness and accent—everything screams "poor country bumpkin."

"Genji's baby," Mrs. Kao said, her voice now dreamy like a doting mother. "He spares no expense on this room."

It was obvious. As soon as we entered the apartment, Genji had herded us to the bedroom with his open arms. But I still got a glimpse of the living room. It was sparse and neat like a soldier's barrack.

"How much?" I asked in a quivering whisper. This room would be my paradise, my American Dream come true. But I dreaded the answer. A room like this in Rego Park would cost at least $500 a month, almost my entire monthly earnings from waiting tables seven days a week.

"Four seventy-five," Mrs. Kao said quickly, leaving no ground for negotiation.

My heart sank. After the rent, I'd have twenty-five dollars left for food, subway, books.

I told myself to leave, but my feet were glued to the floor. Genji's room was melting my willpower into a puddle. The mere thought of the mousy pellets in my bed made me sick.

Genji nudged closer with a big smile, his gold tooth glinting in the light. Was he trying to tell me something? Perhaps I could negotiate with him? He was the owner of the apartment, after all.

"Too much for you?" Mrs. Kao whispered at my ear. "Listen. Why don't you come to my house. We have a spare room for you, seventy-five dollars a month."

I pretended not to have heard her. I knew exactly what kind of room seventy-five dollars could buy. A windowless closet in the basement, a perfect nest for rodents and insects. No, thanks. Now that I had a glimpse of paradise, I was not going anywhere else.

"It's on the second floor, two windows, a little smaller than this, but decent size. And it's quiet. My husband goes to work during the day, and my kids go to school." Mrs. Kao said loudly, her pointed chin jutting in my face.

I stepped back. She didn't like me the minute I entered her restaurant. Why was she trying to rent me a room in her house at such a low price? It didn't make sense.

I eyed Genji's mahogany bed, his dresser, and his antique vases. If only I could crawl into the bed and sleep under its down quilt!

But Mrs. Kao's offer was too seductive: I could save $400 a month, $4,800 a year. That would be ten years' salary in China.

"One hundred fifty dollars good for Miss Wan?"

We both jumped. For me, this was the first time I had heard Genji speak. His voice was small and listless, too soft for a man thick like a stone wall, with muscles bursting through his T-shirt. Mrs. Kao shouted in Japanese, jabbing her finger at Genji's nose. Genji smiled, palms on his heart, and bowed to Mrs. Kao.

She shut up and turned to me.

"Today is your lucky day, Miss Wan. My chef took a fancy to you, for whatever reason. I guess beauty is in the beholder's eye. So when can you move in?" she mumbled in Chinese.

Dumbfounded, I stammered in English. "One hundred fifty dollars good?"

"Rent on the first day of the month," Mrs. Kao snapped. "Five dollars fine for two days' delay, and ten for three days. Understand?"

"Electricity included?" I had to make sure, my eyes on Genji's golden moon.

"What do you think?" She snarled. "Genji has given you his only bedroom for nothing. Why would he go cheap on the electricity bill?"

"Where is he going to sleep?" I turned to Mrs. Kao. In my excitement and eagerness, I forgot to notice that the apartment had only one bedroom.

A dark shadow suddenly eclipsed my jubilation.

She pointed to a cot in the living room. It crouched behind a rice paper screen that separated the door and the bedroom. On top, a white quilt and pillow were folded neatly.

"Perhaps I should sleep there?" I waved at the cot.

"No, no, Miss Wan young girl, need privacy. Me, Genji, old man, like simple, like space. Open be good."

"Thank you, Mr. Genji," I bowed with relief.

Genji beamed. "Miss Wan move in tomorrow? Genji no work. Genji help."

I looked at Mrs. Kao, knees trembling. This was all too good to be true.

She sighed. "Did you bring your rent and deposit?"

"Tomorrow. Tomorrow. No deposit necessary. Just rent and Miss Wan for Genji," he chirped merrily.

"Whatever you say, Genji. One thing I forgot," she turned to me. "Genji hates locks and latches. So don't even think about tampering with the bedroom door, understand?"

Her smile scared me, but it was too late.

"You are not moving into this place," Peng Chen shouted.

"Why?" It was startling to hear him shout for the first time. And worse, he was shouting in front of the doorman, who was picking up the phone to notify my new landlord and roommate that I was downstairs.

"Isn't it obvious? Genji is a Jap! A Jap!"

So? I wanted to say, but held my tongue. Peng was sweating hard. He had spent the whole morning moving my books and clothes from my basement into his red Cherokee, from his Cherokee into the lobby of Genji's building.

"Why this fuss now?" I said finally, trying to make peace. "Why didn't you say something earlier?"

"Well, Miss Tight Lips, I've tried to ask several times who will be your roommate, but you said it'd be a big surprise. Remember?"

It was true. Subconsciously, I must know Peng would object to me moving into Genji's place. He'd hinted many times that I should move in with him.

"It's too late, Peng." I looked at the boxes and bags around us on the marble floor. "The doorman is waiting."

"I won't allow it." He dropped the bags. The plastic burst. Hemingway, Kerouac, and Shakespeare spilled and scattered.

"You're not giving me orders, are you?"

He looked stunned by my tone of voice. Then he shouted, "Yes, I am, because I love you, because I'm your fiancé!"

I squinted into his eyes. The sun lingered behind his back. His shadowy face was the color of pig liver. His statement scared me. He had said it many times before, but I'd always laughed and brushed it off as a joke. But this time, I couldn't laugh. The weight his voice carried told me that he meant it, every word, every syllable. But why? Why on earth did he want to go out with me in the first place? I had nothing to offer: looks, status, money; whereas he, on the other hand, was rich, hot, and always surrounded by beautiful women. When we started dating, Jeanne Shin had given us three weeks, maximum. Peng, the playboy, she declared, had shown interest in me only because he was tired of the beauties on campus. He needed a change of flavor. That was all. Everyone had believed her prophecy, including myself. But it'd been half a year now, and we were still together. Whenever Peng introduced me to his friends as his fiancée, everybody laughed hysterically.

This time he was not joking. Not at all.

"Since when?" I whispered. How I wished to place my fingertip on the space between his eyebrows, so wide and smooth, unlike his deeply wrinkled forehead and the crow's feet in the corners of his eyes. This was what a prairie should be like, where cows, horses, sheep, and other animals graze freely under the blue sky, where I could lie down for a rest.

This was the same impulse I had had five months ago, when I met him the first time in the school library.

"You must be the Communist Virgin," he had said, his shadow hovering over the copy of *The Tempest* I was reading for my Shakespeare class. My nose tickled from a heavy perfume. I looked up. In front me was a tall man, broad-shouldered, tan and well-groomed, dressed in black from head to toe, hair combed back and held in place with spray. He was smiling ear to ear, a faint scar from the forehead to the temple. Two foxy girls in heavy makeup stood behind him like bodyguards.

And you must be the famous playboy Peng Chen that Jeanne Shin raved about, I wanted to say, but I was too shy. His face mesmerized me. A grassland face like that didn't belong to a playboy.

"Do I know you?" I said finally. I couldn't stand his gaze, and I hated being called the Communist Virgin, the nickname Jeanne Shin had given me on our first encounter. It seemed to be spreading like cancer.

"Peng Chen," he said, taking my hand as if plucking a fruit from his backyard tree. "New to the city? Allow me to take you around sometime. No city is like New York, greatest food and fashion, best looking girls. My mother doesn't want me to get involved with anyone here. AIDS, she said, and all other disgusting diseases that would blind my eyes and rot my nose. But she is really terrified that I may bring home a hairy blonde or a Communist iron maiden from the mainland."

He broke into hearty laughter, eyeing me slyly as if he were expecting me to laugh with him.

I wanted to laugh, but didn't dare. My hand burnt in his palm. He had fire, lots of fire.

He squeezed gently. "Don't worry. Her whip is too short to reach New York. So what's your real name, beautiful?"

"Wan Li," I said. Was he mocking me or just being silly? I had planned to remain silent, but I was curious. There was something innocent about this playboy's ranting.

He kissed my hand before letting go. "Peng Chen Wan Li, we belong to each other by destiny."

This time I laughed. A lousy pass, but not a bad sound play on our names. With the right intonations, *Peng chen wan li* could mean *a roc's flight of 10,000 li,* a symbol of mighty glory and bright future. I looked into his eyes—big and slightly bulging, set far apart from each other. They made him look like a gentle cow with a bull's body. I was about to laugh again when I noticed the disgust in the eyes of his "bodyguards."

"I've got a class," I murmured, gathering my books.

"Hey, Virgin, can I call you tonight?"

"I don't have a phone," I lied.

He grabbed my shoulders. "Where are you going, my slut girl?" he whispered.

I couldn't believe what I had just heard. He was so close I could feel his lips tickling my earlobe. The girls were sneering. How much could they hear? I should have slapped his face for what he said. But he was locking my shoulders from behind.

"You're as much a slut as I'm a playboy," he sang in my ear, his breath hot like steam out of a boiling kettle. "Let's be together and live happily ever after."

I kicked him in the shin and broke away.

"Oh, she's tough!" he laughed. I ran as fast as I could. "I'll be in touch," he shouted after me.

That evening Jeanne Shin called. "You hit the jackpot, Wan Li," she said. She tried to display her usual coolness, but her voice leaked sour pickle juice. "What do I mean? You know exactly what I mean. Peng Chen is not only the best looking Chinese man on the campus, but also the richest. His family owns lots of land in Taiwan. Space on the island is measured and purchased with gold by the square inch. Now what does that have to do with you? Are you really this stupid or are you just acting? The most wanted bachelor has fallen in love with a country bumpkin. How odd! What did you do? Perform some witchcraft?"

The phone rang as soon as I hung up. It was Peng. I dropped the phone in my lap. How did he get my number? I was still upset that he had called me a slut. How dare he? I'd never dated anyone in my life, never been touched, a virgin inside and out, but I kept this a secret when I came to New York. In the city of desire, being a virgin was a joke, a sin. Jeanne Shin nicknamed me Virgin the moment we saw each other, but I doubted if she knew it was for real. I wanted to hang up and unplug the phone, but didn't dare. It belonged to my landlords, a couple from Taiwan. They were chatting quietly in their bedroom. If I hung up, Peng would call back right away, and the landlady would be upset for sure.

I picked it up. Peng was chatting away like a magpie, oblivious that I wasn't even there. He was planning to take me to dinner in the best restaurants in New York, bars, shops on Fifth Avenue, malls in New Jersey. I laughed and told him that his plans sounded divine, but I had to work during the day, and go to school at night.

"What about weekends?" He cut in before I finished.

"I work seven days a week."

"Even God rests on Sundays."

I told him that I had never been chosen by the Lord, therefore I had to go to bed to rest my aching bones and get ready for the next day's work. "Please don't call so late again. My landlords have a curfew on nightly phone calls."

He called back the next day, and every day the following week, making the same offers and plans. His patience scared and flattered me at the same time. What did he see in me that was worth his effort? He could get any woman he wanted on campus, not just Asian, but also blue-eyed blondes. Was he really tired of beautiful women and wanted something different?

Having failed to convince me to go out with him, Peng had his sister hire me as a host at her Chinese restaurant in Greenwich, Connecticut. "So you don't have to work at three different places and fall asleep during class," he said. How the hell did he know I nodded off in class? That big-mouth Jeanne Shin! Still, I was touched, even though I was suspicious of his real motive. Since I didn't drive, and couldn't afford to take the train to the restaurant, Peng offered to drive me back and forth. On the way home, he stopped at a SoHo café, claiming he was craving sweets. Thus we began our dating.

I hosted two Friday and Saturday nights, made two hundred bucks, and never went back. The money was great, but I couldn't stand the way his sister eyed me with suspicion, the way she lectured me on how to dress as a hostess, how to please her customers. She saw me with Jeanne Shin's eyes: a hopeless bumpkin, a dead product of the Cultural Revolution.

"What a waste for you to be in this country," Jeanne Shin sighed whenever she failed to convert my name to Lily, or LeAnn. "Someone younger and smarter could have used your quota." Jeanne had been trying for years to bring her sister to New York, but her visa application was rejected each time. "She's just too beautiful. She could easily attract a rich man, get married, and never go back. Those consulates have trained eyes. They could tell at one glance who is an immigration suspect, and who has no chance of settling down in America."

I cringed as she eyed my hair and my red, blotchy face. But she had a point. In New York, the ocean of wealth and luxury, I felt no gratitude or excitement, only the sensation of choking and drowning. Shopping malls gave me dizzy spells. Fancy boutiques and restaurants upset my stomach. The idea of me smoking, drinking, or dancing at discos made me sweat. I even felt guilty lying on the grass in Central Park. Only lazy bourgeoisie did things like this. Peng finally lost it one day and called me a nutcase. Sure, girls played hard to get, but no one in his book had ever turned down jade, perfume, French cuisine, weed, or sex.

"Perhaps I was wrong about you," he once eyed me suspiciously. "Perhaps you *are* a real virgin."

I kept my mouth shut.

"Throw a long line to catch a big fish," said Jeanne Shin. "You might be smarter than you look, Wan Li. Watch out, though, the big fish may go after something else if you play the game too hard."

I said I knew nothing about games. I was just nervous. His big red jeep, his fat wallet, brand-name clothes, and restaurants with menus that did not list prices . . . too much, too much. Perhaps I had been more thoroughly brainwashed by the Communist dogma than I thought. Perhaps I was too old to change. Or did I even want to change? I stopped short of telling her that I had been a Communist since I was sixteen. On my visa application, I had to lie about my political status, and had kept it a secret ever since.

"What are you doing in America then, if you hate the good life, hate dating a rich man?" she screamed, her pretty eyes fiery with frustration.

In the sunset, Peng's scar glowed like hot iron. He wouldn't tell me how he got it, or how he lost his pinky. Rumor had it that he belonged to a gang. I suspected he came from a humble background, and he had grown up doing hard labor, his missing pinky nothing but an injury, an accident. Taiwan was full of nouveaux riches when real estate exploded with new economic growth. People who owned land could get filthy rich overnight. Peng was too sweet by nature to be a gangster. His tough and slick look couldn't hide his innate kindness, but it had taken me months to realize this. If we had started differently, if he had opened his heart, would I have fallen in love? Did I love him? If not, why did I ask him to help me move? True, a car was easier than taking the subway with bags of books and clothing. But I had done it many times, hadn't I? Part of me wanted him to know where I was going to live, what kind of place.

The doorman came over. "Miss Wan? Mr. Genji is coming down."

Peng grabbed my arms. "Promise you'll be careful? Promise?"

I rested my head on his chest. Out of the heavy cologne, I detected the salty ocean and the musky earth. He was a farmer's boy, a fisherman's son. His heart beat strong and steady.

"I'll call soon," I said.

"This is heaven," I said to myself when I woke up the first morning in my new room. Everything was soft and shiny clean: the goose down quilt, the satin sheets, the geisha's nape and snow white breast, the cream-colored roses on the nightstands. The sunlight poured in, melting me in snow-white comfort. Outside the window, a blue jay sang among the maple leaves.

My eyes and nose swelled suddenly. I sat up, sank my face in the comforter, and moaned. My body was hurting as if I'd been tied from head to toe all night long. Every breath was a struggle. The pain had started when I came to New York, but I had willed it into numbness. Once my boss asked me why I kept breaking his glasses and plates. I said my inside felt all knotted together. "I'm tight, really tight inside." Everyone laughed. My boss patted me on the shoulders.

"I know you don't mean it, I know you're a nice girl," he kept saying, winking at other waiters.

I was still puzzled what I had said to make the waiters and clients laugh like maniacs. All I knew was I must not feel or complain. All I had to do was to hold my breath and tough out the first year in New York then everything would be O.K.

I'd landed in heaven, but the pain returned screaming.

Someone knocked on the door twice, and pushed it open. Genji appeared with a tray. He looked at me with concern.

"Miss Wan nightmare? Miss Wan not like room?"

I dried my face quickly with my T-shirt. "No nightmare. Room very nice, like paradise. Thank you so much, Genji. I'm happy, too happy."

He smiled. "Hungry? Breakfast?"

I smelled egg and pancake. "Starving," I said.

"Come eat," he pointed to the tray and closed the door.

As I got dressed, I felt a sense of loss. I looked around my new room: the bed, the dresser, the desk with my books stacked neatly. All intact, all beautiful. Then I realized I hadn't dreamt during the night. I was a heavy dreamer. Strange things came to me whenever I closed my eyes, wherever I was: bed, subway, classroom, standing, sitting, lying down. Bloody dreams of floods, massacres, nuclear explosions, the end of the world . . . And lots of movement: flying, eating, laughing, crying, killing, fleeing, searching hopelessly for a bathroom. I kept a journal, recording my other world. Horrifying as they were, my dreams had become a part of me. They made my nights shorter and less lonesome.

Had I lost my dream because my wish had come true?

I walked into the living room. On the dining table, golden pancakes piled next to a jar of Maine maple syrup, but my eyes were immediately drawn to the silver plate where strawberries, raspberries, and blackberries were arranged into a tri-colored rose. Cubes of honeydew, kiwi, watermelon, and apples lined up neatly as a montage in the shape of a heart. A black chopstick cut through diagonally, its tip punctuated with a strawberry. It took me a few seconds to realize it resembled an arrow.

"How beautiful!" I shouted into the kitchen, where Genji was frying eggs. He pointed to a chair with his spatula for me to sit down. I gasped as I turned to it. On the back of the chair hung an orange silk dress and a blue cashmere jacket. I knew nothing about brand-name clothing, and had refused to be educated by Jeanne Shin and Peng. But Genji's clothes were a different story. They took my breath away. The colors were bright but not loud, the lace exquisite but not frilly. They came from a designer who had great taste, who knew what an Asian woman really wanted, her most secret desire.

Genji brought the eggs to the table, beaming. "Try, Miss Wan," he gestured at the clothes, wiping his hands on the apron.

I backed away. If I put them on, I would never be able to take them off.

"Miss Wan not like them?"

"Too much," I said, trying to tear my eyes away from the garments.

"Try then. Genji ordered from Japan, special for Miss Wan."

I shook my head with difficulty. "I don't take things from strangers."

"Strangers, Miss Wan think we strangers. Oh, Genji hurt so much." He moaned. Suddenly he grabbed the clothing, dumped it in the can, and lit a match.

"What are you doing, Genji?" I lunged and threw myself on top of the can.

"Miss Wan not want it. Genji burn it." He held the match like a torch, his face contorted.

"O.K., I'll try, all right?" I brought down his fist and blew out the match, then fished out the jacket and dress from the can. My hands shook terribly. I'd never seen a person change moods so rapidly. One minute, he was all smiles, the next he was ready to burn down the whole building. The garments came out clean. Genji must have just taken out the garbage and put in a new bag.

I went to my room and changed into the orange dress. It fit perfectly. I glanced in the mirror. Was it me? This thin waist? The swelling breasts and butt? My body was not as flat as an airport runway, despite what Jeanne Shin had often told me. "You've got curves like distant islands on the horizon, do you know that?" Peng once said, after a few glasses of wine. I had dismissed it as a drunkard's nonsense.

I looked away from the mirror. It was embarrassing to stare at oneself. When I was in China I never owned a mirror, not even a hand mirror. There were bathroom mirrors in the apartments I had rented here, but they were small, filthy, cracked, and blurry. This was the first time I had looked at myself so shamelessly.

I looked down at the dress. It hugged my waist and stomach like skin. I straightened my spine and felt like a new person. Could a simple dress really transform me? Wasn't beauty supposed to be skin deep?

Suddenly I froze. How did Genji know my size? How many weeks did it take to order things from Japan? Two weeks at least? And we had met less than forty-eight hours ago. There was no way he could have ordered the dress after we met. He must have bought the clothes before I arrived. How could he have possibly predicted that I'd be his roommate?

I opened the door. Genji waited outside, holding the jacket open. I stepped into it, then turned around, arms raised like a grown chick testing its wings before the first flight.

Genji reached out his hand and tucked the label into the back of my neck. I stood still. This tender gesture was too much. His fingers lingered on my skin, then I felt his wet, meaty cheek on my nape.

"My moon fairy, you're home again. Genji dream about you many years, many years."

My inside was knotted all over again, tighter than ever.

"Ah, Miss Wan moved again. I'd better use a pencil this time. Where's Rego Park?"

I watched Professor Dickey cross out my old address in her book and pencil in the new one. Every gesture was dramatic and exaggerated as if she were on a stage. Her green hat bobbed as she scrawled. How she loved hats! Wide- and narrow-brimmed, feathered, beaded, flowered, embroidered, felt, velvet, leather, straw ... she never wore the same hat twice. With her dramatic hats and southern drawl, she strutted around like a peacock. People in the department called her the Texas Bitch, behind her back, of course. No one would dare confront her. She could quickly change from a diva into a beast at the slightest provocation. She wasn't talking to any of the faculty in the department because she had had ugly fights with each of them. No student would choose her as their advisor because she was famous on campus for her eruptions of anger and insults. I was her only advisee. For some reason we got along. She had waived my tuition when I had no more money to continue my M.A. Instead of kicking me out when I nodded off in her evening class, she brought chocolate bars and brownies to keep me awake. Once she handed me a box of clothing she had worn when she was young. They were flashy with loud colors, lacy collars, and flowing skirts, and were three sizes too big. I dragged them with me from one apartment to another, not daring to throw them away. Her tenderness was flattering and disturbing at the same time. What did she see in me that attracted her attention?

I described the area, my apartment, and my landlord.

"Sounds like a good deal," she said. But her penciled eyebrows rose like a cat on alert.

"Is he a waiter, a cook?"

"He makes sushi at Little Sakura, and he used to be a banquet chef at a place in Central Park, something like green tavern, red tavern?"

"Oh my God, you don't mean Tavern on the Green!"

"Yes, Tavern on the Green. He showed me the pictures of the banquets he made, the bald eagle and Eiffel Tower carved out of ice, the animals and plants. When he makes breakfasts and dinners for us, he turns everything into the shapes of flowers and birds."

"Us?" Her eyes opened wide. "Are you telling me that a banquet chef from Tavern on the Green cooks for a tenant?"

"He wants me to feel at home," I said quickly, my face burning.

Professor Dickey tapped her painted nails on the desk. She didn't look convinced. On my way to her office, I had seriously considered not talking to her about Genji, his elaborate dinners and gifts, his crying on my neck, his calling me moon fairy and mother. But I had to now. She'd say that I was crazy to share a room with a pervert. She would order me to move out immediately.

I couldn't blame her if she did. Everything seemed bizarre and suspicious, a young woman sharing a room with a middle-aged chef from Japan, who suffered violent mood swings.

Professor Dickey broke the silence. "So, why does a big-time chef from Tavern on the Green work at Little Samurai?"

"Little Sakura, Professor Dickey."

She shrugged. "How's the food there?"

I shrugged, too. I had never tasted Japanese food. At home, Genji cooked only Chinese, Italian, and French. Peng loved eating out, but had always avoided Japanese restaurants. I worked seven days a week in Chinese restaurants and tried to eat there as often as I could to save money. I was trying to put away two hundred dollars a month, after rent, transportation, food, textbooks, and other necessities. Some of my savings went to my parents and grandparents in China, and the rest to my emergency fund.

Her green eyes sparkled suddenly. "I know what we should do. Let's go eat there sometime soon. I'm curious about your new landlord. Would you reserve a table for two? It'll be my treat."

"Nice outfit. Made in Japan, eh?"

Peng tugged at the label in the back of my nape. His fingers were rough, full of anger. We were sitting inside the Sichuan Palace on Queens Boulevard. I called Peng two weeks after I moved into Genji's apartment and he came over immediately and took me there. He seemed to be a frequent customer. The owner and waitresses welcomed him like a prince.

"Haven't seen you at school lately," he asked.

"I've been busy."

"Busy with whom? Your landlord? He got you this?" He yanked my jacket.

I turned away from his burning eyes.

"Hmm, what happened to Miss Mighty Principle? I thought she did not take things from men."

My face burnt with shame. How could I explain myself? Peng had taken me to a New Jersey mall soon after we started dating. "Buy whatever you want," he said, waving his gold American Express card. I stood still in the sea of glittering things, feeling like Alice who had just fallen through the hole and arrived in another world. "Go ahead, Virgin, don't be shy," said Peng, giving me a gentle nudge toward the nearest stand. I peeked at the price of the black lace lingerie. My eyes popped. One tiny flimsy thing would cost me a week's salary. In China, I'd have to work a whole year for this item. I ran to the door, feeling sick. "Why aren't you picking out clothes?" Peng asked as he followed in bewilderment. A security guard came and asked if everything was o.k. "Just need some fresh air," I said. He nodded. "Lots of new immigrants had the same reaction when they first stepped in the mall," he said. Peng got red in the face and before he opened his mouth, I dragged him to his car and made him take me home. The next day, he brought me a bottle of Chanel N° 5, Shishedo moisturizer and facial scrub, jewelry, and a Ralph Lauren dress. I refused to take them, citing my mom's warning: all gifts from men are bombs coated with sugar.

"But you're in America now, my Communist Virgin." Peng laughed.

I told him it was against my principles. Period.

Peng drank Tsingtao silently. I looked at his sullen face and knew that I owed him an explanation, no matter how lame it was.

"Please, don't be mad. It's a different situation. He went crazy when I said no. You should have seen his face when he lit a match to set fire to the clothes and burn down the building."

"That's good to know. Should I adopt the same policy from now on?" He grabbed my wrist.

"Don't be an ass." I slapped his hand off.

My stomach tightened with guilt and remorse. He had a reason to be angry. If I could accept Genji's gifts, why couldn't I take his? If Peng's gifts were sugar-coated bombs, what about Genji's? Peng's intention was clear: he wanted to get me into bed. But I wasn't sure about Genji. He let me live in his apartment for token rent, and showered me with elaborate gifts and meals every day. Yet he had never showed any interest in a sexual relationship. True, he had cried on my shoulder like a baby and called me Mama. But there was nothing sexual about it at all. I might be dumb with men, but a few months of dating Peng did give me some clues about what men wanted from a woman. Getting into my pants was the last thing on Genji's mind. Was it why I felt I could accept his gifts?

I sighed. How could I explain all this to Peng? I should have taken off Genji's dress before coming to the restaurant to meet Peng. I wasn't trying to aggravate him on purpose; I simply forgot. I hadn't seen him for two weeks, and I had really missed him. During that time, the dress and jacket had become part of my new identity. They had transformed me from a toad into a swan. That was what everybody had told me. Beauty was addictive.

I took Peng's hand and stroked the jagged scar where his pinky was missing. It looked as if it had been mangled and torn by a machine. What kind of pain had he gone through? What secret? My heart was filled with tenderness.

"Genji is my landlord, and you're my . . ."

"Landlord, what kind of landlord? Forcing gifts on his tenant? How much did you say your rent is? One hundred fifty dollars? Do you know how much he pays for his apartment? Do you want to know? Eight hundred a month at least. And he pays your electricity and phone bills? What a landlord! How can I find such a deal?"

I sipped tea to keep my mouth shut. Peng had become a different person since I moved into Genji's place. What would he say if he knew about our room arrangement and the no-lock deal?

"Are you his tenant or his kept girl?"

I dropped his hand and turned away. I should have slapped his face, or given him a tongue lashing, but how could I defend myself?

He grabbed my shoulders and turned me to face him. "I'm sorry, sweetie. I didn't mean to insult you. I'm just worried. A girl like you sharing a room with a Japanese sex . . ."

"Please, you haven't even met him. He's quiet and polite and very kind to me. Yes, he likes to give me things, but not for sex. Don't ask what he wants from me. I don't know. I don't think he knows himself. He's just lonely, and who's not? We live in New York, for heaven's sake. What am I supposed to do, anyway? Move back to the filthy basement? How come you never worried about me sharing a rat hole with three men?"

"How do you know I wasn't worried?" he growled, grinding his teeth. "I kept a close eye on those filthy waiters. Had they dared to touch you, I was ready to beat them to a pulp. Wan Li," he tightened his grip on my shoulders, "I've asked many times, and I hope you'll take me seriously this time. Move into my place. I have an extra bedroom, and you can live there for free, or pay whatever you can if it makes you feel better. Let me take care of you. Let me make your life easier, please? I won't bother you, I swear to God. It's a gift, like Genji's, and I'll never threaten you with fire."

One by one I unlocked his fingers.

"You want me to be *your* kept girl then," I murmured.

"No. I want to take you home. I want you to be my wife, you fool!"

I felt faint, my ears buzzing with strange noises. What was going on these days? Suddenly all these offers and promises heaped on me. When Peng asked me out, everyone, including myself, thought it was a joke.

"Why?" I asked in a stupor.

He laughed sadly. "You've asked that question so many times. I love you. Can't you see?"

"But why?' I insisted.

"Because you're my Communist Virgin."

I blushed. He had stopped calling me that after he discovered that it was for real. When Jeanne Shin gave me that nickname, she had no idea she had accidentally put her finger on two secrets: I had joined the Communist Party at sixteen, and I had never been with a man. As the nickname spread on campus, I became more and more nervous. I had lied to get into America, and if someone reported me to the INS, I'd be sent to prison and deported. Soon, I realized that nobody had taken it at face value. People called me "Communist Virgin" because I came from Red China, still dressed like a peasant, and still looked uptight and awkward. Peng had gotten a big kick out of it, especially when he called me it in public and my face turned red. He had found it cute and endearing, until the truth came out.

It happened on my twenty-sixth birthday. When Peng discovered that we were born on the same day, same month, and same year, the year of the dragon, he went wild. "I knew there was something special between us the moment we met," he shouted, and insisted on celebrating our birthdays together at his sister's restaurant. She closed her place for the evening and gave us a banquet. After the banquet, Peng invited me to his place for a drink. He had made the offer many times before. This time, I agreed. He had been so happy at dinner, and I didn't have the heart to disappoint him. He took me straight to his basement bar. Unlike the basements I had lived in, this one smelled good and looked slick. It was equipped with leather-topped swirling stools, laser lights, and a state-of-the-art acoustic system. He put on a CD. "*A Love Supreme,* my favorite," he said as he poured a glass of orange juice and slid it toward me. He poured more orange juice into another glass, then added vodka. "Screwdriver," he said loudly, taking a sip. "Perfect with Coltrane."

We drank and talked. Somehow my face started burning. Hives broke out everywhere. "You're not allergic to my orange juice, are you?" Peng teased. "I think I need to lie down. I think I drank your screwdriver by mistake," I croaked, pointing at the two drinks that looked exactly the same. My throat started swelling too. Peng carried me to his bed upstairs. He found some old Benadryl, thrust one into my mouth, and gave me water. He held my hand until my breathing became normal. Then he lay down next to me, scooping my head on his chest. I listened to his heartbeat. It was beating wildly inside. We had never been this close. He started kissing, first my hair, then forehead, nose, cheeks. When his lips enclosed mine, my whole body started burning as if I were having another allergy attack. His tongue slipped in between my teeth, timidly at first, then charged with force. The bed had suddenly disappeared under me and I was sinking, sinking. Peng unbuttoned my shirt, cupped my breasts with his hands.

"You have the most beautiful breasts," he cried. I cringed when he held my nipple in his mouth.

"Did I hurt you?"

I shook my head. I had no words for what I was feeling. It was overwhelming, like being tossed into the eye of a typhoon. He resumed kissing, moving down to my stomach, belly button. I became an uprooted tree, tossing about in the wind. I waved my arms to grab at things, but there was only air. I got something. It was his hair. I pulled. It made him kiss harder.

Suddenly I froze. Peng had just unzipped my jeans.

"Are you nervous?" he looked up, his eyes burning with passion.

I croaked. I couldn't say a word.

"Oh, come on," he laughed. "Now don't tell me you're a virgin. You've been with men, you must have."

I shook my head. *I was a virgin, a real virgin,* I wanted to scream, but was too ashamed. I remembered what he had called me on our first day. Slut.

This time he froze, staring at me in utter disbelief. He tried to laugh again. "You can be really funny, Wan Li. But it's bad timing. There's no such a thing as a virgin nowadays. Not in New York."

I was suddenly aware of my nakedness.

"Please don't stare at me like this," I cried silently. "I'm not a monster. Please take me and make me normal like every other girl!"

"Oh, my God," he moaned, kneeling at my side, burying his head in my stomach. "What have I done? What have I done?"

I struggled to sit up, covering my chest with my arms. My shirt was under Peng's knees. He embraced my waist, face buried in my lap.

"I'm sorry," I touched his hair. It was wily like mine. Strands of gray hair glistened at his temples.

He sat up, cupped my face with his hands. "*I am* sorry. I should have known. I knew you were different from the others. But I didn't expect this. Who would have believed? I almost ruined a rare treasure. Will you forgive me?"

I closed my eyes, not knowing what to say. Growing up in China, I'd been told that since I wasn't good looking, my virtue and brains would be my best assets. In New York, however, everyone talked about how many lovers they'd had like they were counting their trophies. *Virgin* became a taboo word, a curse, the butt of a joke. Most of the time, I felt like a dinosaur, a living fossil.

He pulled out my shirt from under his knees and draped it on my shoulders. "I want to take you home someday," he said solemnly, before he stood up and walked out of the room, closing the door behind him.

"I don't know why," Peng whispered, his eyes half-closed as if he were sleep-talking. "I wanted to take you home the moment I saw you, sitting on the library bench by yourself, so quiet and forlorn, so out of place, yet so lovely. You looked like an alien, an angel from the sky. I'm not laughing at you. Not at all. You looked exactly like the virgin I had been seeing in my dreams, only I dare not say it, because such a thing no longer exists in this ocean of desire, on my island at least, where I grew up, or on this island, Manhattan." He opened his eyes, looked around, looked at me as if I were a stranger. "When I discovered your secret, I couldn't believe my luck. I wanted to take you home right away, to bring you to my mother. But I was afraid that you would vanish if I brought you out into the open air, like the ancient terra-cotta soldiers. I was afraid of your eyes. I see my ugliness, my silly past."

"No, I'm the ugly one," I said. How could he be scared of me? How could anyone?

"Shhh." He put his fingers on my lips. "Trust me. I've seen women. You don't know how beautiful you are. And that's the way it should be, isn't it? If jade knows its own value, it's no longer jade."

He paused. A wave of sorrow passed his face. "But the jade is soiled. It is soiled by a Jap . . ."

"I'm still a virgin," I cried, but my words stuck in my mouth as I remembered my drawer filled with bracelets, necklaces, handbags, earrings, broaches, gold, silver, pearl, jade, all Genji's gifts that had somehow settled in my room. I was indeed soiled, no matter what excuses I'd given myself. My body started itching. The orange dress was suddenly growing thorns from inside.

"Wan Li," he called, holding my hand.

I remembered the way he said our names the first time: *Peng Chen Wan Li, we belong to each other.* I had brushed it off as a dandy's flirt. Why couldn't I believe that he loved me? Did he really? What was it like to not be a virgin? Part of me wanted him to invite me back to his place and give me another screwdriver. But I didn't know how. Peng seemed more respectful, but also more distant since he discovered my secret, treating me like a queen, a doll made of fragile jade. No more crude jokes, no more groping or licentious words. I used to get annoyed, but now I missed them. Alone in my bed, I had all kinds of fantasies based on the memories of our birthday night. Once face-to-face with him, everything vanished, with only the residue of anxiety and helplessness lingering. My life seemed to be a bottomless well without water or light. The day I moved out of Jeanne Shin's sublet, she called me *si mian geda,* a lump of dough that had died somewhere in the process of fermentation and had no hope of ever rising again. *What could you expect from a product of the Cultural Revolution?* she yelled as I dragged my last bags out the door.

"Wan Li," Peng said again. "Come home with me, before it's too late."

I shook my head, hating myself. What was wrong with me? What was it like to fall in love? What was it like to stop fighting and let go? And what was I fighting for?

His face went ashen. For a split second, I almost told him that I was an ex-Chinese Communist, his government's number one enemy. If we got married, he could forget about his ambition to become a senator in Taiwan.

"Not till I find my own place," I said slowly.

"At any cost?"

"At any cost."

Peng opened his mouth and cried. He cried like a baby with a broken heart. I pressed my palm against his temple, his scar. People in the restaurant gawked, but we couldn't care less. Amid his wailing, I suddenly realized what I'd been searching for: an equal footing with Peng, with everyone else in this country. But before I settled down in a place I could call home, I could easily become a charity case, a "kept girl," and I would have no ground to demand equality. Peng would laugh if I told him, and remind me that we were already in the land of freedom and equality. You are so cute, so brainwashed by the communist doctrine that you can't even see what you have, he'd say.

"I just want to know, before I go. Do you love me?"

I closed my eyes. His question had lifted a gate and I was flooded from within. Nobody had ever asked me this question, no one had said "I love you" to me till Peng came along. And I had never said the words to anyone, not even to my parents. I didn't know how.

"I've never been with a man. You are my first, probably my last." My voice started choking. "I wish I were more experienced. I wish I were not this ignorant."

"Oh, my virgin." Peng took my hand and pressed it against his lips for a long time. "Let me know when you figure it out. Take your time, but not too long. Call when you need help, please? I know a few things about Japanese. I grew up watching them swarm over our island chasing teenage girls. Now they go to the mainland, and Thailand, of course. I'm not saying Genji is one of those sex-crazed men. But if I were you, I'd ask myself questions. Nothing is free in this world. Nothing!"

He stood up to leave.

"Don't worry. I'm an iron maiden from Red China," I said to his back.

He turned and gave me the saddest smile I'd ever seen. I tried to chuckle at my own joke, but my voice came out as broken sobs.

"Why peel skin like that, Miss Wan?"

I jumped from the couch. Genji stood at the door holding a takeout container. He was still in his chef uniform, a white bandana wrapped around his shiny scalp. He stared at my bloody toes in disbelief.

I hid my feet between the cushions. "It's only eleven o'clock, Genji. Did the restaurant close early today? You're not sick, are you? You look pale."

"Genji O.K., just stomach pain, probably from fish, last night leftover. Bad habit, can't throw away food. Mrs. Kao say Genji must go home and rest. Tomorrow very busy day, three banquets for lunch. But tell Genji why Miss Wan hurt herself?"

He knelt down and held my feet in his palms. He had rough fingers, callused from holding knives six days a week, twelve hours a day.

"I don't know." I pulled my bleeding toes out of his grip and hid them under my buttocks, wishing I could throw the book I had been reading over the dead skin on the floor. This thing had started after I moved in. Whenever I sat down on Genji's couch, I would pick at my toes, peeling skin layer after layer, digging into the grooves around the nails with a pocketknife. My feet looked as if I had just escaped from a torture chamber. And I always forgot to clean up, leaving yellow flakes all over the couch and the floor. Genji had several talks with me, and I had promised him never to do it again, or at least to clean up after myself.

"Let me do it," I said, jumping up from the couch. Genji had already swept the skin flakes into his palm with a piece of paper.

"Can I make some tea for you?" I offered, my heart burning with shame. I couldn't see his face, but the top of his scalp was grayish pale. He was not well.

"That nice." He sighed as he sank down on the couch, his hand in a fist, holding my skin flakes inside.

I was taken aback. He'd never let me do any chores since I had moved in, not even my own laundry. "Miss Wan must keep hands clean and smooth," he'd say and wave me away if I tried to grab the sponge or the broom. "Genji old man, rough hands O.K., no problem." After a while, I just read or watched TV as Genji cleaned and cooked.

I got up and brought him the garbage can and a wet hand towel. I returned to the kitchen to boil water. It felt good to be useful again. As I watched the gas flame licking the bottom of the kettle, it occurred to me how uneasy I felt to be waited on like a princess.

Genji rested his head on the couch, eyes closed. I put his tea on the coffee table. "Come sit with Genji." He patted the leather.

I sat down. He nestled his head against my shoulder and inhaled deeply.

"Ah, Miss Wan smell good. Genji feel like home, like rest with Mama."

I touched his scalp lightly. It was soft, like a baby's cheek. Genji nestled closer, his husky body curling into a ball.

"Mama, Mama," he moaned.

I held my breath. It's O.K., it's O.K., he's just sick and wants his mommy. "Where's your mother?" I asked.

"Gone, long gone, no more Mama."

"Poor Genji." I held his head in my palms. How many times did he shave each day to keep his scalp so smooth? "Why Genji not get married or find a girlfriend in America?"

"No more girlfriend for Genji," he cried, hitting his chest with his fists. "Genji heart broke. Girlfriend die, motor accident, Tokyo. Oh, my moon fairy."

"That's terrible. I'm so sorry, so sorry."

"Seven years. Genji can't forget. Love too much. Genji lonely, Genji homesick. Who help Genji?"

He was writhing under my feet. I slid on the floor to hold him. His pain was contagious. My nose and eyes felt swollen, but I didn't want to cry. Once I started, it'd be all over. I wanted to pick up the phone and dial Peng's number. Had I known I would miss him this painfully . . .

"Please, Genji, don't give up. Never give up. You'll find somebody just like your old girlfriend, perhaps even better. O.K.? I know some girl from Shanghai, nice and pretty. Do you like Chinese?"

I was thinking of Jeanne Shin. She and Genji would make a good couple.

"Genji loves Chinese," he mumbled. "Miss Wan nice, smell nice, look nice, heart nice, just like Genji's mama, like Genji's moon fairy."

I patted him gently on the back, pretending I hadn't heard what he'd just said. Soon he started snoring lightly, his breath sour like over-fermented rice. How strange to have a landlord in my lap like an infant, a sick animal! I looked down. My feet had stopped bleeding. It was 2:00 a.m., and the air was chilly. I wanted to get a blanket, but didn't want to disturb Genji. Even though he was the sick one, his body was still warmer. I nudged closer. Something was stirring in my stomach. It was hunger. I was longing for Peng, longing to hug him the way I hugged Genji. How wonderful it was to give! And to take. To take and give with grace, not with guilt or shame. Did I still have hope? Would I someday stop fighting myself, and stop fighting Peng? Would I ever learn to accept his love and love back?

Old Heaven, I prayed silently, let this lump of unleavened dough rise someday!

"Would you please bring us the menu?" asked Professor Dickey as Mrs. Kao put down tea and ice water on our table. "We've been sitting here for ages."

I avoided Mrs. Kao's eyes. She didn't need to serve at all. Her waitress could handle us easily, since we were the only early birds in the restaurant. She was treating us as Genji's guests.

"You don't need a menu. Our chef is making a special dinner for you."

"Oh, oh, how terribly sweet!" cried Professor Dickey. She leaned over and whispered in my ear: "Is it a kind of scam? How much will it cost us, you think?"

"Not a penny! You're our chef's guests," Mrs. Kao said.

Her voice was polite, controlled, but the contempt seeped through. My face was burning. I stole a glance at Genji who was spreading rice on a sheet of seaweed. His hands danced on the counter with grace.

"Oh my," exclaimed Professor Dickey, "what have I done to deserve this honor?"

"Because you're Miss Wan's guest. Isn't it right, Genji?"

Genji was sharpening his knife. He waved, his gold tooth glittering in the soft light.

I turned my head away as soon as our eyes touched. We had been avoiding each other's eyes since the night we slept on the living room floor, even though nothing had happened. I woke up alone on Genji's couch the next morning smelling fried eggs and pancakes in the kitchen. We ate in silence. Genji seemed to have recovered from his stomach pain, but he looked flustered, as if he had been caught wetting his bed. He brightened up only when I told him my professor wanted to eat his food at Little Sakura.

Professor Dickey gave me a nasty look as if I had robbed her pleasure at being my patron. I wanted to tell her I had nothing to do with this. I just booked a table as she had told me. But I kept my mouth shut. The more I explained, the angrier she'd get.

"So what's for dinner?" she asked, looking slighted.

"It's a surprise. Have some tea and relax. The appetizer will arrive soon." Mrs. Kao poured green tea into our cups and left.

I played with the jade bracelet around my wrist. I had stopped wearing Genji's clothes since Peng and I broke up. But today I put on the bracelet Genji had given me, a gesture to thank him for what he was doing for me. He had started preparing for the dinner a week before.

What would Peng say if he saw this? But it wouldn't happen. Peng hadn't called for twenty days. He kept his promise. He had given me up. Was he seeing someone else? Should I call him? What excuse could I use? I was settling down in Genji's "paradise," getting used to his comfort and luxury. But could I really call the place my home?

Mrs. Kao brought Age Dashi Tofu, edamame, and soft shell crabs. The bean curd's tender yellow crust made the soy pods enticingly green. I savored the colors with my eyes when Professor Dickey plucked a pod with her fingers and popped it into her mouth.

"What is this? So fibery. Hard to swallow." She chewed like a horse.

"Soybeans. You eat the inside only, like this."

I opened a pod and revealed the plump beans.

"Ha, I guess I'm just another Western barbarian." Laughing, she forked a piece of tofu.

"Hmm, not bad, not bad at all, the texture, the flavor. I hate tofu, so bland and rubbery. But this, hmm, your landlord is a good cook indeed." She sucked air to cool her tongue, and before she swallowed it, she stabbed her fork into the belly of the crab.

"Such a tiny crab. How do you peel the shell?"

I laughed. "You can eat its shell. It's soft. Try it."

But Professor Dickey hardly needed any encouragement. She jammed the whole thing in. Claw tips jerked between her lips as if it were being eaten alive.

"Hmm, I like this the best, crispy like fish and chips! Hey, guess what I've found out about your landlord. You won't believe it." She leaned over.

I looked at her anxiously. Professor Dickey thought she was whispering, but even her softest whisper came out louder than my shout. We were close to Genji's counter, no more than ten feet away, where he was making us an elaborate dinner, for free. Out of his own pocket, most likely; Mrs. Kao is a frugal owner. Did she have to talk about Genji right now? I had no idea what she was going to say. But from the glee in her green eyes, it couldn't be good news. I was very fond of Professor Dickey, and grateful for what she had done for me, but at that moment, I wished I could have gagged her big, thin-lipped mouth with a napkin.

"Your landlord belonged to some underground organization in Tokyo. He must have done something pretty bad; they've been after him for the past seven years, the cops, his gang bosses. They got his girlfriend, I think. She died in what appeared to be an accident. But no accident is an accident, know what I mean? He escaped to America and worked in New Jersey and Connecticut before Tavern on the Green. They must have tracked him down there. That's why he had to quit and why he hides in this no-name joint."

She paused, checked my face for reaction. I sat motionless. The tofu in my mouth was turning into chalk. Why was she telling me this? Where on earth did she get this?

"I did some investigation." She tapped her crimson nails on the formica table. "Not that hard nowadays. A few hours on my computer, a few phone calls, a pleasant afternoon tea at Tavern on the Green, and I pieced the puzzle together."

I stared. Had she investigated me? Had she discovered my secret membership in the Chinese Communist Party?

She knocked on the table with her knuckles.

"Hello, anyone home? Did you hear what I just said? Your nice, generous landlord is a gangster, got it?"

"Chasing the Dragon," said Mrs. Kao, her face a mile long as she dropped a plate between us with a thud. A row of eel wrapped with rice and avocado zigzagged through the pickled ginger, shredded turnip, and horseradish. "Enjoy, and don't let the bones get stuck in your throat." She gave me a piercing look before she turned away.

"Got it?" Professor Dickey snatched the head off the dragon and threw it into her mouth, her eyes biting me.

There was a loud buzz in my ears, and my temples pulsed furiously. Another migraine was on its way. How could I connect the smiling, moaning-like-an-infant landlord with a gun-waving gangster?

"Wake up, girl, you're living with a mobster."

I shushed her, shooting a sideways glance at Genji. The smile had receded from his face, and his cheeks suddenly collapsed, empty like a winter beach. He continued making a sushi roll, but his hands moved like a robot. Oh, what had I done?

"Hey, don't stare at me like this. You need to look for a new place, now."

"What for?" I clung to the table.

Professor Dickey looked at me with pity. "It's none of my business, but since you are in my program with my scholarship, I need to know. You're not sleeping with a gangster, are you?"

"Hell, no," I said, pressing my fists against my temples.

"No offense, please. Just checking for your safety. You're alone in America. Your family is in China. This is a great country, America, full of opportunities, but full of dangers, too. Loonies and perverts everywhere. You're a smart girl, but gullible. Some advice from an experienced woman won't hurt you. Perhaps this is what you like? Perhaps you find it exciting, no? Quite a mix, I have to say, a top-notch chef and an ex-mobster on the run. And the perfect victim, young, nice-looking fresh meat from a third-world country, intelligent with a touch of innocence."

I hiccupped violently.

"Oh, dear, drink some water, and eat a piece of the dragon. It'll open up your channel. Ah, here comes the entrée. We seem to have a new waitress. She has a nice smile. Look at this food. How magnificent! The color, the shape, arranged so neatly like a checkers game. Come, let's eat, drink, and enjoy the dinner. It's not every day we can taste food prepared by a banquet chef from Tavern on the Green."

Our table was covered with food, but I couldn't eat a morsel. The only thought I had was how to shut Professor Dickey's mouth, how I could flee. Finally she noticed my agony and asked if I had a migraine. I nodded. She sighed over the leftovers and called the waitress for boxes.

"Hope I'm not spoiling the girls," she muttered as she pulled out a five-dollar bill from her wallet.

Mrs. Kao chased us to the door, the bill pinched between her fingers.

"This is not necessary, Professor."

"Suit yourself." She shrugged and put the money back into her purse.

I stared at the ground. Would Mrs. Kao force the waitress to return the ten-dollar note I had slipped into her hand on my way out? This would be the worst insult one could dish out to a Chinese, worse than spitting in the face or punching in the stomach.

"Meet me outside your building in an hour, Miss Wan," Mrs. Kao said to my back, her voice sub-zero. "We need to talk."

At 11:00 p.m, Mrs. Kao arrived in her Buick. Genji got out and passed by me without a word.

I got into her car, trembling with fear and guilt. What was she going to tell me? Was Genji really an ex-gangster? Was he mad at me? Would he throw me out of his place? I wouldn't blame him if he did, but where could I go after this?

She pulled her car over in front of a Chinese restaurant. I wiped sweat off my forehead and followed her inside. People greeted her like they were old friends as we passed by tables. She nodded and chanted greetings in her melodious Taiwanese dialect, her shoulders relaxed as if she had arrived home. A young waitress with dancing eyebrows and bright eyes rushed over. She greeted Mrs. Kao first, then gave me a wry smile.

"Long time no see, Miss Wan."

I recognized the waitress and the restaurant. Mrs. Kao had taken me to Peng's favorite place, Village Wok, a place that specialized in Taiwanese cuisine. Her name was Connie. She and Peng had come from the same village on the island. I had once asked Peng why he didn't go out with her. They seemed to be so fond of each other, flirting and laughing heartily without reservation. Peng just shook his head and said that she was like a sister.

Connie took us to a corner table and walked back to the kitchen. Soon she brought us dish after dish: stinky tofu, fried intestines, roasted anchovies, lamb stew, hollow-hearted green.

Apparently she knew what Mrs. Kao wanted. Mrs. Kao filled my plate with food, and waved at me to eat. I sat still, hands between my knees. The strong smell of the tofu was churning my stomach. It used to be my favorite snack. My grandma even nicknamed me the Stinky Tofu Princess, as I always begged her for a dish of the sizzling hot, smelly delicacy from street vendors.

"What do you think you are, a princess?" Mrs. Kao exploded finally, stabbing into the intestines with her chopsticks. "You think you're better than Genji just because you lick some white professor's ass? Who gave you the right to bring that old bitch in to insult my chef, right in front of his face, in front of my face? Have they stuffed so much shit up your ass that you lost your heart? Are you Chinese or a devil's running dog?"

I bowed my head. Even if I had ten thousand mouths, I couldn't have defended myself.

"Say something! I haven't chopped off your tongue, for heaven's sake," Mrs. Kao hissed, attacking the dishes furiously but not getting anything. The other customers were staring. Connie was on the phone near the kitchen, glancing at us discreetly. Was she reporting the scene to Peng? Amid the murmur of the dialect I couldn't comprehend, I suddenly understood why Peng kept coming back to this place in Flushing. He was homesick, like Mrs. Kao, like me.

I started weeping. Tears splattered into my rice bowl. I heard Connie gasping, "Oh my God, she's crying!" So she *was* talking to Peng. Would he change his mind and call me? Why had he suddenly become so stubborn and proud, like me? I wiped my face with my sleeve. My paper napkin had become soggy with tears. Mrs. Kao handed me hers with a growl.

"Not here, for heaven's sake! You've disgraced my restaurant and now you have to make a mess here? This is the only place I can relax, O.K.? So stop this nonsense, now!"

I dabbed my cheeks with her napkin.

"I knew this would end badly, I knew," she sighed. "I warned him, many times, but he wouldn't listen. His heart is set. Predestined, all predestined, what else could it be?"

"Whose heart?" I looked up from my napkin. For a second, I thought she was talking about Peng, then realized they had never met. So it had to be Genji. Why was his heart set for me? And what did it all have to do with predestination?

"Thank Heaven and Earth, Miss Wan finally opens her jade mouth," she mocked. "You know exactly who I'm talking about. He fell for you hard, the moment you walked in my door. Why? Only God knows! All the girls I have introduced him to, more beautiful and sophisticated than you, each one of them, but no, he wouldn't give them a second look. I don't know how you did it. He worships you like a goddess. Must have owed you big in his previous life. How else can I explain it? He'd have died for you. You must know. You're not stupid, with all the books you've read. But what have you given him in return? Nothing but grief."

The air became tense again. I felt overwhelmed as if I had once again walked into that New Jersey mall for the first time. I had not a single clue of Genji's feelings toward me. True, our relationship went beyond the normal landlord-tenant relationship, with the token rent I paid him, the gifts and affection he heaped on me, and our moments of intimacy, hugging, and crying in each other's arms. But who was normal? Just look at me, a dumb virgin at twenty-six, my only boyfriend left me because of my stubborn ignorance. What was the use of my education if I couldn't read the most basic book of life—love?

"Genji told me he lost both his mother and fiancée," I said.

She scrutinized my face with an odd expression. "True, you look exactly like his girlfriend. He showed me her photo. Spooky, isn't it? He said you sound and smell like his mother. Now that's a bit of a stretch."

"Why did he come to America?" I wanted to ask if he was a gangster, but I knew better.

"Why did you come? And why did I?" she snapped. "Who wants to leave home and start a life from zero? You sound like one of those white demons. They always ask: how did you come to America and why! As if I came here to steal their land or something. As if they'd done me a huge favor to let me work my ass off keeping my restaurant open with a huge debt. Oh, you're making me mad again!"

I touched her trembling hand. "I'm sorry, Mrs. Kao. I didn't mean it that way."

She exhaled and gazed at me long and hard.

"Everyone makes mistakes in life: you, me, him, her. I don't know what Genji did in Japan. I don't care. All I can tell you is this: Genji is a good man. I give you my personal guarantee."

I looked up at Mrs. Kao. Her face was tender, motherly.

"What do you want from life? Really, when it comes to the bottom line, isn't it all about finding a good man or a good woman? Life is hard. You need friends, love, and family, more so if you live away from home. When it comes to family and love, you can't find anyone better than Genji." She paused, waiting for her words to sink in. "He's the best chef in town. I say best not only because he has great skills, he also has a big heart, as big as the sea. Why do I need to babble on? You live with him, you should know. Besides, he has a green card. Just that alone . . . "

"I have a boyfriend already, Mrs. Kao."

Light broke into my heart as the words came out. Things seemed clear all of a sudden. *I love Peng. I will call him when I get home. We will start over on new ground.*

"Since when did you have a boyfriend, or friends?" she sneered. "How many phone calls do you get a day? Zero!"

Not true. Jeanne Shin had visited me a few weeks ago. But I said nothing to repute Mrs. Kao. I wasn't sure why Jeanne Shin had come over the day after Peng and I broke up. I thought she had wanted to comfort me. But she stayed less than ten minutes, didn't even sit down on Genji's comfortable couch and open her chatterbox like usual. She just looked around and showed great interest in the apartment setting, how Genji and I shared the space. I had urged her to stay longer. It was Genji's day off. He was out shopping for an elaborate meal. Apart from wanting her company, I was hoping secretly that she and Genji would like each other and start dating. But Jeanne Shin rushed away.

How did Mrs. Kao know that I rarely had phone calls? Was she spying on me? Or was it Genji?

"I don't need to follow you around or bug your phone to find out." She waved her hand. "It's written on your face, Miss Wan. You've never been popular at home or at school. You were born a loner, doomed to suffer. I know because," she paused, "because I'm a loner myself."

I wished I could crawl into her arms and cry. She knew me, this shrewd restaurant owner, and recognized me as a bird of the same feather. Perhaps I could tell her some of my secrets, ask her what to do about Peng.

"How long have you been in New York? Ten months, Genji told me that. Yet you still don't wear makeup, your earlobes are yet to be pierced. I've seen people from the mainland, young, middle-aged, old. Yes, they're stubborn and awkward, but they adapt quickly. They want a good life in America just like everybody else. But you, what do you want from life? Look at your face, tight and closed-in like a beetle trapped in amber. You look like a virgin from the last century. My God, don't tell me you are one!" she gasped.

Part of me wanted to flee from the shame, and the other half wanted to hear what else she had to say about my past and future. What did I want from life? In China, I had really believed I was marching toward a communist paradise with my fellow countrypeople, sacrificing everything we had along the way. Then I came to New York in search of a new paradise, a real one, but only drifted from one basement to another until I ended at Genji's place. And I was still not happy. Worse, I was making people around me unhappy.

Mrs. Kao sighed loudly.

"I should have trusted my instinct. But who would have believed . . . That's why I didn't want you to become Genji's roommate in the first place. You are too much alike, though his loneliness comes from a different place. He needs someone warm, outgoing, and practical, to tease him out of his shell."

I wanted to tell her that I'd done that. Genji could talk like a chatterbox. But something suddenly dawned on me.

"Is that why you tried to rent me your place for seventy-five dollars?"

She nodded.

"Is it your idea to find him a girlfriend through his apartment rental?

"It was stupid, O.K.?" She turned red. "I realized it as soon as he wanted you to be his roommate. I had thought a nice girl from Taiwan might cheer him up. And if he was happier, I would be able to keep him longer. You know how hard it is to keep a restaurant open in this town? Too many restaurants, too few decent cooks. Everyone tries to steal chefs from each other. Money helps, of course, if you can afford to pay a sky-high salary. But what could I offer? Debt that goes all the way to my nose? Genji dropped in my lap like a pancake from the sky. I still can't believe my good luck. I can't pay him a big salary, and he doesn't seem to care. I think he just wants to be left alone to mope over his mother and fiancée. It breaks my heart to see him sad like this. So I came up with this plan. You were the first one who answered the ad. When you walked in, I knew everything would be shattered, my hope for Genji's happiness, my plan to make my Little Sakura big. You, you're my ill star."

That's not fair, I protested silently. She couldn't have meant it seriously. I looked at Mrs. Kao, her tightly knit eyebrows over her burning eyes.

"I'm sorry. What can I do?" I said gently.

"Be his girlfriend."

Tears swelled my eyes. I fought not to let them fall.

"I cannot do that, Mrs. Kao."

"I know," she gave me a sad look.

"It has nothing to do with Genji. I really like him, and respect him, but I can't be his girlfriend, because I'm . . ." I wanted to say in

love, but she would just laugh. Was I capable of love? The realization
hit me hard. "I'm, I'm . . ." I stammered. The word "impotent" came
to the tip of my tongue, but I couldn't say it. The word belonged to
men. "I think I'm useless. I think I'm scared."

"I know."

She gazed at me with such pity that once more I wanted to col-
lapse on her shoulders and cry my eyes out. For some reason, her
pity didn't bother me the same way it did when Professor Dickey
had showered me with sympathy.

"She lives alone, that professor of yours, yes? I bet on my restaurant she does."

"I have no idea," I murmured, feeling ashamed. I knew practically
nothing about Professor Dickey, though I'd been seeing her two or
three times a week at school. Once I asked her where she lived, and
she stared at me as if I had asked her if she was constipated.

"She's a very smart woman, and was once beautiful. She had her
ambitions, wanted more than a normal, mundane family life. That's
good. But time went by fast. Before she knew it, she became a spinster."

I shuddered at her hinted warning. I felt I had already become a
spinster, a dinosaur fossil.

She picked up her chopsticks and piled more food on my plate.
"Let's eat. This is our fuel, our tie to . . ." She chewed the intestines
as she searched for the word. "Never mind. Health is the ground for
happiness, especially when you live away from home."

Suddenly she laughed. "That professor of yours, Dick, Prick? She
can eat! Such a rice bucket, a bottomless pit. Do you know how
much food Genji made for her? Enough for a troop. It almost made
her likeable. I love to watch people eat to their hearts' satisfaction."

We laughed together. Mrs. Kao had a very handsome face when
she wasn't frowning.

Before she let me out of her car in front of Genji's building, Mrs.
Kao said, "I'll leave the matter to you and Genji. Have a good night's
sleep and tomorrow morning you two can talk things out, O.K.?
Perhaps you can still live together as friends, for now."

I nodded and turned to leave when she grabbed my hand. "Stubborn girl, you'll have endless bitterness to eat, but you'll find your heart, and you'll do great things with it. Trust this old lady."

The apartment was dark and silent, the only warmth rising from Genji's body on the cot. If I walked a few steps forward, I'd fall into his world of comfort and longing, his scent of rice, fish, vinegar. "Go ahead and be his woman," I heard Mrs. Kao whisper at my ear. "He'll make your dream come true."

But I groped into my room, into my bed, pulled the blanket to my chin, shut my eyes tight. Sleep wouldn't come to me. What was my dream anyway? I had thought I knew. When I boarded the plane to New York, my heart had filled with sorrow and longing: my sorrow for the broken dream I had worked for with blind faith, my longing for a new promise, a new hope to fill the empty space. Nine months had passed, and I was still afloat, still lost between two worlds, two dreams, two men.

The bed suddenly became too big, the mattress too springy. I reached for the space between my legs. Nothing but a dry well. My whole body was a black cavity. What was Peng doing right now? Had he found a new girl? That shouldn't be a problem for him, since he was always surrounded by women.

I picked up the phone and dialed Peng's number. Someone picked it up after the first ring.

"Yelloooo."

It was Jeanne Shin's voice, her particular way of answering the phone. The sexy way, she had said. What was she doing at Peng's place at two-thirty in the morning?

"Hey, is that you, Communist Virgin?"

I held my breath. There was muffled stomping to rock music. A party was going on in the basement.

"I know it's you, Communist Virgin. I knew you'd call after the scene in the Village Wok. Listen, I'm not being a bitch, O.K.? But you had your chance, and now it's my turn. I've been living with him for almost a month. He's picking out a rock for me. You know what that means, right? Or do I need to explain? Never mind. He'll propose soon. Just a matter of time. Understand? We're going to get married and live happily forever. Can you do us a favor? Leave him alone. He's suffered enough for you. You should have seen his eyes after he found out there is only one bedroom in Genji's apartment. He has never talked about you since then. NEVER!"

The phone clicked, went dead.

I turned off the light. Darkness devoured me and my tears. I had lost him. For what? My illusion of paradise? Or my deluded belief that I could keep my independence while sharing a space with Genji for token rent? Everything had a price, as Peng had warned me. And I was paying dearly.

I should have known Jeanne Shin had been interested in Peng. Had she been open about it, I'd never have agreed to go out with him. I'd never have competed with my friend. Was she my friend? Would a friend spy on me in order to steal my lover? If she was a wolf in sheepskin, why did she care about me as if I were her little sister? In spite of her constant mocking, I had really felt her love when she dropped food and clothes in my lap, when she tried to pierce my ears so that I could wear the pearls her mother had given her, when she lectured me on how to beautify myself to get ahead in society, especially when I insisted on calling her her Chinese name, Ji Xing, lucky star, and watched her stomp her feet like a little girl. She looked so lovely and real when she dropped her guard. Behind her tough vixen's mask, she had a tender spot for me. She had made me laugh with her wise quirky quotes from some ancient book. Considering how she hated reading, except for magazines like *Mademoiselle,* it was double funny when those tough, military sounding quotes slipped out of her rouged lips.

I'd once asked Peng why he didn't go out with Jeanne Shin. She was a real Shanghai girl: sophisticated, metropolitan, and beautiful, someone who knew how to dress, eat, and entertain. Peng had shaken his head and said Jeanne Shin was every man's mistress.

When I asked him what that meant, he just smiled and changed the subject.

Suddenly I felt sorry for Jeanne Shin. She was living in her own dreamworld. She had moved into Peng's in his moment of weakness and anger, but soon he'd wake up and realize his mistake. Peng Chen would not marry her. Even if he did, he'd never love her as he had loved me.

"Miss Wan?"

I jumped. It was too dark to see, but Genji was in the room, very close to the bed. I could feel his body heat, his breathing on my hair, and his longing weaving me into a cocoon.

"Is that you, Genji?"

I turned on the lamp. Genji shielded his eyes with his hand. He was stark naked, his body shockingly white and hairless.

"What are you doing here?" I asked gently. I wasn't scared; naked Genji looked like a baby beluga stranded alone on a beach.

"Genji not sleeping. Genji want talk." He shivered and shifted his bare feet back and forth.

"Sit down, Genji. Are you cold?"

I was hoping to get him to put on some clothes with my hint, but he jumped onto the bed instead. I pulled up the blanket and wrapped it around his shoulders.

"Sorry, Miss Wan," he bowed. "Genji fail. Dinner not good. Miss Wan touch nothing."

He couldn't be serious! I was the one who should apologize, who should prostrate before him and beg for forgiveness.

"Oh, Genji, please don't make me cry." I put my hands on the back of his neck. His skin was softer and smoother than a woman's. "I shouldn't have brought Professor Dickey."

He looked up, his head shaking like a rattle drum. "No, no, no, Professor Dickey important, help Miss Wan get good education. Genji wish help as much. But Genji too ignorant. Genji no schooling."

He moaned bitterly as he knocked his head against the headboard. I held him still in my arms. The blanket had slipped off.

"Listen, Genji, please listen. You're just as good as any professor in my school, if not better. Believe me. Education isn't everything. Look at me. I have a degree from Fudan University, and I'm going to graduate school. But I still say stupid things all the time, make foolish mistakes, and live off you like a leech."

"No leech, Miss Wan pearl, true pearl for Genji." He tilted back for a better gaze. "Genji lucky, live with beauty from ancient time, hair so black and thick, eye so bright, neck so slender. Genji make a sculpture someday."

He reached for my face, tracing eyebrows, nose, lips. His callused fingers tickled and scratched. I shivered. The sensation of pleasure was almost painful. My ground was slipping away as he reached for my collarbone, but I caught his hand.

"You're an artist, Genji. If you learn to speak better English, imagine how many great opportunities you'll have."

I stopped short as his hand balled into a fist. What nonsense was I saying? He'd been a banquet chef at Tavern on the Green. How much more successful could he be? So why did he leave that restaurant? Why did he leave Japan?

"Genji too old learn English. Genji help Mrs. Kao success, Miss Wan happy."

"What about *you*, Genji? What makes *you* happy?" I shouted.

Startled, he moved his gaze from my face to the books piled on the nightstand.

"Miss Wan make Genji happy. Genji feel like home again, like Tokyo."

I kneaded open his fist. "Genji, would you let me teach you three English words a day? In a month, you'll have ninety words, and in a year, it will be how many?"

He buried his face in the blanket between his knees. "Genji grateful. Genji promise work hard."

I stroked his neck. It was early spring. The predawn air was quite chilly. But his body steamed with sweat.

"Genji, how do you keep your skin so smooth?"

He looked up. "Genji have skin disease."

I laughed. "You're joking. You have the best skin I've ever seen. Soft and hairless."

He patted his shiny scalp and cheeks. "Not joking. Genji hairless. Hair fall when girlfriend died, lose all when mother died."

I stared. No wonder he looked so open and vulnerable. There was not a single hair on his scalp, face, chest. No mustache or beard, not even eyebrows. He blinked. No eyelashes to protect his eyes. How could I have been so blind?

"Your heart is broken, is that why? Did you see a doctor?"

"Many. Chinese, Japanese, American. Genji lost job in Tokyo, then Tavern on the Green. Boss worry about hair in food. Genji wear hat, but hair fall all over, handfuls. Genji feel shame. Genji broke. Hide for a year before work for Mrs. Kao."

This was a very different story than what Professor Dickey had told me. Who was telling the truth? I really wanted to believe Genji. His explanation seemed to fit his personality. If someone else had told me that Genji was a gangster, I'd have laughed in their face. But why would Professor Dickey make up such a story? True, she loved drama, and she exaggerated things. Still, to smear someone so harmless was a bit outrageous.

Genji shivered. I touched his scalp gently. It was clammy like a wet palm. "Are you cold, Genji? You want a sweater?"

He bolted up and ran out, covering his groin with his hands. When he returned, he had put on a pair of sweatpants and a T-shirt. "Genji so sorry. Genji don't mean scare Miss Wan. Genji shame."

I laughed and tried to tease him out of his embarrassment. "So Genji, do you mean your entire body has no hair? Including your nose, armpits, your midsection, you know, down there?"

He beamed at my tease, his thumb on the waist band. "Want check out again?"

"No," I shouted. And we both laughed.

"I thought you had come in to do something bad, Genji," I said. The crisis was over. Now we could chat.

"Like what?" he looked up, twinkles in his eyes.

"Oh, you know, like rape or something." I waved my hand to dismiss the topic. Suddenly I felt I had said something wrong, seriously wrong.

"What rape mean, teacher?"

"Gee, it's like violating, oh, never mind. It's like forcing someone, forcing a girl to have . . . Hey, you're giving me a headache, Genji." I whined and slapped his arm, hoping to distract him.

He jumped up with a smile. "Wait a second. Genji get dictionary."

I wrapped myself with the blanket. How was I going to get myself out of this mess?

"How spell rape?" He opened his leatherbound dictionary.

"Genji, can we do this tomorrow? I'm tired. I want to sleep." I faked a big yawn.

"Genji want first lesson."

I sighed. Perhaps the Japanese definition for the word wouldn't be as harsh. Perhaps he would go back to his bed after this. Next to the fully dressed Genji, I felt naked in my see-through nightgown. What the hell were we doing here, at this hour?

"R-A-P-E," I spelled.

He knelt on the floor, licking his fingertips to turn the pages. "Word too small. Genji too old, need glass," he chuckled as he lifted the dictionary closer to his eyes.

"What you mean?" He looked up, face twisted in disbelief. The gentle, smiling teddy bear had suddenly turned into an enraged grizzly.

"It doesn't mean anything. I mean, I don't mean that at all. Please, Genji, no!"

He leaped onto the bed, pushed me down, pressed his dictionary on my chest. The edge of the book cut into my throat. I managed to turn my head to the side to get some air.

"You want Genji raaape? You have it. Here, here!"

He thrashed like a stranded whale on the beach.

I curled up and kneed him in the groin.

He crashed down, his bulging eyes an inch away from me. "Raaape, you want this, right?" He grunted as he kneed my legs open. The blanket got in his way. He jumped up and yanked it off, tossing the dictionary in the air. It landed on the nightstand, knocked down the books and the lamp. The antique vase shattered, but the bulb, protected by the pleated shade, still shed light from the floor. Genji held up the sheet like a war banner.

"Books teach this? Crooked heart? Crooked mind? Genji treat Miss Wan like pearl, and you think Genji raaape? Think Genji a monster? You got a monster."

I shut my eyes, held my breath. If I couldn't see, if my body turned into a breathless corpse, then I would be all right. He would not touch me, just like a bear would not touch a dead animal.

And he came down like a landslide, his penis hard like a rod. A few minutes ago, it had hung softly like a little tail, shy and gentle and harmless. Now it was poking furiously between my legs. But my vagina was a closed gate, rusted before it had a chance to open. Genji struck harder with each failure. The pain became unbearable.

My stomach heaved, my whole body heaved. It wanted to expel the pain, the shock, the humiliation.

My vomit landed on his face, a pinkish goo of half-digested intestines, squid, stinky tofu, noodles, and other food from Village Wok.

He jolted up and froze. I fled to the bathroom, closed the door, and vomited the rest of the food into the toilet.

There was silence in the apartment, heavy and unbearable. I wished I were still retching so that I didn't have to deal with the silence, didn't have to open the door and face Genji.

I cleaned my face and checked my body. My groin was tender, bruised, but there was no blood. He didn't break me. I was still a virgin.

I started weeping, broken by an unspeakable sorrow. Where could I go? Where was my road?

Then I heard *him* sob, loud and uncontrollable, sobs like tidal waves that swept everything, good and bad, along the path, leaving no trace.

I opened the door and walked to the bedroom with a towel. How could I hate or fear this sobbing man? He was a lonely lover, a lost child, just like me.

In a fetal position, Genji knelt in the vomit, arms around his head as if he were blocking his own sound, his own sorrow.

I started cleaning him with the towel, first his shoulders, arms, face, then the bed. His body opened up at each touch. So did mine. Soon I stopped trembling, and he stopped wailing.

"I didn't mean it that way, Genji, not at all," I said when I finished. He was still in a fetal position, but relaxed and clean. He had broad shoulders, muscles bulging like a professional body builder. He must have weighed more than 200 pounds, and I had just moved him around like a newborn.

He trembled slightly, but said nothing.

"I guess I'll move out."

Once the words were said, my chest opened up, and air rushed in. It wasn't as scary as I had thought. For a month and a half, I'd been living in a dream, an illusion. Now the dream was over. When the day broke, I'd take the subway to Chinatown and get the *World Daily*. There would be a place for me. Somewhere.

Genji mumbled, his old voice returned, thin and listless. I bent over to listen.

"Genji fail again. Genji fault."

I pressed my swelling eyes against his shoulder.

"Not Genji's fault. Not my fault. Not anybody's fault."

Another wave of sorrow pulled me under. Whose fault was it then? And how could every good intention turn sour? What had I lost in the search? What had we both lost?

"Genji wish meet Miss Wan next life. In Kyoto or Shanghai," he whispered.

"So you're going home tomorrow," I said.

Peng was standing behind me. He had entered through the hallway soundlessly, but I knew it was him. I could smell him a mile away.

The student center was deserted at dusk on Friday. I'd come there straight from work to wait for him. Last night when I got home from the law office where I was working as a temp, I saw the blinks on the answering machine and pressed the button. Jeanne Shin's voice came on. It had been two years since I had spoken to her on the phone. Both she and Peng seemed to have vanished completely from campus. Since Peng's department was in a different building, it was understandable that we might not bump into each other. But Jeanne Shin and I had been taking the same classes, and her sudden disappearance didn't make sense, unless she had quit and transferred to a different school. I heard a rumor that she had gotten married. I assumed she had married Peng and they had been busy and happy with each other. I wasn't surprised to hear her voice. I knew we'd be talking again. I wasn't surprised either that she had found me. I had moved a few more times after I left Genji's place, and was now working as a temp from one office to another in Flushing after I got my Master's degree. Jeanne Shin was perhaps the most resilient and resourceful person on earth. What surprised me was the content of her brief message. I had to play it three times to convince myself that I had heard it right:

"Hello, Virgin, long time no see. Hope all is well with you. I just want to let you know that Peng received an award of excellence for his Master's thesis on Taiwan's democracy and he's going home tomorrow with his mama to marry a real virgin on the island."

So Peng didn't propose to her, after all, as I had predicted. Why hadn't he tried to contact me? What was he doing here? What was I doing here?

Peng put his hands on my shoulders. I turned around. We gazed at each other without a word.

He had aged, his forehead wrinkled like ripples. His cow-like eyes, having lost their glint of overstimulation, were calm and moist with a hint of sadness. He was still clad in black from head to toe, but the material was home-woven cloth instead of slick, shiny mock leather.

He looked exactly the way I had seen him in my dreams.

I inhaled. No more cologne or perfume from his foxy "body-guards." Only the familiar smell of the island in the East China Sea. I was homesick again.

"Congratulations on your double joy!" I whispered. His silence calmed me like the ocean.

He reached out his hand and pulled a hair from my head.

"You've got this." He lifted the white hair he had just plucked. It shone in the twilight.

"I've got quite a few," I said.

"Wait till you see mine." He raked his fingers through his hair, making a face.

I laughed. It was good to see the playful Peng again. We sat down on a bench, and we watched the sunset through the glass wall, his arm around my shoulders. My eyes stung with tears. There was no lust in his hug. Had I lost him for good?

"You look lovely," he said.

I blushed.

"I'm working in a law office now. There's a dress code, sort of. My boss's girlfriend took me shopping at the Gap. There was a big sale. She picked out a bunch of stuff for me."

I was talking so fast I began to choke on my own words.

"Wan Li," he turned to me, "You haven't changed, no matter what you wear."

I lost my words. I wished he'd call me Communist Virgin, just one more time.

He lifted my white hair again to the last light of the setting sun. It flickered against the night sky.

"I wish you had plucked it two years ago," I said.

My cheeks burnt. Peng was engaged, ready to get married. I had no right to discuss regrets and wishes with him. I had come here to say good-bye. So had he.

He cupped my face in his hands. We were close, our lips almost touching. His breathing became faster.

"I have my own place now, a big room in a nice house on Farrington Street, in Flushing," I whispered. I ordered myself to stop talking, but my mouth didn't belong to me.

"Oh Wan Li, my Communist Virgin," he cried, hugging me to his chest. "Why do you have to be a communist? Why?"

So he knew, but how? I hadn't told a soul about my secret identity. I untangled from his embrace and looked up.

"Jeanne Shin told me. But I had already guessed. You emitted communism from every pore. I mean it as a good thing. Communism isn't as stinky as the propaganda makes it. It's about utopia if you look at its origin and main principles, but we're not ready for such a thing. We're selfish by nature. That's why capitalism is so attractive. It feeds on our greed and fear. I grew up poor as a child. I know what poverty does to a soul, and I also know what wealth can do to a person. But you, you seemed to have come out of a vacuum, from the moon, so clean and uncorrupt. You're perhaps the last communist virgin left on the planet."

"I'm not clean any more. Look at me. I've been living in New York for almost three years. I took Genji's gifts. I'm wearing Gap clothes. I wish I had listened to you."

He covered my mouth with his hand. "It has nothing to do with Gap or Genji or New York. No matter what you wear, where you live, you're my virgin."

I slid to the floor, leaning the back of my head against his stomach. I kissed the scar of his missing pinky. If my identity didn't bother him, then why couldn't we start all over again? Why had he never called or looked for me?

"I have never met my father," Peng said, his voice low and tired as if it had traveled a long distance. "His fishing boat was supposed to return on my seventh birthday, but a typhoon came a day earlier. Not a single fisherman made it back. My mother sat on the beach waiting for his boat to appear on the horizon. No food, no sleep. Her hair turned gray completely. On the seventh day, she stood up, took us home, and cooked us our favorite breakfast: porridge with thousand-year-old eggs. After we licked our bowls clean, she said, 'Let's work.' And we went to the marsh to harvest reeds and wove baskets with them to sell on the market. She also sold her embroidery and knitting. My father's two younger brothers tried everything they could to force her to remarry so they could inherit our house and the marshland. But she stood her ground. She didn't know the value of the land. Nobody knew at that time. She just didn't want to marry again. A woman was cheap, a remarried woman was worthless, and her children from the previous marriage were nothing but garbage. We three stay together in this house, dead or alive, she told the matchmakers, holding a knife against her throat to show her determination. Finally they left us alone. We worked hard, the three of us. When Mom went to the market, my sister would clean the house and take me to the streets, not to play, but to find food and fuel, cast-off vegetables, coal, and twigs along the railroad. We had street fights daily. That's how I got this scar on my face.

I went on a fishing boat as an apprentice when I turned twelve. My mom tried to stop me. But that was the only way I could make decent money. I did it for four summers until my finger got caught in a pulley when I tried to save the fishing net in a storm. Mom said that if I wanted to go back to the boat, it would be over her dead body. I stopped. My sister quit junior high school and found a job in a factory so I could go on to high school, then college. I owe everything to my mom and sister."

Dusk had arrived. One by one, buildings across the street lit up. Around us, the flickering lights of Manhattan winked and beckoned with irresistible charm. Peng had slid down to the floor to sit behind me, his arms wrapping my chest, his thighs and legs around mine. I held onto his hands, my back pressed tight against his thumping heart. If only the night would last forever. If only the sun would never rise in the morning.

"Then our village became an industrial development district. Suddenly our land, thirty acres of salt marsh where nothing but reeds grew, became a gold mine. Money came so big and fast it was scary. Before we learned what to do with it, we were swamped by relatives asking for help. We gave as much as we could, but the more we gave, the more we were hated. My relatives felt they were more entitled to the marsh than my mom, who had been sold at fifteen to my father. My sister and I begged her to leave. We could have gone anywhere with that money. But she was stubborn. She loved the rough sea, the muddy coast, and the salty marsh. The place reminded of her home, a fishing island across the East China Sea, on the mainland, from where she had to flee with her mother to Taiwan when her father died fighting Mao. Her mother, my grandmother whom I have never met, remarried after years of wandering in poverty. Her new husband didn't want an extra mouth under his roof. For a bushel of rice, he gave my mother to his friend in the fishing village. He was twenty years older, but she grew to love him and the land. She wanted to be buried next to her husband.

Eventually, my sister left. She came to New York with her husband. They opened a restaurant in Flushing, then moved it to Greenwich. Business flourished. My sister was a great chef and manager. She brought me over five years ago, once I had graduated from college, hoping I'd get a Master's in business management and help her launch things other than her restaurant business. She planned for us to make big money. I tried for two years and failed several courses. I was partying hard to the point of going mad. Of course I'd go mad. For a thirsty drunk, New York is a giant cellar with the best collection of wine and whiskey. I had nothing as a child, and I wanted my compensation.

Still, I was ashamed of my F's. I was a straight-A student from elementary school to college. When my mother asked me when I would get my degree and return home to deal with the local representatives who had been pestering her to sell the last chunk of her land, I got an idea. I wanted to be a politician. It wouldn't be hard to beat those stupid men in our town campaign, especially when I have money and an American degree. If I won, and of course I'd win, I'd run for the National Assembly. So I changed my degree to political science. I was going slow. I was not ready to return to the island yet, though I knew I had to. I'm the island's son. Before I go back, I'll extract as much fun as I can from this city. Once I become a politician back home, I'll no longer be free. So I was playing hard until I met you."

He hugged me. My joints cracked. He was still strong after all these years drinking, screwing, taking drugs. I trembled in his arms. This sudden outpouring of his past. The story was not a complete surprise. I had felt the weight of his childhood, its harshness. Why hadn't he opened his heart earlier? Why was he telling me now?

"You jolted me out of my drunken stupor. I still remembered the moment when I found you here, kneeling on this very bench. You were reading, your head bent low like a praying child, and your hair spread on your back, so thick and black, shimmering in the twilight like the wings of a flying bird. I was stunned for a second. You looked different, yet familiar, as if we had known each other from our previous lives. To tell you the truth, I had come here for a good laugh. Jeanne Shin had described you in great detail, your awkwardness, your bookishness, your terrible clothes and look. I had asked her to come along, but she wouldn't. So I came with my other friends.

"I know you don't believe me. I said lewd things to you that day, acting like a jerk. But inside, I was cursing myself. This is not you, Peng Chen, not your true self. But I couldn't stop. I'd been playing the role of playboy for almost two years, like a mask I'd been wearing for so long it stuck to me and became my own face. I blew it. I made a terrible impression on you and I wanted to change it, but I didn't know how. So I did the only thing I knew at that time: bought you gifts, took you out—things that would delight normal girls. But you were not normal. The more I spent, the less you trusted and respected me. And I wanted you to love me so much it hurt."

He wept, his tears soaking through my hair.

Why didn't you come to me earlier? Why didn't you? I wanted to scream. Instead I pulled his arms tighter around my chest. The clock handle on the wall was pointing to nine. We didn't have much time left. When the sun rose, he would be gone, forever.

"Then you moved into Genji's apartment, and I just lost it. How could you live with a Jap, after what they did to us Chinese, on the mainland, in Taiwan? I know I shouldn't judge like this. Genji is a nice man, I'm sure. He shouldn't bear the blame for his nation. I just couldn't stand the thought of losing you over him. Then Jeanne Shin visited your apartment. She offered to check out your new place for me. I should have known better, but I was going mad with rage and jealousy. She came back, said there was only one bedroom, and that you two were definitely sleeping together. 'What a pity,' she said, 'that your virgin turned out to be a whore!' I told her to shut up and get out. I didn't believe a word she said. But suspicion had poisoned my mind, and punched holes in my heart. When you rejected my gifts, I had tried to accept it, even admired you for it. But what made you take his stuff? Was he better than me? Did you like him better? And then you didn't bother to change Genji's clothing when you came to see me in the restaurant. You looked so dazzling, but my last hope was blasted away, together with my dignity. I had to get away, or I didn't know what I'd do to you or myself. I went home sick, couldn't get out of bed for days. Jeanne Shin came to take care of me, then moved her stuff in. How I wished it had been you instead of her! Every day, every night, I was hoping you'd call. I couldn't call you because of my pride. If you had just called to ask me how I was doing, I'd have forgiven everything, everything. But you never did, and Jeanne Shin bugged me for a ring, a ring with a big rock. When I said no, she would scream and cry and threaten. Finally she wrote to my mother telling her that I was in love with a communist.

"I don't blame or hate her. She wants a good life like everyone else, a life she missed out on growing up in China. She's lots of fun when she stops scheming so much. But she can't help herself. I don't know what happened to her when she was a child. Her whole mindset is that she's alone against the world, that she has to be on guard twenty-four hours a day. She's a good fighter, I have to say. Even my mom admits it. But a good fighter doesn't always win the war, especially in the war of love."

He sighed, fingertips raking the roots of my hair tenderly. I was about to ask what made someone win the war of love when he continued, "Not money, either. It helps to lure certain kinds of people, that's all. Or brains. Scheming and strategies often backfire. Jeanne Shin is jealous of you, which she will never admit. I think it was jealousy and rage that made her write to my mother. When my mother came, she cleaned the house, getting rid of the clutter, including Jeanne Shin. I don't know how she did it. Jeanne Shin is a tough fighter, but she's no match for my mother. Not at all. I didn't know where she went. My mother had total control of my mail and phone calls. Soon I heard she quit school and married a professor's son who was going to MIT. You know the professor. He teaches Shakespeare in the English Department.

"'No more monkey business, son,' my mother said after Jeanne Shin was gone. We both set to work. She cooked, washed, cleaned, walked me to school and the library. She made sure that I attended classes, worked a good six hours a day on my thesis, and slept eight hours at night. I was her baby boy again, safe and warm in her bosom. It was embarrassing, but I needed her to kick my habits, get rid of bad friends, and finish my school. And I did. I completed all my incompletes and requirements as well as my thesis. For two years, I talked to nobody except for my professors and advisors, never went out to bars or discos. On Saturday nights, I went to my sister's house with my mother, and we played mahjong till dawn. I didn't miss the old days, not a bit. But I missed you. I knew when you moved out of Genji's place, when you lived in the apartment of your Korean classmate's sister, when you had a quarrel and she threw you out. I knew you moved around to a few more places until you settled down on Farrington Street. I knew it all, and the phone numbers. My hands would grab the phone and dial your number. But my mother watched me like a hawk. She'd take the phone out of my hand and unplug the cord. 'Over my dead body,' she said. 'You know I hate communists, who killed my father and his entire family, who exiled me when I was six.'

"When I finished my thesis, she presented me the photo of a young girl from the island. She looked twelve years old in the picture. Mother promised me that she had a high school degree, was an excellent cook and embroiderer, and had never traveled outside her mountain village.

"'She'll be your wife and the mother of your children,' she declared.

"What could I have done but obey? I am a mama's boy, as Jeanne Shin called me, a creature of habit and comfort. If you had been with me, I would have had some strength to fight, but not alone. I'm not blaming you. No. I blame myself. I'm not a man. Not any more. I have loved you, Wan Li, with all I had. Oh, God, why did you *make* us when you can't let us *be* together? Am I blaming God? Yes, I am. If you don't mean for us to be together, why did you let us be born on the same day, same month, same year? Why did you let us meet on this damned campus, in this damned city? Why did you make my girl a communist?"

And he bawled, a man with a broken heart. I turned around and took him into my arms. I hugged, kissed, rocked him back and forth. I took off his jacket and my shirt. Our skin touched and melted into each other, arm to arm, shoulder to shoulder. We moaned. In pleasure and pain. I unzipped his pants, took his penis into my hands. It lay still, lifeless. I held it between my palms, between my lips. It tasted slightly salty, like a fish just out of the sea, as I had imagined. Slowly it expanded, a desert flower unfolding its petals after a rain, a dried-out sea star thrown back to the ocean, absorbing my saliva, my love. Then it jumped to life, throbbing with ferocity.

I removed my shoes, my stockings, my underwear. The clock pointed to midnight. A new day was beginning. I straddled him. I was riding a horse. I was riding a dragon. We were two dragons born in the same year, same month, same day. Under the early summer sky we soared. The stars were bright and silent, their pointed fingers nailing into our flesh, crimson, sharp, and lovely . . . and we screamed.

Genji found me on a train going to Manhattan.

I was dozing, dreaming stars and ocean waves when I opened my eyes and saw him beaming at me across the aisle.

"Genji!" I jumped up. "Why didn't you wake me up?"

"You look peaceful! I feel happy just watching."

He still looked the same, round and hairless. But something had changed about him, greatly.

"How have you been? Still in Rego Park?"

He nodded. Slowly a pink blush spread on his cheeks, forehead, and the space between his bare eyebrows. "Miss Wan, I got married."

"Congratulations! Who's the lucky girl?"

My heart beat fast, not out of jealousy or anger, but from joy. It was nice to see him again, to see him happy.

"Her name is Fangfang. She lives in Shanghai. I went there to meet her last month and we had our wedding in a grand restaurant on Nanjing Road. Hundreds of her relatives and friends came to the banquet. It was just glorious."

"A Shanghai girl, eh? She must be beautiful," I said. Genji had never looked so confident! "How did you get to know her across the ocean?"

"Mrs. Kao put an ad for me in the paper, and Fangfang was the first to respond. Oh, I must get off. I'm so late for Sakura. I missed my stop waiting for you to wake up. By the way, our restaurant is no longer little any more. Mrs. Kao made it big. We made it big. Call me please. I'll invite you to dinner when Fangfang comes to America. She's waiting for her green card."

He lunged for the door.

It dawned on me that Genji no longer spoke in the third person. He didn't ask a single question about my past few years, didn't notice my thick waist bulging with a life that had been seeded seven months ago in the library. I hadn't talked to Peng since he went back to Taiwan, and had no plan to.

"Hey, Genji, you're speaking good English!" I shouted to the closing door.

"I've been taking lessons," he shouted back from the platform, his gold tooth lighting up the dim station.

The train moved on, slowly first, then fast, taking me into the heart of Manhattan, the city where I had found love.

A flutter in the stomach, a twitch of a finger, two fingers, then a tap, a punch, light and playful, followed by a kick, a somersault. The life inside me was waking for some action.

I put my hand on my belly. "Hey, girl, you want to meet Auntie Jeanne Shin soon? Her real name is Ji Xin, lucky star, my lucky star, and yours, too. She'll give you a blue bird, and we'll fly home together on her back."

FORAGE

So Virgin called, and my peace of mind is gone. How did she find me? Not by accident for sure. She hates window shopping. As far as I know, she has never walked along Fifth Avenue and I bet she has never heard of Bergdorf Goodman. She must have done some homework to track me down here. But WHY! I asked her right away, and instead of giving me a straight answer, she just made that old prissy virgin-whore giggle. It used to drive me nuts. Not any more, though. Working at B.G. has finessed my social skills. Believe me, to be a good salesperson here is an art few can master. Most people can't even get their foot in the door, like Virgin. Even though she has two Masters degrees, she would not last more than four hours in the department. She wouldn't be hired in the first place.

"I miss you," she said on the phone.

When the fox says Happy New Year to a chicken, you know there's only one thing on the fox's mind: dinner.

Still, I can't believe my legs are shaking from the little voice of a good girl with eyes so translucent as if she were giving you her heart and soul unconditionally. But anyone who has seen a few things in this world can detect the nymph beneath that smooth skin, which is nothing but a painted mask, even though she never wears makeup— a cosmetic virgin. Is that why she sucks men in like a black hole?

No, it's the beast behind the mask, and only I can smell it. When it comes to grades, I suck. My best score at Hunter College was a C from a young adjunct poet who would have given me a B or A had

I opened my legs for him. But I was busy fighting Virgin for Mama's Boy. Besides, I don't give a shit about grades. I have no desire to get a Ph.D. Even a Masters degree was a total waste of my time. I did it for my visa, which allowed me to live here legally. It's not that I have no brain or I'm antieducation. The things they make us pay such an enormous price to learn are totally useless in real life. And what do those four-eyed professors know about instinct or the sixth sense for survival? On the streets or in the jungles, they'd be the first to perish, I bet, and no fancy degrees or deep knowledge can keep them warm or fed. The sixth sense, you either have it or you don't. It's a gift, like a good singing voice or fingers that play instruments. I hate reading, and I'm tone deaf, but I'm the queen of seeing people's minds through their masks. I haven't met a rival yet, except perhaps Virgin, who doesn't know what she has. Doesn't even know who she is really.

The moment I set my eyes on her, I smelled the beast and knew it would jump out and tear up everything I had built.

It's been eight months since I saw her in the student center with Peng Chen, Mama's Boy. What secrets in that midnight darkness! And what horror! Everything I had feared came true: that Peng Chen loved her, loved her more than he ever loved me; that Virgin was a slut, a slut so wild that she'd do it in a public space.

For eight months, I've been trying to block out what I saw that night. Faces in rapture, exploding like a big bang. I've seen men and women reach climax. Not pretty at all. Faces pinched, bodies twisted and entangled in the stink of their come. Phew! I had a glimpse of myself once as I was coming: pink, wet, wrinkled, and messy like a giant clam. My ecstasy turned my face into a vagina. I removed the mirror from the bedroom after that.

But how they moved in perfect harmony, two angels dancing in God's courtyard, an ecstasy that comes only as a heavenly gift!

I backed out, tears in my eyes. I'm a born warrior. I don't fight often. But once I get into a battle, I have to win. I win by guts and craft: strategic planning, the understanding of the enemy and myself, the careful and daring maneuvers, and the patience, yes, the patience and speed and perfect timing of a hunting beast.

Yet I backed away from this game—my first and last voluntary withdrawal since the Shrew, Peng Chen's mother, moved my things out of the apartment and changed the lock. Even though I quickly moved on and got married to get my green card, I still considered myself in the game. As long as Chen loved me, I still had hope.

After the scene in the student center, everything changed. How could I compete with the blessed?

I cried, not because I had failed, but because I thought I still loved him, that lady's man, that mama's boy. Of all the men I've collected in my jewel box, he was a small gem with big stains, yet I loved him without logic or shame. To win his attention, I used every strategy I learned from *The Art of War*, the yellowed book that passed from my great-grandma to my mama then to me, on the night before I left Shanghai for New York, wrapped in blue silk that had seen its years.

"Why this, Mama?" I asked. I had heard of this book. A must for all politicians and military men who need to know how to fight and kill. There are classics that teach girls girly things and women womanly things, but no one read them anymore. I was hoping for a Chinese-English dictionary as a farewell present. It would be more useful, I thought.

"Oh, Xing Xing, my lucky star," she whispered in my ear, her fragile body quivering in the autumn breeze. "It's time to know something about your mother's family. You're going far away, and I don't know when I'll see you again. Listen carefully, my girl. This book freed your great-grandma from a brothel in Shanghai, helped her climb all the way up from the lowest rank of concubine to a warlord's first wife. And my mother, your grandma, could have stayed home and enjoyed a luxurious life as a general's daughter. But the book taught her how to predict where the wind would blow. So she joined Mao's army in Yan'an, when they were besieged and chased around as bandits by the Nationalist armies. She married a peasant who quickly became a commander, then the head of the district in Shanghai, and she herself enjoyed enormous power as the head of the district education department. Had she stayed home, she'd have been exiled, even executed after Mao liberated China in 1949. One single move, and life was changed forever, for her, for me, and for you."

Imagine how stunned I was to hear I was the great-grand-daughter of a famous courtesan. Suddenly everything made sense, my sexual history starting at my thirteenth birthday, things men would shout into my ears as they came. But how could it explain my mother, who wants nothing to do with men or politics, who seems to float on earth waiting for the chance to return to heaven? The only things that tie her to the earth are me, my sister, and her aging mother, my grandma, a hardcore revolutionary, who still believes in shedding her last drop of blood for the cause of communism. Both have had only one man in their lives: their husbands, both short-lived. One divorced his old wartime wife and married a Miss Shanghai, and the other, my father, died of lung cancer when I was nine. They've raised us with love and strict rules. Had they known what I've done behind their backs . . . I can't imagine the dire consequences.

"As for me, your useless mother," she continued with that dreamy look in her eyes, "the book weathered me through the Cultural Revolution. I would have been tortured by the Red Guards, exiled to a remote labor camp, and you, my child, beacon of my life, would be wasting away toiling in the fields as a peasant's wife instead of going to New York. So treat this book as a treasure. Read a page a day, over and over, and memorize it until every word is branded in your memory, the way I memorized Mao's Little Red Book during the Cultural Revolution. It will help you get a foothold in the new city, where you have no roots. Remember Sun Tzu's number one rule: to know the strengths and weaknesses of yourself and your enemy. If you know the enemy and know yourself, you need not fear the result of a hundred battles. If you know yourself but not the enemy, for every victory gained you will also suffer a defeat. If you know neither the enemy nor yourself, you will succumb in every battle."

Perhaps my mother is not as fragile as she appears. Perhaps she knows more about me than I let myself believe?

How well the book has served me! I came to New York with twenty-six dollars, the maximum we were allowed to take out of China at that time. I didn't know a single person except for White Tiger. We had met in the Peace Hotel on Nanjing Road, where I worked as a tour guide. The night I arrived in New York, I slept in the basement where his son used to live. At dawn, he came to my bed. No word passed between us. This exchange was understood from the very beginning of our encounter. He was fierce, a surprisingly good lover, much better than any man I had had in Shanghai. Later he showed me his collection of magazines and videos, hundreds of them in his living room closet. He liked to do it while watching the tapes. Never had I imagined such impossible positions for sex, and the orifices one could use! It was embarrassing in the beginning. I couldn't look at the screen, didn't know where to put my limbs. But soon I got used to it, and got bored, to tell the truth. Every scene in the videos is the same, meat pumping against meat over fake moans, nothing else. I asked why he wasted his money collecting those dumb movies. He laughed and said that if I were a man, I'd understand. Well, I don't need to be a man to understand his needs and fears. He may be a tiger in bed and business, but inside, he's just as frightened as a rabbit banished from the nest. At least I can be alone for days and months; I have no need to go through sex partners with the speed of an assembly line. And I'd never ever bother anyone with endless phone calls the way he harassed his ex-wife who left him with their son for a white man. Never! When he told me a new girl from Beijing was coming in a week, I packed my stuff and left without a word.

Well, that's the way it is. He's not a bad man, really. He got me out of China, trained me in bed and on the streets. His favorite chant: Want success in America? Work like a dog, fight like a tiger, and trick like a fox. His discipline and will are harder than steel. As soon as he was done with me on our first night, the first morning, actually, he got up, took a shower, and drove me to his antique store on Broadway. "Dust the vases, answer the phone, make sure to write down the numbers and names, and page me if someone wants to buy," he said before he took off, just like that, as if I was his fucking secretary. It was 9:00 a.m. I was still reeling from my first airplane ride, my first jet lag, my first night away from Mama and home. I had just turned twenty-two, already felt old in this strange city in a strange country. A man in a brown uniform rang the bell. I buzzed him in. He handed me a package and clipboard. What's that for, I asked, putting on my cutest smile. Where are you from, the moon? he growled.

People at Bergdorf Goodman call me Moon Girl because of my smooth manner with customers. They would never have guessed that this shimmering, mysterious, and slick-looking me was a country bumpkin eight years ago who threw up pizza on her boss and didn't know what a UPS man was. Nor do they have an inkling that I'm shaking inside and rambling like an old hag who lost her bag— all because of a phone call from Virgin, foe from my previous life.

I'm coming to see you, she said.

He who knows when to fight and when not to fight will win.

Should I follow old Sun Tzu's teaching? Should I tell my boss I'm sick and have to lie down?

It's not a lie. I feel queasy as if I were two months pregnant. My knees wobble like I have had diarrhea for three days straight. It happens every time we're close, within a half-mile range, this reeling, this sick loose bowel sensation.

Even before she shows up, I'm losing my center. I'm no longer the exotic, sexy China doll men drool over. All my expensive attires, my Gucci purse, Chanel perfume, Japanese pearls, Armani dress, even my beloved Jimmy Choo stilettos, turn trashy in front of that nerd, that bookworm, that one-hundred-percent country bumpkin who knows nothing about fashion, who wears no jewelry or makeup, who cuts her own hair because she's too cheap to go to a salon.

It doesn't make any sense—the power she has over me. I'm supposed to be a warrior, but now I'm planning to run like a chicken. Where can I go, anyway? This is my place, my kingdom. I worked hard to get here: from Blue Dragon Antique, sweatshops and restaurants in Chinatown, to shoe stores and boutiques in SoHo, then Macy's, and finally, Bergdorf Goodman—a path paved with sweat and semen.

Yes, semen. I'm a woman of scattered brains and a broken family. My body is my biggest capital, and every man wants a share. So I make the best use of it. I'm used to sex. I've been used to it since my beloved uncle took me to the park behind Shanghai Opera House on my thirteenth birthday and whispered *whore my little whore I want to fuck you to death my little whore* into my ear as he tore into me and apart. How many more men have I had since that starless night in the bush? Only my lacquer box knows. It is filled with rings, sleeve cuffs, coins, pins of Chairman Mao, Che, Clinton, the Beatles, Pink Floyd, Led Zeppelin, and other crazy shit—keepsakes I have collected from the men I befriended. Do I enjoy sex? I don't know. I do know I can please. Too many men have gone crazy as they thrashed on top of me, inside me, wishing to eat me up as they melted into a puddle of sweat. Had you been born a hundred years earlier, White Tiger once said after he came, shuddering violently, you'd have been the most sought-after courtesan in Shanghai. Thank you, I said, and kept smiling. Only after he went into the shower did I allow myself to sob. Once a whore, always a whore, as the Chinese saying goes. But what does my great-grandmother have to do with me? I've never met her, never heard about her story till I left Shanghai for New York. My mother, the weakest link of her family, as she calls herself, is as clean as an angel could be, and so is my grandma, a pure-to-the-core communist. Had they known my sexual history, they'd have fainted, disowned me, strangled me, burned me alive . . . and I wouldn't blame them.

Perhaps it is in my genes, my great-grandma's flesh and spirit. Mama said she was quite famous for her singing and dancing, one of the most prized girls in Shanghai. Did she ever fall in love as I did over Chen the Mama's Boy? Probably not. When you're in love, you become weak, irrational, out of control. Did she get attached to men the way I felt about White Tiger? I knew from the beginning that White Tiger was a business transaction. Still, I couldn't help myself. Not just because he gave me my first orgasm. Sure that counts. But what counts more are the things he taught me in order to survive in the jungle, the way he handled me when I barfed pizza on his crotch.

Yes, pizza on his crotch. What did he expect? He left me alone in his dim musky store for five hours on my first day in New York. By two-thirty, the only thought I had was to go home and curl up in my mama's arms. Then he showed up with a flat white box, pungent odor leaking from it like poison gas. Lunch, he said, revealing a round dough, bloody and gooey like a thousand men's snot congealed together. He tore off a piece and handed it to me. I turned my head.

"You want to make it in New York, learn to eat pizza first," he said. "It's fast, nutritious, and affordable. And it's available everywhere. You asked me what the typical American food is. Well, here it is, pizza New York style. There're hot dogs and hamburgers, of course, but pizza is the real deal. You'll eat hundreds, perhaps thousands of slices before you can start eating French, Italian, or Japanese gourmets, the expensive ones. But you'll be there someday, I can tell."

I took a bite, chewed, swallowed, holding my breath like I was taking pills. Suddenly, the volcano inside awakened. I ran to the door.

"Where are you going, Jeanne Shin?" He grabbed me, shouting the new name he had given me. "Hold it in, just hold it in."

I lunged and my insides erupted.

When it was over, I knelt and scooped the mess into a plastic bag with my hands. There was so much. I had puked everything: food, organs, blood, my whole being. I wiped his shoes and pants with the yellow skirt he had bought me in Hong Kong, which I had saved for the first day in America. I sobbed as I cleaned. Everything had to go: my past, my soul, my body, my old name. I had to empty myself in order to begin a new life. He stood still as if I had turned him into a statue. I got up and stood face-to-face with him.

He held out the pizza.

"Rule Number One: you do not cry. Rule Number Two: you do not cry. Rule Number Three: you do not cry in this city."

I took a bite, then another, my face dry and hollow, burning like a torch. The cold pizza tasted like dog shit, but I swallowed it as if I were taking one-hundred-year-old ginseng that would give me strength, courage, and magic. This was my first test. More would come. And I would pass them all until I reached my destiny.

Here I stand, in the most expensive store in the most fascinating city on earth, selling pearls, diamonds, ruby, onyx, sapphires, and other precious jewels that light up the eyes of the rich and the poor. You think nothing dazzles those who get anything they want in a blink of an eye, whose senses shut down from overstimulation? Wrong! Raise a good old diamond ring in front of those flashy athletes, movie stars, CEOs' wives and mistresses and daughters, old-money heirs, you'll see how their eyes sparkle and how their breathing quickens. It always works. It's human nature to forage, our old animal instinct. We used to forage food for winter and famine, now we hunt for money, fame, diamonds, gold . . .

And the housewives from the suburbs of Connecticut, New Jersey, Long Island, they are my favorites. I can hear them climb the subway steps in their pumps and stilettos, smell the odor of their mediocre perfume and the hunger for the dream that drifts hopelessly away as they age. They stop at the door. They always do, as if to adjust themselves to the magnificent beauty of Bergdorf Goodman. Then they strut in, fake Gucci bags tight under elbows. They loiter around the designer jewelry first, the cheap kind that sell at three- to four-digit prices. As they lean against the counter pointing to this and that, their eyes glide across the smooth-talking clerk, and land on me, no, on the diamonds and pearls and the sparkling stones behind the glass. Soon, they come over, shoulders slouched as if the luster from the precious jewels were hurting them. They point to a black pearl necklace or a diamond ring, eyes burning with the rush. I unlock the glass door, raise the stone to the light, turn it this way and that, watch them melt away by the longing, watch their hearts crushed as they steal glances at the price tag. They hope for a sale, a big markdown. But B.G. rarely marks things down, and never in the precious jewelry department. The high price is the secret, apart from the top designers and quality materials. The higher the price, the higher the value, the more desirable it becomes.

It's a game that makes us feel more beautiful, more desirable, more upper-class. A game no one escapes.

Like 3-J, Jane Jackson from Jersey, who shows up every Friday, 10:00 a.m., thunder or snow, and leaves at 3:00 p.m. Nothing stops her, not even the death of her mother. And she buys, always one item in the middle-range price, the maximum of her B.G. credit. You'd think she's my best client since she buys from me only. You're wrong. She buys, then she returns it the next Friday. Get it? She returns what she bought the week before then buys another so she'll have something new to wear for her Saturday night outing. My colleagues hate her. Here comes 3-J again, their eyes will say as soon as she appears at the door and shuffles her way to my counter, since I'm the only person willing to deal with her for hours every Friday for a sale that doesn't earn a penny of commission.

My colleagues call me a saint. My boss hints that I'll be promoted soon as a reward for my patience. I laugh to myself. They have no idea. I'm not doing this out of kindness or charity. No way José! Charity is not in my dictionary. 3-J has been teaching me everything I need to know about the business: even the ugliest girl on earth, even the bag lady on street, dreams of becoming a beauty queen.

She's the soil for my secret plan—a high-class shopping empire on Nanjing Road.

The seed, however, was sowed by MaryAnn, the biggest catch in my career at B.G., pinnacle of all my victories.

I noticed her the moment she strolled in. To other salesgirls, she looked just like a normal client: designer dress, designer shoes and handbag, lush blonde hair fluffed into a perfect coif, creamy skin made up just so. She looked immaculate, well-to-do. But she was not a kept woman like most of the ladies-who-lunch-at-B.G. She had earned every scrap of cloth on her gorgeous body with her hands and mind. It gave her something that others don't have: confidence—not the kind you buy with money and brand names, but the kind that springs from within, from having seen and lived through the ugliest side of life, yet still loving it, still enjoying it a great deal, like a child who cries hard from a bruised knee but five minutes later starts playing and laughing again as if nothing had happened.

At the door she gave a quick glance at our floor, then walked toward my counter. I stood at attention. This was no ordinary client, definitely not one of the lunch ladies yapping on cell phones about their hectic social schedules while squandering their husbands' money. This woman had a purpose. She knew exactly what she wanted, where to go. No one else noticed it. Not even Big Al, our very alert, very experienced security man. But I knew, thanks to the *The Art of War.*

With one look, she had inspected the terrain for her mission.

"How can I help you, Madame?"

My pure British accent stopped her for a second. Astonishment rippled through her perfectly made up face, but she quickly resumed her posture like a skillful general who conducts his army as though he were leading a single man. From the twinkle in her eyes, I could tell her adrenaline was pumping and she was ready for some excitement.

She was facing a worthy opponent, and she knew it. I bet she had never lost a single battle in her career. A superior schemer, per-haps the most talented I'd ever seen. Her body radiated confidence to the point of arrogance, which would be her Achilles heel. If she saw through my mask, I might not have a chance. But my skin color fooled her. How could a yellow China doll outsmart a blonde fox?

Good! Let's find out who's superior.

"I'd like to see a few rings, Jeannie."

Superb first move. By calling me by my name in an intimate way, she made it clear who was the boss. Good. Let the illusion fool her. Who gets the last laugh laughs best. She had a bewitching voice, rich and creamy and dark and sticky like melted chocolate in bubbling butter and sugar. It's hard to believe it came from such a waif-like body. What a waste of a heavenly gift! She could have been an opera diva instead of a jewelry operator. But I should give her the benefit of the doubt. I might be wrong. For the first time, I hoped I was wrong. I would hate to send her to jail.

"Anything particular that strikes your fancy, Ms. . . . ?"

With my voice still trailing in the air in an uplifted tone, I looked into her eyes in such a way that no one could refuse to give me their name. She sighed, pointing to a carved diamond ring.

"Please, Jeannie, call me MaryAnn. May I try this?"

"Ah, Jude Frances, elegant taste, MaryAnn."

I unlocked the oak-framed showcase and took out the eighteen-karat gold ring studded with diamonds. This was my favorite of Jude Frances. The patterns were elaborate and intricate, but very subtle and tasteful, with the diamonds set seamlessly in the white gold.

She slid it on. Her manicured hands looked agile and strong. She raised the ring to the light. It sparkled like a soldier's bayonet in the sun.

"A bit too loud for me," she sighed. "May I look at that cross band?"

Another Jude Frances. The cross looked horribly wrong on most of the women who tried it on, but it somehow fit MaryAnn's slender finger just right. Her eyes lit up and she stole a quick glance at the price tag: $2,310, one of the low-price products. She put it down slowly. I suggested the heart-shaped band, also a Jude Frances. She shook her head and turned to Yossi Harari's line. Those were extremely loud rings, each with stacks of twenty-four-karat gold bands of red stones and diamonds that gave the illusion one was wearing a dozen rings. Was she losing her mind? Was she distracted? I looked again at Harari's products and realized what was going on. Next to Harari, Big Mama, our $36,000 diamond ring, sat in her throne of a black velvet case.

I was relieved. Once I spotted her target, I no longer needed to keep a close eye on the counter passively. I could watch her from a higher position, predicting her next move. Sure enough, after trying on a few Harari rings, she asked to see Big Mama casually, together with a few others. The counter was now scattered with rings, and I was swapping them in and out of the cases at a dizzying pace. MaryAnn slipped a ring on, raised her hand to the light, walked to the mirror across the counter to get a better look under different lighting before she tried a new one. She had me do the same so she could see what it looked like on my finger, in order to get a more objective view. The pace got faster and faster, but I remained centered. As long as I didn't lose sight of Big Mama, I'd be fine. She came for her and for her only. Nothing else was worthy of her attention.

Finally, MaryAnn heaved a big sigh and pulled the Jude Frances cross band from her right middle finger. "Lots of choices, Jeannie. I need to think about it over lunch. May I come back?"

"Surely you can." I gave her a big smile, watching her turn and walk to the door, Big Mama in the deep of her black Valentino satchel. First-rate skill, first-rate control, I said to myself, hand on the phone. All I needed to do was lift the receiver, and she'd be destroyed. And I needed to catch her before she stepped outside the revolving door. Once she got out, she'd be gone, forever. Through the window, I could see a cab waiting on the curb across the street, its engine idling. She had her exit route planned. I had to act soon, in a few seconds, if I wanted to keep my job at B.G.

But the receiver felt heavy and sticky. I couldn't lift it up. I couldn't send her to jail.

"Ms. Mary . . ."

She stopped at the door, turned halfway as if she were ready to sprint out if something happened.

"Take your time over lunch, MaryAnn, and please watch your steps at the door."

Her green eyes grazed me like teeth.

"Ever heard of this saying, MaryAnn? 'O divine art of subtlety and secrecy! Through you I've learned to be invisible, through you inaudible; and hence I can hold the enemy's fate in my hands.'" I chanted, word by word, so she could hear clearly. If she knew Sun Tzu, she'd turn around.

She turned pale, blood leaving her face like waning tides. Then, a tiny smile spread on her face, the smile of recognition of comrades in a foreign land. She turned on her heels and walked to me in big strides.

"You know what, Jeannie, I don't need to think about it over lunch. I don't even eat lunch. Diet, you know." She gave me a wink. "I've made up my mind on the cross band. Here's the credit card. Let me try it one more time, though, before you swipe it."

"Are you sure, MaryAnn?" My heart beat fast. Big Mama was safe now. So was she. I was relieved and awed at the same time.

"Absolutely! You're the best salesperson I've ever met, Jeannie. If there were more people like you in the business, I'd be broke in a month or two."

She winked again and burst out laughing. I joined in heartily. It took a genius to recognize another genius. I'd miss her when she was gone.

"I don't lunch, but I do enjoy a good dinner, particularly with good company." She leaned over, whispering. "Would you care to join me tonight at the Four Seasons for some duck and wine?"

Before I could answer, she took my hand and planted something cool and smooth into my palm.

Big Mama.

"Good," I said. "See you at eight."

Bizarre, right? I was supposed to alert security, supposed to get her arrested, and testify in court to get her locked up in jail. Even if

I let her go, I should just let her go completely. Instead, I spent the evening dining with a jewelry thief. But I'm a girl who loves to break rules. I follow them only to start a game, and always end up bending and breaking them in order to reach my goal. I didn't let MaryAnn go out of kindness. I was curious. She's perhaps the smartest fox I've ever conquered. And I wanted to find out how she got into this, who trained her.

I wanted to know her for my own sake. Deep down, I felt a connection with her. Can a fox trust another fox? No. Can a fox form a temporary liaison for some hunting? Perhaps. I didn't know what I wanted from her at that time. It wouldn't be stealing for sure. That's never my game. I just wanted to keep the door open so when the time comes, when I need her, I can find her.

Or she can find me.

I have never asked where she lives. She comes to me whenever she has played a trick somewhere in Paris, London, Greece, Switzerland, San Francisco, Las Vegas, Dallas, or wherever big diamonds beckon. She finds me in B.G. and we go out to dine in the finest restaurants in Manhattan. Just as B.G. draws few but always rich clients, MaryAnn tricks sparingly but always with success. She never talks about it. But I can tell from her radiant face and relaxed hands, her body that pours satisfaction through every pore. All we do together is sip wine and eat delicate French cuisine that has no prices on the menu. Whenever a line from *The Art of War* slips from my mouth during our small talks, her hazel eyes sparkle and turn the color of jade. That's how I know she must have learned Sun Tzu by heart as I have, and I laugh. No wonder she's so good in what she does, far superior than any other professionals I've seen in my career. She's slippery, her tactics unpredictable like water that shapes its course according to the nature of the ground over which it flows. And she's disciplined and calm as she awaits the appearance of disorder and hubbub among the enemy. But most important of all, she's not greedy. For her, it's no longer just about money, but more about play. It's about the art of the game, the art of the war.

Once I asked her what made her come back and buy the Jude Frances cross band, which she still wears on her middle finger. She gave me a look and turned her face away.

"Your voice, the way you called my name. You wanted me to go back, just like my mother, whom I haven't seen for years. Oh, by the way, ever heard of this?" she started chanting: "To lift an autumn hair is no sign of great strength; to see the sun and mòon is no sign of sharp sight; to hear the noise of thunder is no sign of a quick ear.'"

We laughed. I told her she'd be a first-rate general had she been born a man.

She grabbed my hand. "Let's team up and have some fun."

I shook my head. I have four more years to become a citizen. Before that happens, I must not give the immigration bureau any reason to deport me. Besides, I'm not interested in her games. The tactics I've picked up from the book are not ends but means to reach my ultimate goal: to become rich, immensely rich, so that my mother and grandma can enjoy the rest of their lives in luxury and peace, so that I can have my name carved on the marble walls of the Metropolitan Museum, Opera House, City Ballet, and other places in Manhattan, Shanghai, Beijing . . .

MaryAnn's game will never get me there. Besides, I don't want to end up in jail, to which she's doomed. She doesn't know. She thinks she's invisible and untouchable. But her fate is already written in her face: to die in prison. She hasn't been caught yet, but she will. It's just a matter of time.

Unless, of course, she changes her course.

Working as a sales girl at B.G. won't take me anywhere, either.

I have my plan. It's not through men. I've had enough of them. I should thank Chen's mother the Shrew. I hate her for foiling my plan, but she also pointed out my path as she threw me out of her son's apartment.

You're not cut out for this, girl. You're too smart, too crafty, too ambitious. You know exactly what you want, and you go after it relentlessly. Men will never trust you with their money. They are not worth your talent, anyway.

They're chickens, most of them, my own son included. The rest are bullies, the worst kind of chickens. So don't waste your time. Go find your own path. You'll do well.

Her words were thunderbolts that jolted me out of my spell. I had started going after Peng Chen with two clear goals: his money and a green card. Then Virgin joined in, and things got out of control. Was I blinded by love? Afraid of losing the battle to Virgin? Or was it something else completely? For whatever reason, I'd forgotten my mother waiting to be reunited with me, forgotten my immediate goals, my ambitions. I had no more time to waste.

To start on my own path, I would need a green card first. So I married Dave, my Shakespeare professor's son, who'd been chasing me while I was chasing Mama's Boy. Dave knew I wasn't in love with him, but he got what he wanted from me—sixteen months of the best sex. We parted as friends once my green card came through. He had his own dream to pursue—to become a politician or diplomat, and he would need a woman of his own kind for his career: blonde and white. After the divorce, I took speech lessons and got the job at B.G. Since then, money has been trickling in like a singing brook. Men still want me like mad, but I've lost the appetite. What I saw in the student center eight months ago—lust, lechery, deflowering, celestial mating, whatever it was between Virgin and Mama's Boy—did some number on me. My sex drive has plummeted to that of an eighty-year-old lady.

MaryAnn grabbed my hands. "Perhaps we can go to Shanghai together and do some tricks. That's the only city I haven't touched yet. I'm saving her for the big moment of my life."

No, MaryAnn, I shouted inside, *you shall not touch Shanghai with your paws.*

But an idea hit me and suddenly everything became clear.

To get rich, I must look beyond Manhattan. There's not much room to move around on this island. The market is fully mature, filled up. But Shanghai is a different story—the city I'd vowed never to return to when I boarded that plane but have never stopped dreaming about for the past six years. I've been watching closely what's been going on there. It's once again turning into a paradise, yes, a paradise for capitalists and foreign investments, a paradise for fashion and beauty. It's a city where women are willing to starve themselves to death for fashionable clothes, shoes, bags, jewelry, anything that makes them look feminine and beautiful. It's in our blood, coded in our genes. We want to look beautiful at any cost.

It's all about survival. The most beautiful get power, money, social status, food, sex, health, even longevity. It's Darwinian: the more beautiful, the better fit to survive and succeed. Just look at the animals and birds. The ones that have the most colorful feathers and biggest horns get laid. Do I need to go into details? Same thing with plants: roses, tulips, and apples. They spread all over the world with their appearance. Beauty conquers. That's right, more powerful than guns and bombs.

That's why we'll do everything, anything to have it—budget payments, credit card payments, the biggest moneymaking machine that turns people into slaves, millions of them. They make dreams within reach. Just swipe the card, and you can have anything you want. Pay back little by little, have your blood sucked dry drip by drip, but who cares! To me, the smartest thing B.G. has done is to open B.G. credit cards. Why let the banks get fat? We work hard to make our clients happy, so we deserve to reap rewards, big rewards. Just imagine the interest we make every day from each purchase. We take cash, of course, which doesn't happen so often except with the new arrivals from China who have become fat from taking bribes and have to flee from the occasional government investigations to appease the robbed mass—the impoverished, furious mass. And they come here with big cash and buy the shiniest and most expensive items they see as if they were free.

The suckers!

I don't like them at all, even though I've made a small fortune from their desire to look American as quickly as possible, a down payment for a two-bedroom condo on the Upper East Side, even though they speak the language that comes to my dreams and makes me weep upon awakening. They always come to me, the only yellow face among the girls dressed in black from head to toe, our unofficial uniform. The slick, metropolitan color doesn't necessarily win respect from the rich, but it does scare away some of the unwanted gawking tourists.

With my yellow countrymen and women, however, my black dress alone won't do. As soon as they see my face, fear and awe vanish from their eyes, and they immediately resume their confidence that they can buy the whole world with the money they've robbed from the poor. Hey, Miss, they bellow, their fat fingers pointing to the watches and jewelry behind the glass. And I silence them with my three-thousand-dollar British accent. Yes, I paid that amount to a professional linguist who remolded my tongue, nose, and mouth to talk like a prissy Brit. On my first lesson, when she asked whether I wanted an American accent or British, I burst out laughing. She reminded me of my handsome gynecologist. After the procedure he performed for me, my last one, he said firmly that I should be on pills, and asked with a straight face if I preferred the brand that would make my breasts larger. My linguist was not much to look at, bad complexion, beady eyes, and hooked nose. But she had a voice that could send men into instant orgasms. And that's what I was paying for, the power to get what I wanted with my voice and words. And I can tell you it was worth every penny of the three thousand dollars I spent. I was practically hired on the spot after I talked to B.G.'s personnel manager on the phone for half an hour. The face-to-face interview was just a formality. Of course, my body and apparel were all part of it, but those wouldn't do without my accent. I had tried before, several times, and each time I'd been told to learn more English. In fact, Mr. Roger was dumbfounded when I showed up in his office. "Oh my, Miss Shin," he said, looking me up and down with an undisguised curiosity, "I think you'll do just fine here."

I do more than just fine. I'm the most sought-after salesperson in the department. I have the longest list of loyal clients who guzzle up my advice like fancy chocolate bars—all due to my impeccable English.

Never would I have thought my accent would work the same magic on my countrymen. The shock in their eyes when I open my mouth! A fucking little Jap, one mutters to his comrades after the initial shock. Perhaps an ABC, American-born Chinese? Another suggests, looking me up and down suspiciously. When they talk to me again in their stuttering, broken English, no one dares use that careless tone of voice like they own me, body and soul. But I can still feel the contempt bubbling up in their darkened hearts. No matter how good my English, I'm still a service girl.

Maggots. Wait till I open my B.G. on the waterfront of Shanghai. Their dirty money will flow into my pocket in exchange for diamonds, gold, designer shoes, and clothes.

Shanghai is exploding with new money and desires, yet it doesn't have a single store like Bergdorf Goodman.

It will change soon.

I made a promise to MaryAnn. "We will make it to Shanghai, MaryAnn. We will do something big."

I've been planning quietly. I know what I want for a luxury department store in Shanghai. It will be elegant and classy, with lots of woodwork to give it the tasteful look of an expensive old-line Manhattan apartment, and of course, intimate, to make the customers feel comfortable and royal. The first floor will be devoted to jewelry, perhaps cosmetics and perfumes. The second floor, however, will be for shoes only, all top designer shoes like Manolo Blahnick and Jimmy Choo. You'd be surprised how shoes work on people's psyche and sex drives. A woman can never have enough shoes just as she can't have enough diamonds. Gems and gold make her feel rich and aristocratic, but shoes give her the womanly power to hook a man's soul, the secret that Chinese women have known for over a thousand years through their foot beautification. Above the shoes, I'll have two floors for clothing, then another floor of shoes and bags. Have I mentioned that one can never have enough shoes? On that floor there will be a café that serves the best cappuccino and latte in China. Then another floor of clothing. The top floor will have things like fine glassware, tableware, pens, chocolates, and a few appliances, and of course, a restaurant that serves the most sophisticated French cuisine.

I'm almost ready. I've been talking to a few venture capital bankers who can't wait to dip their hands in the Huangpu River. I have the ideal representative for marketing—MaryAnn. She's blonde, the hottest hair color for girls in Shanghai nowadays. She's white, the skin color that no girl in Shanghai would get no matter how much powder they sprinkle on their pumpkin faces. She's thin and pretty and classy. But most importantly, she makes one feel included; that is, she gives the illusion that you can belong to that class if you wear her clothes, her shoes, and her jewelry. Will she join me? Sure she will. Once I point out her immediate future in America, which is getting dimmer and dimmer, and once I show her the potential fun and gain in our play in Shanghai, she'll jump in screaming with delight. To tie her hands with a string, I'll give her some company shares. Only a fool will steal from her own rice bowl or pluck feathers from her own body. And as a company representative, she will appear everywhere. On TV, billboards, magazines, web sites. Her face will be a public domain, recognized wherever she goes. I'd like to see then how she can still perform her old tricks, ha!

She'll be my left hand.

I haven't revealed my plan to her yet. *It is the business of a general to be quiet and thus ensure secrecy; upright and just, and thus maintain order.* Ah, here goes Sun Tzu again. A good general must mystify her officers and soldiers and keep them in total darkness in order to ensure success.

And the location, the key to success. I've secured a building on Nanjing Road, in the middle of the busiest street for shoppers and tourists, a few blocks from the waterfront, Peace Hotel, and No. 1 Department Store of Shanghai. With that location, my success is guaranteed. Its value can't be measured with gold. And you can't buy it with money, either. Connections only. Through my uncle. Yes, the same uncle who took me to the park on my thirteenth birthday.

When Mother suggested I talk to him, I almost threw up. But I had to put that water under the bridge. I need him to bring my vision into reality. No matter who rules China—emperors, nationalists, communists, or capitalists disguised as communists, one thing remains the same—nothing can be done without a good network. And my uncle seems to have established an elaborate web with the government in Shanghai as well as in Beijing. He's eager to help, a bit too eager. I guess he wants the money. He has the mind and guts to see my vision: a department store like B.G. in Shanghai could reap millions, even billions of dollars, if it's managed right. Perhaps he also wants to repair what he did to me twenty years ago? I don't know.

Of course I'm nervous. I don't know what I'll do when we're face-to-face. I've killed him in my dreams, over and over, yet he always comes back, more alive than ever.

That's not, however, what keeps me from going back to Shanghai.

I'm waiting for a sign. I need one more person to launch the business—someone I can trust, someone I don't have to play games with, someone I can share my life with with ultimate ease, safety, and in joy. It won't be a man, I know for sure. I said I've washed my hands of them. The Shrew is right: men are either chickens or bullies, which are basically the same thing. Will it be a woman? I'm not sure. When the person shows up, I will know.

11:28 a.m. In thirty-two minutes, Virgin will arrive. She's riding the subway, the pristine green number six. I can sense the vibrations of her body, smell her particular odor of baby powder and musky earth. When the clock strikes noon, she'll enter like a damn German train pulling into the station, punctual to the second. I still have no idea why she is coming to see me. Should I treat her like a customer? Should I show her some earrings? She has the most gorgeous earlobes, perfect size, shape, and skin tone to be adorned by pearls and diamonds, to be held on the tip of the tongue. If I could persuade her to have her ears pierced this time . . .

Here comes Mr. Hong in his dirty jacket and unwashed hair. He looks like he just jumped off the ship, clutching a bulging leather bag, eyes shining with super confidence. He's here to buy the necklace his hooker mistress picked out yesterday. Great! Now I can distract myself for a while. When Virgin arrives, I'll be busy, very busy. I'll make her wait, give her a headlong blow before she has a chance to talk. Poor Mr. Hong, he can't wait to have his blood sucked dry. Yesterday he stepped in the store with this woman, obviously intimidated and at a loss where to go, what to do. When he saw me, a big smile opened on his face, and he shuffled over quickly. The giant diamond ring on his finger showed off his wealth, but his weathered leathery face, his coarse hands, and the heavy accent from the western region of China betrayed his origin from some backwater province. God knows how many people he robbed to get here. But I didn't scare him away with my British accent. Instead, I welcomed him in Chinese. I don't know why. He looked so gullible as he hovered around this woman as if she were a queen, not knowing she was a second-class service girl with self-dyed hair and cheap perfume. She wanted this estate necklace of black pearls from the African coast. It is an ugly piece, to tell the honest truth. Too many large stones and pearls and diamonds. Every gem from the necklace is priceless, but when they are piled together just for the sake of showing wealth, it becomes a hideous thing. If it were mine, I'd take it apart and make a necklace with the pearls alone, a few pairs of earrings with the gems, rings with the diamonds. The hooker wanted it because it was the most expensive item, a good six-figure price.

Mr. Hong looked devastated when he saw the price tag. He didn't have enough cash. Of course he didn't. No one in his right mind would go around Manhattan carrying such an enormous sum unless he hired an armored truck. The real wealthy people don't carry cash. Just a swipe of plastic or a phone call to the bank would do. "Why can't you get credit cards like a normal American?" whined his hooker mistress. Mr. Hong hung his head as if he had just lost his manhood. I suggested he open a B.G. credit card and pay it off in ten months. I was trying to save his fat ass. In ten months, the little hooker will show her fox tail, and Mr. Hong may wake up from his dream world. But the hooker wriggled her snaky body against Mr. Hong and her pale knobby hands massaged his pot belly until his knees buckled and he promised her to return the next day to get the treasure.

"Good morning, Mr. Hong. How did you get here?"

"By train. It's clean and fast. Why?"

"Did you swallow a leopard's gall bladder, Mr. Hong, carrying this kind of cash in the subway?"

He took out a big wad of hundreds from his bag and stroked it gently, eyes glassy with lust. "My pretty Miss Shin, when you're in love one day yourself, you'll know the taste of a gall bladder, too. Thanks for your concern, though. I'm not as stupid as I look. Who will bother to rob a man who looks like the biggest country bumpkin in the whole town, hahaha? Can I look at the necklace again, by the way? Just want to make sure everything is still together. I'm just carrying out my woman's order. Isn't she smart or something? She wanted to come with me, but I made her wait at home. I want to give her a surprise tonight, over dinner and wine."

"You bet, Mr. Hong." I bent over to open the showcase, glad to get away from his greasy face, which is making me sick. His hooker is bleaching his pocket and spreading syphilis in his body and he calls it love? He can't be too stupid if he is capable of stealing so much money, slipping it through the government security and getting himself into the USA. Imagine all the fish in Shanghai and the rest of China, bigger and even more gullible? I'll not feel a slight tinge of guilt to see them take my bait. If the hooker can bleed the sucker, why can't I?

I need to take action before it's too late. But where is my sign?

Nesting quietly next to the loud necklace is a pair of Penny Preville earrings—eighteen-karat white gold with 1.32 cut diamonds and an emerald-cut center stone, small, delicate, no longer than an inch. Perfect for Virgin's earlobes. Are they still covered with those very fine down hairs? Is the skin there still tinged with pink? When she comes, I'll put them on her. I'll ask her to guess the price. "Five hundred," she'll whisper, taking a deep breath as if in awe of the number she has just uttered. I'll laugh my head off. Once a country bumpkin, forever a country bumpkin. Doesn't matter how many books she's stuffed in her big round head, how many degrees she has earned and keeps in her drawer. Why doesn't she hang up any of her shit on the wall? I would if I had any.

"Think big," I'll say, enjoying the shock in her eyes. She looks like a kid and an old lady at the same time. Child Crony, a perfect name for her, just like the Virgin Slut I nicknamed her when we first met on campus. This one fits the best, even though it is the Communist Virgin that spread on campus. Virgin Slut. Quite a contradictory mix. But that's her, Wan Li, the Sphinx Simpleton, the enigma and pain in my butt, my destined foe and love.

"It's five figures," I'll say, after a long pause for suspension. She'll give me this look as if I were speaking Korean or Swahili and I'll have to refrain from smacking her on the nose so it will no longer snub me with its high bridge, as if it were fake, like the fake noses nowadays in China. Had I been born with a nose like hers, I'd have become an admiral, a millionaire, a movie star, anything but a book-worm.

See what Virgin can do to my mind? Turning it into a wild horse in the clouds. I must concentrate, must hold my ground, no matter what. I have *The Art of War*. I'm in charge of the estate jewelry section at B.G., the crown of the luxury store in Manhattan. I'm dressed from head to toe with top designer brands. I speak English flawlessly. I'm the most charming girl at Bergdorf Goodman. I have nothing to fear.

"Miss Shin, hmmm, Miss Shin, lovely earrings. I'm sure my girl will love them. Perhaps next time? Today she wants the necklace, just the necklace, please."

"I'm sorry, Mr. Hong. I'm getting it for you right now."

Then I feel her presence.

It's her and not her. The field is the same, but the energy is different. The old Virgin was tight, rigid, inward, and closed. This one bursts like a fireball, no, a volcano, its lava melting trees and houses and rocks and sins along its path.

"Miss Shin, I say, Miss Shin . . ."

I look up. Before me, a bulging globe clad in a blue silk shawl: source of the heat and smell and light of a new life . . .

I close my eyes. Inside the globe is a bird, blue, lighter than the blue silk, almost violet and much more lovely. Blue Bird. That's it, my store, our store, has a name now. Blue Bird, blue phoenix, the mythical bird that fetches food for the Western Queen, symbol of good luck, courage, kindness, hope. The sign has come.

How ironic! I tried all kinds of tricks to get pregnant from Peng Chen. Every night except for my bleeding days. I wanted a baby with him so badly that I even drove the stud into exhaustion. When his mother showed up in his apartment from Taiwan, he happily moved into another room. But despite all my efforts, nothing happened. My stomach remained as flat as an airport runway. With Virgin, it only took one shot. How do I know one shot only? Because I saw him deflower her in the student center, saw Mama Shrew pick up her boy a few hours later and escort him directly to the airport. I followed them there to make sure he got on the plane because if I couldn't get him then nobody else would. At least no one in New York City. When I got home, I collected everything that had to do with Mama's Boy and Virgin: photos, perfume, rings, necklaces, suits, bed sheets, pillows, everything except for the fake pearl earrings Virgin got me for my birthday. I took them to a dumpster in a schoolyard and burnt them all. The smoke from the pile was dark and rancid. I cried. I had lost the war. I was damned for what I'd done in the past.

Who'd have known a seed sprouted in Virgin's womb that night?

I should have known. There were signs all over. Mama's Boy vanished from my dreams completely that day, and Virgin showed up every night, always with a halo and a mysterious smile, always accompanied by a blue moon over her head, a blue bird perched on her shoulder. I have been too busy hating the Shrew and his son and myself to notice this sign, to realize how I've loved Virgin since the moment we met.

"Ji Xing."

I used to hate it when Virgin called me by my Chinese name. I would yell all kinds of names at her and demand that she call me Jeanne Shin.

"The first step to make you an American," said White Tiger when he gave me the new name upon my arrival.

"But why?" asked Virgin with wide eyes. "Ji Xing sounds lovely, like the ringing of a bell from a distant star. I also like the meaning—lucky star. Isn't it what your mother wanted—to wish you good luck every time your name is called?"

I stamped my feet, called her stupid bitch, superstitious witch, country bumpkin, and a bunch of other names. I was determined to sever my past. Why did she keep dragging me back?

"Xing Xing," she calls again. She wants to tell me something.

Shhhhhh. I put my fingers to my lips.

She laughs and takes my hands into her palms. I open my eyes. Virgin's face is a blossoming peony. Faint folds run across her forehead like the veins on flower petals. She smells like peonies, too, the scent that comes from her skin and the baby in her womb. Virgin never wears perfume. It gives her violent allergy attacks. Her palms are rough and chapped. The cuticles need a manicure badly. But they're warm like a stove, the coal stove I used to light at 4:00 a.m. in the dark alley every day once I turned six, the stove that cooked breakfast, lunch, and dinner for my entire family that I loathe and dream about every night. First a layer of newspaper, then a few precious trinkets found from the streets, trees, neighbors' yards, then coal balls made from scratch with bare hands. The fire, so tiny and seemingly weak, kept us warm and alive nevertheless.

Tears well up in my eyes. For the first time, my name no longer sounds like a mockery or curse. Xing, the ring of a star from far away. Ji Xing, a lucky star. Xing Xing, a new star rising.

I try to say something to Virgin, something smart and funny and wise and powerful. Perhaps a quote from *The Art of War?* I summon my old Sun Tzu, but he has vanished, completely and totally, not a single trace left in my brain cells. Impossible! I've been chanting his words every day like a religious fanatic. He can't abandon me like this.

Then Virgin speaks. She speaks in the dialect we were both born into and grew up with, the dialect I've shunned for six years but now is breaking every floodgate in my heart.

"I'm going to Shanghai, Ji Xing. Would you go with me, with us?"

THE HOMECOMING OF
AN OLD BEIJING MAN

Just ten years, and the city is gone. Old square yards with elms and wisterias, gone; narrow lanes patrolled by sharp-eyed, tiny-footed ladies from the neighborhood committee, gone. Skyscrapers shoot up into the sky like bamboo shoots. Highways, streets, alleys, and sidewalks are covered with cars spitting fumes into air. No more blue sky. No more dirt or weeds. Everything is smoothed over with concrete. My shoes never get muddy; my collar stays clean for a whole week, quite unlike the old dusty days. Restaurants line up along the street like sparrows on wires, and beautiful girls lean on doors, their sweet voices snatching souls, their painted eyes making knees tremble. What choice do I have but to enter and sit down at a table? I've never eaten out so much. Four times a week at least: roast duck, lamb fondue, pig's feet, donkey's ass, and fish that costs eighty-six yuan a pound, half of my monthly salary before I retired. I eat and drink till my stomach is about to explode, and then stroll into a hotel for a whole body massage to digest the meat and wine. If I'm not too tired after that, I go to a karaoke bar with my son for more drinks and fun. Six months in Beijing, I just eat, drink, and sing, going to places in my son's 2004 Mercedes or my daughter's Audi. I put on thirty pounds. What a lucky old man I am!

I didn't mean to stay this long. I had promised my youngest daughter I'd return to Minnesota in a month, as soon as I finished this monkey business with my son-in-law in Beijing. "Ba, your home is in Minnesota," my youngest daughter reminds me almost every day on the phone. True, for ten years I've lived in Minnesota with her and her kids and my old wife. Three years ago, I became a naturalized alien. That's what the paper says. I guess I'm a natural American citizen now, head to toe, inside and out. And I have a really nice home in Minnesota—a big house on a crystal clear lake full of fish and five acres of rich land. The property is worth at least a million now. My daughter is a great businesswoman. The first thing she did when she came to America was go to school at Hamline University. She had to study harder than her classmates because her English was bad. I don't quite get it. Her English was good enough to get her a job as an interpreter for foreign tourists in Beijing, and to get herself a great husband. Anyway, she got her MBA and now stays home managing the stocks her husband left behind. Still, she needs me: her kids still young, and her mother, my old wife, still wanders outside and gets lost all the time. For almost ten years, I've been the only man in her household. I don't speak English or drive, yet, but I'm a man, the pillar of the house. I promised her I'd go home after the Mid-Autumn Festival, as soon as I had a chance to eat the Muslim-style moon cakes. How can any filial daughter deny an old man such a simple request?

But my son and daughter in Beijing come up with all sorts of ways to get me to stay one more week, then another. Soon one month becomes two, and two turns into three. Then it's Thanksgiving and my daughter starts marinating three fat chickens with garlic, soy sauce, and tea leaves for roasting, so what else can I do but stay another two weeks? In the blink of an eye, Christmas arrives. My son insists I should experience how Chinese celebrate Christmas nowadays. It has become a big deal, almost bigger than the Spring Festival. He takes me to a church on Christmas Eve. Nice music, short service, and a big feast. I've never seen so much food in my life. We eat and drink till dawn. By then, everyone is singing and dancing and making merry. I'm sure Lord Jesus himself is smiling happily from the sky. That's the way to celebrate his Lord's birthday, anyone's birthday.

When life is good, time flies.

Beijing seems to have become a paradise for the rich. They dress well, eat well, and travel to Paris, London, New York and other nice places for vacation. They are loaded with money. Just look at my son's apartment in the heart of the city, six bedrooms, 250 square meters, all for himself, and his rotating girlfriends. Do you know how much a place like that costs? Ten thousand yuan a square meter. Go figure. I worked my ass off my entire life. All I got was a crummy apartment with less than twenty square meters, no kitchen, no bathroom, no water. A rat hole, as my son called it. In that rat hole, I raised my three kids plus my adopted son, who later became my son-in-law. And you know what? I was much more content than my rich playboy son who constantly complains about his place being too small and out of fashion and is looking to put two million yuan down on a mountain villa at the foot of the Great Wall.

Same thing with my daughter. She has an apartment just as big as her brother's place for her family of three—herself, her son and husband (before she kicked him out after his affair with a seventeen-year-old). What a sin! I often wonder how she feels when she drives by the slums where migrant workers and unemployed people congregate. She used to be such a conscientious girl, giving and generous, hardworking like her husband. When she turned eighteen, she joined the Party, a young promising member and an ideal companion to her husband, the most hardworking and honest man I've ever seen. I knew what I was doing when I did the matchmaking.

But ten years later, both she and my son-in-law joined my son's camp of ruthless greed. Now she's buying another apartment in my name, just because she can. She hates to see her money rotting in the bank. An apartment in the city will triple its value within a year. Why in my name? Not because I'm moving back to Beijing. No. She doesn't want her husband to get it if they get a divorce. You see the kind of brain she has?

I try not to ask how on earth she got that kind of money. As far as I know, she's still a good daughter, filial and capable. When I left for America ten years ago, she was working as a government employee making sixty-five yuan a month, not enough for a cup of tea these days in Beijing. And my good-for-nothing-son didn't even have a job. You may ask why I didn't find a job for my only son. I did, a dozen at least, in my own department, in my friends' departments. All office jobs, no manual labor, unthinkable for someone who didn't even have a high-school diploma. But my boy couldn't hold anything longer than a week, couldn't stand being shut in a cubbyhole from nine to five every day, six days a week. Just couldn't. I thought he'd end up on the street as a beggar. Instead, he became a millionaire, richer than his sister.

I don't know how they made their fortunes. I don't want to know. They're grown-ups. I taught them what's good, what's bad. They surely work hard, but not the way I worked for the Party. For forty-six years, I never arrived late or left early a single time, never stole a fen, never had an affair. You bet I had opportunities. Too many. I was the secretary to the minister of hydraulic power. All the dams we built for the new China. Big responsibilities, big money deals, and always surrounded by beautiful girls. But the idea of pocketing a penny never entered my mind, let alone glancing at a girl who was not my wife. That's how we were, the pure, dyed-in-the-wool communists. Our only dream was to build a paradise where everything was just and everyone was equal and happy. Most of my buddies are dead now. Those still alive have quit the Party. They're sick to death over what's going on. Everyone steals. The big shots steal big bucks, and the small potatoes steal pennies and nickels. Those who refuse to steal can't hold their jobs for more than a month, because they make the thieves look bad, and they get rid of the good guys in order to steal with ease. Sure, the government tries to intervene. Every year they catch a few and kill them to send a message. Last year two lieutenant governors and the vice chairman of the People's Congress were shot, the biggest chickens ever killed, to scare the monkeys. Have the monkeys gotten the message? You bet your ass they have. They started stealing more and faster. Grab as much as possible while you can, before you get caught, that's the mantra. And what's the chance of getting caught anyway? Less than a plane crash a year, less than being hit by lightning. Besides, there's always the escape route to America or Canada or Europe. With the millions of dollars they've stashed away in Swiss banks, they can live anywhere like kings and queens.

Would I be corrupt like them if I had stayed in China? I don't think so. I'm old-fashioned, a die-hard communist. I would have quit the Party too, like my buddies. I miss Mao, miss our good old days. Sure we had only one pair of pants and a jacket in those days, had meat to eat once a week at most, and a one-room apartment to raise kids. But we were clean, our souls full of fire for a better society. Now we live in big apartments and go around in nice cars and eat out every day, but my conscience is ill. The rich are so rich they don't even know how to squander. The other night in a karaoke bar, I saw a guy throw out two stacks of hundred-yuan notes for his waitress. I asked my server if it happens often that a client leaves a ten-thousand-yuan tip and she said,

"Grandpa, that's not a ten. That's a twenty-thousand yuan tip, and it's the norm in this bar."

How I wish I could have smacked that smirk off her fox face!

Instead, I fled. Twenty thousand yuan to a hooker bitch? No way!

When a worker is laid off, he gets two hundred yuan from the government, if he's lucky. That tip could feed two hundred poor workers and their families for a whole month.

Let me tell you how the poor live in Beijing. One morning I couldn't sleep, so I went for a walk. In the dim light, I saw a man picking food from a garbage can. "Rotten Egg's son, what the hell are you doing here?" I shouted. Of course I knew exactly what he was doing and why, from his hollowed cheeks and patched clothes, from the stale cabbage leaves clutched in one hand, and the plastic bag with empty Coke bottles in the other. He looked up. For a split second, I thought I had the wrong man. Rotten Egg's son was the same age as my oldest daughter, forty-two, and this man looked older than me. But the old man answered in a choking voice.

"Uncle Wu, Uncle Wu, I can't believe you're still alive! I can't believe you still remember me!"

I started weeping myself. Of course I remembered him. His father, Rotten Egg, had shared the same office with me for twenty-five years. We were drinking buddies. We played cards every weekend. I called him Rotten Egg because he was the biggest cheater I'd ever met and his hands reeked with the odor of bad luck. Whenever we lost, I'd yell, "Rotten Egg, you need to move your ancestors' tombs to a better spot so you can get some luck for once in your life."

Indeed, Rotten Egg was an incarnation of ill stars. His parents died when he was seven. At thirteen, he ran away from his uncle to join Mao's army. With his long years in the army and the Party, he should have been a minister at least, if not a governor. Yet he had never gone beyond being the vice minister's secretary. And his only son inherited the same luck: sent to Mongolia at seventeen where he herded cows and sheep for ten years, he didn't return to the city until his father retired. I used my back door connections to get him a job in the dam construction company associated with the Hydraulic Power Ministry. It was manual labor in the open air all year round, but the pay was good, and the job was secure, considering the kid had no degree or skill or brains. Before I left for America, I found him a nice spinster. Not a young beauty for sure, but a virgin all right. Time for Rotten Egg to hold a grandson in his arms.

On the eve of my departure, Rotten Egg got drunk. "Brother Wu, Brother Wu," he wept. "Who's going to play with me when you're gone? Who's going to take care of my son when I'm gone?"

"Shut up," I yelled. "Can't you say something auspicious before my flight? You and I will live at least twenty or thirty more years. And I'll be back in no time, brother, and we'll play cards again. I promise."

Had I only known it would take me ten years to come back! Had I only known Rotten Egg would be crushed by a car while crossing the street, and his son would end up a scavenger in the garbage!

What could I have done? What could I have done to make things better?

"I'd like to invite you to my place, Uncle Wu," Rotten Egg's son murmured. He sounded exactly like his father, the same nasal whine, same twitching eyes that indicated bad luck. "But I have no chair for you to sit on, no water or electricity to make you a cup of tea."

So we chatted on the street. He had been squatting in his father's apartment after he lost his job. The company was privatized four years ago, and he was dismissed with a two-thousand-yuan retirement package. Couldn't find another job, not even as a temp. No one would hire a forty-year-old man when the city was swarmed with hordes of young peasants willing to do anything for almost nothing. The housing department had been trying to get him out, cutting off water, electricity, and other services.

"Still, I'm better off than most of my ex-coworkers," he chuckled. "At least I still have an apartment. Luckily I don't have a family to support. My wife left when I lost my job. Don't fret, Uncle Wu. It's fate. I want her to live on. No need to hang two people on one tree."

I slipped two hundred yuan into his pocket. "Buy some bread for yourself, son," I said and walked away fast. I couldn't say a word. I'm sure Chairman Mao couldn't say a word either from his grave.

I heard there are millions of unemployed workers like Rotten Egg's son, those who lost jobs and apartments and had nowhere to go, and those who lost their land and poured into cities for a meager living. We're sitting on a volcano.

I said to my daughter one day, "I'm not questioning how you've made your money. I just want to say this: Don't be greedy. Stop when you've made enough for a comfortable life."

"Yes, Father," she said.

Can she quit? Will she? I doubt it. She manages the designer clothes section at Saite, the biggest department store in Beijing. Her floor has over two hundred workers, making huge profits every month, though every other floor loses money. She tried to quit twice so she could spend more time with her son and keep a better eye on her husband, but the company wouldn't let her. They bribed her with a limo, two personal assistants, big bonuses, power. Every morning a handsome young man drives her to an air-conditioned office, her secretary brings her Blue Mountain espresso and the *People's Daily* on a silver tray. She sips her morning elixir, reads the paper, and gives instructions for the day's plan, then takes off, doing whatever she wants. Her days are swamped with lunch and dinner invitations from designers and wholesalers. Their fortune depends on her, and they'll do anything to keep their products on her floor. Should I name some of the gifts piled in her closets? Chanel perfumes, Lancôme cosmetics, Gucci bags, Armani dresses . . . oh, there's her son's college fund, half a million under his name, and the boy is only seven. Unbelievable! But this is nothing compared to what the big shots get: cars, apartments, mansions in Canada and America . . . You ask me why such elaborate gifts? Go figure.

I'm afraid. So is she. We all know we are sitting on a volcano. Our butts feel the heat and quiver. She wants to quit, but can't. She's already on the pirate ship. Around her, nothing but the vast sea. To quit is to lose everything. Without things, she's worthless, better off dead than alive, especially for a woman her age—forty and up. She's lost her youth, her face wrinkled, waist round and puffy. Neither makeup nor cosmetic surgery will ever make her young again. If her husband takes on a few mistresses, what can she do but weep and swallow her tears in silence?

Let me tell you something about Chinese men these days. As soon as they get a few extra yuan in their hands, they run out and find themselves some girls: hookers, mistresses, concubines. Doesn't matter if he is a high-ranked official or pulls a rickshaw. Every man is a rotten egg, including my own son, including my son-in-law, that son of a rabbit. When I took him home to Beijing from Tang Shan twenty-eight years ago, he was nothing but a scrawny country bumpkin. I gave him a home, sent him to school, got him a job in my department, introduced him to the Party, promoted him to the head of the department, and then gave him my oldest daughter. I thought I had an eye for a good man. He had been good, exceptionally good. My kids, at least my daughters, had regarded him as a big brother and role model. And he was the best worker, the straightest person I'd ever encountered. When I was interrogated for corruption, my wife went mad and wandered around the streets for days and weeks without returning home. He came to see me every day in jail, every day for a whole year, bringing me food and clothes and kind words. He was the only one who believed in my innocence, the only one who wrote hundreds of letters to higher authorities to expose the crooks who had put me in jail because I had refused to cooperate in their corruption schemes.

When he married my daughter at thirty-three, he was still a virgin. How did I know? Because my daughter asked for a divorce a year after their marriage. I asked her why. She started crying and said the husband I'd chosen for her was a eunuch. No way, I said. I'd seen his body as we walked those two hundred miles from Tang Shan to Beijing. He had a perfect body, nothing missing or deformed. So I questioned him. He blushed hard, this thirty-four-year-old man, and mumbled that he didn't know much about sex and he'd been hoping I'd give him some advice. So I did, and two years later, their son was born.

My heart broke when I heard he took his secretary, a seventeen-year-old girl, for his concubine.

What turned an old virgin into a playboy?

Perhaps I shouldn't be too hard on him. After all, who doesn't like the tender flesh of a seventeen-year-old? But eating tender meat is one thing, beating your wife is another. A man can have as many concubines as he wants, but he must respect his wife, put her first, no matter how old and ugly, how unpleasantly shrewd. A wife is a wife just as a concubine is a concubine. There's an order in things, a place for everyone. You break that order, society will turn upside down. You'd think that son of a rabbit would know better. But no, he beat up his own dear wife, his son's mother, in front of his little whore. How pathetic! How is she going to live again? How is she going to show her face in public, let alone run a big company?

Before that happened, I'd been telling my oldest to swallow it, just swallow it, for the sake of her son, her own happiness in the long run. She had never been much of a looker when she was young. Now she's past forty. If divorced, how on earth would she find another man? Even if she finds one, there's no guarantee that a new husband wouldn't pick up a concubine. It's the trend of the nation, as old and mysterious as human desires. Old Confucius was absolutely right: when the body is clothed and stomach fed, lust comes racing.

She had called at five o'clock in the morning Minnesota time, weeping like a little girl. Her husband hit her in front of the little bitch concubine. She was going to kill herself because she had lost her face.

"He brought her home?" I gasped.

"No, I followed them to a restaurant. They sat together like real lovers, holding hands even while they ate. I couldn't stand it. He never treated me like this. Never! For the first year, he was nothing but a eunuch, then he was a cold fish. All these years, I slept next to him feeling dry and old and worthless."

"You have your charm and you definitely have a brain." I said, trying to console her. Unlike my youngest daughter, who has fair skin and watery big eyes, my eldest is endowed with a thick torso, short limbs, high cheekbones, small eyes, and a dry flaky complexion. She's lucky she has a husband at all.

"I couldn't stand watching them chat and neck like lovebirds. So I burst in and scratched the bitch's face and pulled her hair. I pushed her to the floor and kicked her in the stomach. And the bastard slapped me."

"Tell him to sleep in his office for a week," I said. "That'll teach the son of a rabbit a lesson."

"I already changed the lock and dumped all his suits into a trash can. He's not coming back."

That was when I decided to go home, after ten years in America, to take care of the monkey business my son-in-law and my daughter had created.

My youngest daughter said, "Ba, you vowed never to go back again. Have you forgotten the year you spent in jail, your high blood pressure? Since you came to Minnesota, you've never been so happy, so peaceful. You can double the size of your vegetable garden if you want, go fishing as long as you want, and I promise I won't say a word about your fatty pork, your grandson won't laugh at your pig feet casserole again. I promise. But don't go back. You'll lose your temper, you'll have a stroke, and . . . "

"Your big sister needs me, and your brother, too."

She cried. "What about me, Ba?"

I sighed. At the hospital, her husband wouldn't let go of my hand. He couldn't speak, couldn't close his eyes until I said I'd stay till my grandchildren grew up. Poor Jimmy, so kind, so intelligent, so loving! You can't find such a gentleman among Chinese any more. Why did he have to be diabetic? Why did he have to die at fifty-seven? My poor daughter, widowed in her twenties, with two young kids and the ferocious relatives of her late husband who called her a vixen and tried all sorts of tricks to strip her rights. Of course I stayed. I'm her father, for heaven's sake, grandfather of a lovely girl and a smart boy. I know my daughter, my pigheaded child. She'll never marry again. After a husband like this, she can't look at another man again. It was love at first sight. He went to Beijing for a conference, and she was assigned to him as an interpreter. She was twenty-two, a flower ready to bloom. He had just turned fifty, had three grown-up kids from his first marriage. But no matter. Before his trip was over, they were engaged. Their love was the kind you hear only in fairy tales or see in movies. How she suffered during the year waiting for her immigration papers! And how he traveled to Beijing every other month to comfort her! I still remember the tears in her eyes when she boarded the plane to America. It was her decision to have a kid to keep their love going.

She knew he would die ahead of her, way ahead. So she persuaded him to let her get pregnant. The first one was a girl. He was thrilled, having wanted a girl all his life. But no, she wanted a son, a son to carry on his name, his spirit, his intelligence, his face. Jimmy wrote to me, begging me to come over. He was about to have his legs amputated, and his wife was pregnant with their second child. The man knew he didn't have too much time. So I came. It was good timing. China had started the reforms, and things were changing fast. The new government was dumping old Party loyalists to clear the path. After I got out of jail, I returned to my old job, but nothing was the same. I was losing my temper every day, throwing things, yelling at my wife, quarreling with my boss, my friends. My blood pressure shot up to two-fifty.

Is America as heavenly as my daughter described? Well, everyone has his own heaven. For my daughter, it was her husband. For my son, it's his Mercedes. For me, it's a good meal over a bottle of *Er guo tou* liquor and a chat with old friends. During my first year in Minnesota, I had no one to talk to. There were only a handful of Chinese in the Twin Cities in those days, and most of them were restaurant workers who spoke only Cantonese, and were too busy to chat with a customer. The streets were nice and clean, so clean that I stopped my spitting habit. No one forced me to. No police or old ladies with red armbands scolded me or gave me tickets like in Beijing. If I wouldn't spit on the carpet in my own house, I wouldn't spit on a street that seemed cleaner than my floor. But the streets were worse than a maze, no garbage can or a store or a person to mark my way home. After I got lost a dozen times, after my daughter drove around searching for me in dark streets and parks, she begged me to stick to Summit Avenue. "Don't go off on other streets, please," she said with tears in her eyes. But I'm a human, not an inmate or a dog to be let out for relief. If I see something interesting, I like to cross the street and take a look. Not that there is much to see anyway, except for trees that don't talk. It took me ten years to like their silence. My daughter and her husband were living in a big condo on Summit Avenue at that time, ten times bigger than my apartment in Beijing, but I was dying from loneliness. My American son-in-law was a cultured man, having held many important jobs in his life, directing museums in big cities. He tried to entertain me with his funny Chinese, and I shouted back with my pidgin English, and we just ended up laughing. He did teach me how to enjoy football and turned me into a Vikings fan. He found a church near the University campus that had a few dozen Chinese followers. The first time my daughter took me there, I talked two hours nonstop with some men, before I got to know their names and where they came from. It turned out they barely spoke Mandarin, but they listened as if they were listening to a sermon. Such good Christian lambs! Since then we've been going there every Sunday. We're not converted. Not yet. I tell my Chinese pastor I am still thinking, just so he won't shut his door on me. I have no interest in the Bible stories or Jesus' deeds. The food there is terrible, but it is free, and I get my salvation—to speak Chinese for a whole afternoon.

After his amputation, my son-in-law bought a house on the lake, a house equipped for wheelchairs, surrounded by five acres of trees. Every day I dig and fish. The water calmed me down, and the garden, too. Since we moved there, we've never bought a single fish or vegetable. Everything comes from the lake and garden. Morning and evening, I play with my grandchildren. Smart, smart kids, just like their daddy, and so good looking, like most of the mixed bloods. When they go to school, I move rocks, fix the fence, plant vegetables and trees, weed, fertilize, feed chickens and goats . . . Yes, I have two goats, one black, one white. Great milk, tasty meat. I would have raised pigs if my neighbors let me.

My daughter said, "Ba, you're a Minnesotan, a true Minnesota farmer."

I nodded and smiled. I was born in a peasant family of many generations. I grew up digging in the fields until I joined Mao's army to fight Japanese devils, then the evil Nationalists and greedy landlords, until we finally threw out those bloodsucking imperialist colonizers from the West and established a new China. My Yellow Plateau and its hard clay soil! How my parents and grandparents would have cried with joy if they had seen the Minnesota land, so rich you can squeeze oil from it! Fate is a big laughing mouth. Sixty years ago, I ran away from home to fight the landlords and American imperialists. Now I have become an American citizen, own five acres of the richest land on the cleanest lake, a landlord a hundred times bigger and richer than those country bumpkins I had helped to execute.

China had become a memory, far away and long ago. And Beijing, my beloved city, came to me only in my dreams, as fragrances of duck feet, cow tongues, pig elbows, and dumplings with pork and white cabbage.

"Ba," my daughter said, "I've never seen you so calm, never seen you get along with Ma so well. America has made you healthy again, and happy."

"Happy, yes, happy," I said.

In Beijing, I eat like a pig, all the fatty stuff cooked with soy sauce my American daughter didn't allow me to touch for ten years, all the delicious things my American grandson scoffed at. Ba is making up for his lost dreams, my Chinese daughter said laughing. She bought me the largest pig head she could find. I gnawed on its crunchy ears, its chewy nose and tongue, its tender cheeks. For ten years in Minnesota, I had to beg like a child to buy meat other than steak or chicken breast, the most boring kind, like white bread. No flavor, no personality, no fat to oil my joints or smooth my intestines. I still can't believe how Americans throw away feet, head, and intestines, liver and heart, and grind them to feed chickens and cows, cats and dogs. My daughter claims it is the American way. O.K., but is it also the American way to cook food either boiled or broiled only, with no salt, sugar, oil, or soy sauce? Only Tartars from two thousand years ago cooked this way.

"It's to prevent diabetes and high blood pressure, Ba," said my Americanized daughter. Well, I'm not diabetic, nor am I barbaric. I'm sick of cooking my meat in the fireplace in the middle of the night when my daughter and grandchildren are sound asleep, sick of not being allowed to use the stove. Chinese cooking ruins the house, she said, all the frying and smoke and grease. Well, she might as well seal up my mouth and give me an i.v. The clean way, the American way.

So I open my belly and stuff myself like a pig. Not just to fulfill my carnal desires, but also to fool that good-for-nothing son-in-law of mine. He called the day I got home, offering to drive me around the city and visit my old friends in his car, offering to take me out to a stand that sells smoked donkey.

"The only one left in Beijing, and the best one, Ba," he said.

Son of a rabbit, the nerve he has to call me "Ba." How could he face me again after he broke my heart like this? When I took him to Beijing in 1976, I treated him like a son, an eldest son. Whatever I gave to my children, he had a share: food, clothes, books, education . . . except for whipping. I never raised my voice to him, never lifted my belt over his head. He owes everything to me, his job, his Party membership, his rank, his home, his wife and son. And what did he give me in return? A slap in my face! As far as I'm concerned, boxing my daughter's ear in public is equivalent to boxing my ear in public. If I had my way, I'd punch his face till he got his senses back. A real Chinese man never shows disrespect to his wife in public, no matter how many concubines he takes in.

I'd also ask him how he changed from a communist into a beast.

But I just mmmhed and aahaaed with him over the phone. I guess I have been re-educated in America, tamed and cultivated by "Minnesota nice." Not really. I just wanted to find out the truth before taking action. I'd only heard my daughter's side of the story. The girl has a tendency toward imagination and exaggeration, a womanly tendency, if you know what I mean. Finding truth takes patience and strategy. You beat around the bush till you find the path. You never confront, never say, "Hey, son, I heard you've taken in a concubine. Is it true?" Of course he'll say, "No, sir, that's not the truth." Of course he'll hide his woman while waiting to weather the storm. So I just eat all day and play with my grandson, who is seven years old and smart as an elf. He spends weekends with his father after my daughter kicked him out.

My son gets more and more impatient. He assumes the only reason I came back was to help him beat the shit out of that ungrateful beast, and he's been pumping his muscles lifting weights and doing sit-ups to prepare for the fight. The moment I took my Tang Shan orphan home, my son disliked him. The boy who saved my life twice dwarfed him in every aspect. When I left for America, I made my son-in-law the trustee. He drew money from my monthly retirement pay and gave my son a weekly allowance. It was humiliating, but what else could I do? My son could not be trusted with money. He would have spent his monthly allowance in five minutes.

"What are you waiting for, Ba," he growls. "His little whore's belly is getting big. If we don't teach him a lesson now, we'll have endless trouble. The bastard is desperate. He wants half of my sister's money. Half! Do you hear?"

That's news to me, serious news. When the baby is born, when the rice is cooked, my daughter will lose her husband, and I'll lose my eldest son, forever.

I approach my grandson.

"What a game, what a brain, sonny boy," I praise the boy bending over the little square machine. That's all he does now, play Game Boy and watch TV. No more talking with his mother or grandpa or anyone else. "Who taught you this complicated game, your dad or his aunt?"

"Aunt Li," he said without looking up.

"Is she as pretty and young as your own aunt?" I pointed to my American daughter's wedding photo ten years ago.

"Not as pretty, but she's fun and laughs a lot. She plays with me like the big sister I've always wanted."

Tender meat, that bastard loves tender meat.

"Is your daddy's new place as big as your mom's?"

The boy shook his head. "Grandpa," he stopped his Game Boy and looked at me with his dark bright eyes. "Can Daddy come back home? He said he was sorry he hit Mommy, but he is entitled to the apartment. He wants to move back with Mommy."

Over my dead body! I shouted to myself.

"Don't you worry about a thing." I stroked the boy's soft hair. "Grandpa will take care of it."

"Let's teach that son of a rabbit a real lesson," I said to my son.

"Finally!" He beamed, his cheeks flushed like a monkey butt. "The old fox has sent his little whore to her parents in the countryside and he himself has been hiding in his company compound. If we show up there, he'll start screaming for help and the security will come right away. So we have to get him on the street. He goes back to his apartment to do laundry Sunday afternoons, after he drops off his son at my sister's place. I just talked to my exgirlfriend, who lives next door. He's home eating duck feet."

"What are we waiting for? Let's go."

His red Mercedes shoots forward like an arrow; much faster than the cherry-colored Ford van my Minnesota daughter drives.

"Good detective work, son," I murmured.

"I learned it on the job. Never thought it would come in handy in this kind of business," he laughed, his nose scarlet from excitement. He'd been bored to death idling at home since the government closed his real-estate agency. He didn't tell me why it was shut down, and I didn't ask. My daughter hinted that he had made millions within two years and I believed it. Just look at his brand new car. I don't know how much it cost, how much his gigantic apartment with the view of Tiananmen Square cost, or his mansion in the suburbs with live-in servants, his Rolex studded with diamonds, his Armani suits in the overflowing walk-in-closet. Don't want to know. Something is not right if a young man without any skill or a college degree can make so much in two years. I'm just worried.

How deep is his connection with Zhong Nan Hai, the center of all power? Maybe he does know a few big shots there. How else would he have made this kind of money? Maybe they closed his agency to protect him and themselves. When the storm is over, they'll let him out. But what if they can't weather the storm? What if the big tree topples? He can go to jail, just like that, get executed without a trial. I suggested that I could get him a green card. He might have to wait ten, twelve years, but he would get it eventually, since I'm a citizen now. A cunning rabbit needs three holes. But he curled his lips.

"I'd rather die a tiger than live in a hole as a rabbit."

True, in China, he is a tiger, though he's been crouching for the past six months. He can have ten girls a day if he wants, goes to the best restaurants, lives in the best apartment, drives the best car, goes to the best gym, and travels to the best places. All these require money. He has money. But he doesn't speak a word of English, and his talent for smooching will go kaput in America. The boy has been a lazybones since the day he was born. Didn't like to work or study or learn any skills. His brain is like a sieve. Nothing holds. But boy he's a charmer! When he opens his mouth, the dead stand up and start dancing for him. People say he looks like David from the Bible, with his six-foot height and broad shoulders, his big eyes and high nose, his deep, silky voice and olive skin, all the features rare for a Chinese that make him a star in Beijing. But in Minnesota he'd be nothing. Everyone there looks like David, to me at least, taller and bigger-nosed. His good looks wouldn't earn him a bowl of rice there.

His phone rang. He pulled it open and started talking. If a cop saw us, we could be fined two hundred yuan, plus a warning. Six warnings a year, and you lose your license. But my son drove as if he owned the city. He must have connections with the cops, too, who are getting rich from fines and bribes.

"Hurry, the old fox is leaving his hole." He accelerated.

The traffic was awful. Before I left China, the streets were crowded, but you could still walk or bike through, at least for the strong ones like me who knew how to push elbows and legs. But what can you do with cars? The way my son drives, he would lose his license on day one in America. No one here follows rules, no one waits for pedestrians. It's the law of the jungle: the fit get their way, the weak get crushed. I see accidents every day. You have to be an Olympic athlete to dodge the flying cars. The government just passed a bill: in any accident that involves a car and pedestrian, the driver takes the full responsibility. There's uproar among fancy car drivers. Go figure! They never slow down, even if you are crossing on the white pedestrian line. The only things they recognize are cars fancier and bigger than theirs. Why? Because they don't want to be crushed.

"Trust me, Ba, I've never had an accident!" A hurt look came over his face when I grabbed the handle to steady myself.

Never say never, I muttered to myself.

He weaved through the traffic as smoothly as he seduces people. He'd been waiting for the moment since my return. His knuckles turned white from gripping the wheel. Suddenly, I began to worry.

"Sonny, we just want to teach that son of a gun a lesson. That's all. No blood or bruises, hear me? You're already in the mud, and we don't want to go deeper."

"Don't worry, Ba, everything will be fine, just fine."

He sped through another red light and turned onto Wood-chopping Lane. I used to come here every Sunday to drink and eat smoked pig's elbows with my son-in-law. The little restaurant that had the best smoked meat had vanished, together with the gray tile-roofed square compounds. We drove by shiny apartment buildings with orange glazed tiles. A two-bedroom unit in those buildings costs at least half a million. My son-in-law wasn't doing too bad if he could afford living in this area.

The car made a few more turns, and suddenly we were in a different world: worn crowded compounds lined an old gray street dotted with shabby Muslim eateries where old men and women squatted smoking pipes, playing with bare-bottom kids next to a tall stove. On top, a giant steamer was puffing white clouds and in the clouds crouched the loveliest, puffiest, whitest mutton buns wafting the most delicious fragrance.

I closed my eyes and inhaled. *This is my home, my old Beijing.* I wanted to get out and buy a dozen buns to share with the old folks and kids. Perhaps I could give my son-in-law a call and invite him here. We could drink *Er guo tou* and talk things over. Perhaps he'd come to his senses, give up his concubine, and go back to his wife and boy.

My son slammed on the brakes. "There he is, the old fox!"

A gray Honda was passing. The driver braked at the screech and looked in our direction. When our eyes met, his face went ashy and I started shaking. My adopted son, my son-in-law. How he had aged—those deep wrinkles that cut into the corners of his eyes and mouth! And the abandoned look on his face as if he had nothing to live for. The fire had died in his eyes, the fire that had lit the pitch-dark night when he appeared out of nowhere and dug me out of the rubble the night 240,000 people perished in their sleep in the Great Tang Shan Earthquake, July 28, 1976.

How many times did I awaken to the same scene—the earth rumbled as it opened its belly and ate us alive. Within sixteen seconds, a quarter-million people died, the entire city was leveled. Many never had a chance to wake up, thank heavens, and many died slowly under the debris. The irony was I had been sent to Tang Shan to meet the leaders there to warn them about the quake. But no one paid much attention, including myself. Tang Shan had never had an earthquake. It was not supposed to. We were in deep mourning: our beloved Premier Zhou had just died, and Chairman Mao was dying in Zhong Nan Hai. Maybe the heavens wanted to bury us alive along with these great leaders as a sacrifice? Only fate knows, just as fate sent this skinny boy to me that deadly morning as I gazed up at the dust mushroom in the sky and prepared for a slow death. In the darkness I couldn't make out his face, only his eyes that burnt like twin stars. Without a word, he knelt in front of me and started digging. He used a thick tree branch first, then used his hands so that I wouldn't get hurt. A beam fell on his head and knocked him down. I reached for his hand. There was no pulse. Don't die, buddy, I prayed. If we survive this, I'll take you and your family to Beijing, and I'll make sure you have a bright future. And he must have heard my prayer. Within minutes, he opened his eyes, jumped up and started digging again with his bleeding fingers.

And I came out of the rubble without a broken bone. We waited for two days in the eerie silence. Most people had died. Those who got out alive just stared into space in a daze. No one came except for a few planes that dropped some water and bread. Finally I said let's get out of here, and we started walking toward home, toward Beijing. The entire city of Tang Shan had been flattened. There was nothing but rubble reeking with rotting bodies trapped under collapsed buildings. We walked by mass makeshift graves. Heavy rains had washed away the mud and the bodies were exposed, some gnawed on by hungry dogs. We walked along the road, joined by those who could still move. We were hungry and thirsty. We had given our water and food to the sick, the wounded, and the kids. The loudspeakers on the roadside blasted the Party's slogan: "Resist the earthquake, rescue ourselves." We heard rumors that this earthquake presaged Chairman Mao's death, that there was a fierce power struggle in Zhong Nan Hai. To show that everything was still normal and under control, the Party had rejected offers of international aid. I held the boy's hand and kept walking. From then on, I was his father. In fact, he looked more and more like my son, my first son who had died before he reached a year old.

On the day he married my daughter, I asked how he found me that morning. I wasn't even supposed to be in that building, the building where my uncle and his family lived. I was visiting them the night before, had meant to tell my uncle about the earthquake warning as a joke. But a few cups of wine opened my chatterbox and we talked into the early hours, and I was so tired I just crashed on the bunk bed with my clothes on. Two hours later, everyone in the building died except for me and my future son-in-law who was staying up late reading *The Count of Monte Cristo.*

"Did you know you were digging the wrong person?"

He looked me in the eyes. "You were the right person. Still are."

"Did you ever realize I was not your father?" I insisted.

He hesitated a moment. "Yes, when you held my hand and prayed for me. My own father never touched me. He only whipped me with his belt."

The gray Honda fled, and we gave chase. We snaked through narrow, winding lanes, sending kids and old people scrambling for their lives. Finally, we nailed him at the end of a dead lane. My son jumped out, shattered the Honda's window with one kick, plucked the hunched man from the wheel, and threw him on the ground.

"What are you waiting for, Ba?" my son roared as he punched and kicked.

I lifted my steel-clad boot. Since I arrived in Beijing, I'd been wearing my work boots every day for this moment. But I couldn't stamp down. Not on the soft body that offered no resistance. Curled into a fetal position, it looked like a giant meatball fallen in the mud. Both were my sons, both my flesh and spirit, the palm and back of my hand. Why did have we have to do this? Why?

"Can we talk it over somewhere else?" I pleaded.

"No!" he screamed. "How can you talk to a filthy pig who sleeps with teenage girls, beats up your daughter, and schemes to rob her apartment? He's not your son. Never! I am your son, your only son."

I looked into his bloodshot eyes. As he was growing up, I whipped him constantly to make him behave like his adopted brother. I had sowed hatred in his young heart.

A big crowd gathered around us. A young boy shouted in a thrilled voice, "Come quickly. Come watch Mercedes beating up Honda! Watch the rich guys beating up a poor bastard!"

Blood rushed to my head.

"This is not some poor bastard," I shouted, pointing to the muddy meatball. "This is my son. He's taken a wrong path, and I'm here to get him back."

And I started kicking. I kicked at his thighs, his butt, and his guts. He writhed in the dust, covering his head with his arms. He had grown so fat I couldn't feel any bones in his body. He used to be all spine and muscle, moving with the force of a tornado, his eyes bright with spirit. For twenty-nine years, he had been my pride, my lost and found son. The great earthquake did not destroy him, nor the aftermath of the Cultural Revolution. But money and sex gobbled him up and spat him out as cow dung. I kicked and punched. I wanted to make him scream in pain. I wanted to scream in pain. Who would give back my son? Who would give me back my old Beijing, my old country?

Someone screamed, "Call a cop."

Blood spurted from the scar on his thinning scalp, the scar from the fallen beam twenty-nine years ago. He had been covering it carefully with his hair, and I had forgotten how long and deep the scar was. Now the reopened wound gaped at me like a hungry mouth.

The ground shook violently under me. There was the familiar muffled roar from the earth's belly, the violent swaying of the sky, the sound of the buildings collapsing, the most terrifying silence as the dust rose slowly like a giant mushroom, like the atomic bomb in Hiroshima, only this one was three thousand times bigger and darker . . .

I pulled him up from the bloodied street.

"Let's go home, son," I said. "Let's go home."

MAVERICK

In the wildness is the Soul Mountain. There are Wu Xian, Wu Pan, Wu Di, Wu Xie, Wu Luo and other great wizards. They go up and down the mountain to pick herbs.

—The Book of Mountains and Seas

This is it, Shan Gui, June 6, 2006. In six hours, the Coffer Dam will explode. The river will rush in and we'll all go under.

The wind is blowing. Clouds are gathering on the Twelve Peaks of Wu Shan. Below us, white water tears through the narrow Wu Gorge, sending up clouds of mist on the steep slopes. In six hours the river will rise to the red mark—175 meters, and everything will go—the gorge, the slopes, the mist, and our home under the dawn redwood. The river will become a lake: tame, servile, voiceless.

Without the river, can you still find your way home, Shan Gui, my mountain spirit?

Tall grasses dance on your grave, whispering our song like seductive girls. But who can sing or dance like you, with your phoenix voice and deer spirit? You are the goddess of the Twelve Peaks.

"Call me *lazi*," you said, head cocking in such a way that always set me on fire. "Not because you got me in your net or because I can swim for days without rest or food. I'm a fish because the river is my home, and I breathe better in the water."

I laugh and call you Shan Gui over and over again. I love the sound and its echo—mountain ghost, mountain spirit, mountain goddess.

You're a seer from the river and sea, and I become one through your amber eyes.

Today is our thirty-sixth anniversary. Thirty-six years ago I pulled you out of the river. The jolt to my hands and heart when I got you in the net still feels fresh. For five days I had been throwing the net into the water and pulling it in. But nothing came to me, not even a shrimp. This had never happened before. My father, a master hunter and fisherman, had taught me everything I needed to know to live with the mountains and rivers. I was delirious with hunger and grief when the net tightened suddenly, and the boat started drifting sideways. I grabbed the rope. The weight was pulling me down into the river. It wasn't a rock. I could tell because I knew every inch of the river like my back yard. It wasn't a white sturgeon—the river elephant as we fishermen called it. Through the water I saw the shadow of a regal body with gold and green scales. My heart pumped. I had caught a *lazi*, a dragon fish, a royal Chinese sturgeon, King of the Long River. A thousand pounds for the green sturgeon, ten thousand for the elephant, as the fishermen's saying goes.

"Wu Pan, Wu Pan," I shouted my name to the sky, "Old Heaven has finally opened its eyes. You are not going to die. Not yet!"

As I pulled in the net, my mind raced. I could sell the sturgeon on the black market and buy enough corn and sweet yams for the winter and spring till the summer crop ripened. I'd even have some left over to buy a piglet and raise it to sell, and then I'd buy two piglets, plus clothes and food. With decent clothes, I could go to the market and meet people, perhaps even bring a girl to my shed.

Then you emerged from the water, shimmering silky green and gold. You curled in my net as if you were lying at home in a hammock. I rubbed my eyes. I couldn't believe what I was seeing. Was I hallucinating from hunger? True, it had been three days since I ate my last yam, but how could I mistake a fish for a woman? Slowly, you stood up, a cascade of black hair to your knees, a green dress shredded like a fishing net that revealed your white belly and pink nipples. Blood rushed to my face as you walked toward me. I had seen this face, this smile, this forest of hair. But where? I closed my eyes. Light came through my eyelids and lit me up from inside.

I started weeping. I hadn't cried like that since my mother vanished in the river and we were forced to leave the town where our ancestors had been settled for five thousand years. "Cry no more and grow up fast, my little son of hope," Father sang as he carried me to the bell tower on his back. I was five, still unable to walk or talk. We lived like cavemen in the mountains. My playmates were monkeys, deer, birds and other animals who came to the shed for the food I had saved for them. I didn't cry when the Red Guards took my father away and called me down the mountain to claim his body a week later, his head purple and swollen from being hung upside down, ropes cutting deep into his ankles.

"Take me home, Pan Ge," you said.

I opened my eyes wide. I had heard this voice, the voice of blue wings laughing in the wind and calling me Ge—brother or Pan Ge—Hope Brother. It had been singing to my sleeping soul for the past ten years. I had tried to hold onto the wings, only to awaken to my father's back at the fire, rings of smoke rising from his pipe.

I looked into your brown eyes where light shines from within. How did you know my name, the secret name only two people on earth knew? "Keep it hidden until you're out of danger," Mother had told me. Father would call me Wu Pan when he was teaching me Wu's secret knowledge. To the outside world, I was known as Gou Dan—dog shit, a common name for sickly children. We are sick because of our past, it is believed, but if we keep our heads low, we may slip through the gods' wrath and live a normal life.

You took my hand, and a door cracked open in my brain. I had a glimpse of a white gibbon with blue eyes, two children hanging onto her breasts.

"Let's go, Pan Ge, before the sun sets behind the mountains."

I followed you along the thin path. You didn't say a word, but every time you bent to pick a flower or an herb, every time you paused to listen to the hushed sounds of the forest, the door opened wider, and things father had tried to teach me came out one by one: the names of the plants, the tunes of birds and insects, the rocks, the soil, the clouds, and the words that link them all together.

You walked fast, your feet barely touching the ground. I had no trouble keeping up with you. I no longer felt the pang of hunger, and my body felt light and swift. You seemed to know where we were going, and I was willing to follow you to the edge of the world.

Before the sun went down, we arrived at the bell tower. I gazed at the tomb under the tree where Father had lain for six weeks. There was no headstone to mark the spot, as he had wished. Grass and flowers already covered the grave. I gazed up at the bronze bell. No one knew when it had been built, how this giant thing had been hoisted to the tree where it hung like a green ear. The chain that hooked the bell to the tree had grown into the trunk.

Father had been ringing the bell six times a day, seven days a week, since we came to live here. Its sound traveled all the way to the brine pit in the valley. There was always someone from the Wu Clan to ring the bell. No one knew how it had started, but since people began producing salt in the valley, workers had been using the bell as their clock to make the salt and to go about their daily life. Father was once trapped in a landslide. The workers missed their cue to add minerals to the salt that was crystallizing, and the whole batch was ruined. When they realized that the bell hadn't rung for a long time, they rushed up to the mountain and dug him out. He continued ringing the bell even after the Red Guards smashed all the ancient salt-making equipment and the workers all scattered. Since his death, I tried to ring the bell every day. It was father's wish: keep it alive as long as we lived.

Under the tree were the ruins of an old temple. Our hut stood among the stones in the shadow of the pagoda canopy. From the back window, I could touch the knotted, shredding trunk. I loved the smell from its brown bark, loved the rumble from its belly in the middle of the night. I used to put my arms around the trunk. Father laughed and said it would take twenty kids like me to circle the tree.

He said it was older than the first man, older than the giant dragons that terrorized the earth for hundreds of million of years, older than the green sturgeon in the Long River.

You didn't say a word. Without looking, I knew you were also looking at the tree and the bell and the things around us—the mountains near and far, the river in the distance.

"We're home, Pan Ge," you said.

You took my hand and walked to the hut. As soon as you stepped in, the dim humble place became a paradise. You wiped, cleaned, and washed as if you were home. You laughed as you caught my gaze, and then pushed me to the fire pit. I lit the fire. Through the heat and smoke, I watched you move here and there like mist circling the mountains. As a child, I had often gazed at the Twelve Peaks across the river and daydreamed of climbing the slenderest peak—the famous Wushan Goddess. The more I looked at you, the more you resembled that goddess. Was I in a dream? I pinched my thighs. I heard you laugh. Then I smelled the dinner—a fish and rabbit grilled to a perfect golden brown served on a blue slate.

I've never questioned how you got the fish. You are the river goddess. Fish run to you just as the river runs to the ocean. But how you captured the rabbit remains a mystery. The mountains had become barren since trees were cut to fuel the furnaces to melt steel, grow oranges and corn. Only Father, the master hunter, could bring game home. He never touched it himself. He hunted only when *I* needed meat. When the Red Guards took him away, all the animals and birds left suddenly, as if they had followed him to heaven.

After I licked clean the slate, you put a crown of flowers on my head. We walked into the open air. We floated in the clouds. And suddenly I started to sing. I'd never sung in my entire life. I didn't talk till I was six. Those who visited Father for medicine hinted that I was possessed by evil spirits, and something should be done about it. Father told them I would speak when I was ready, and I did. But I couldn't learn the sacred chanting for the gods and ghosts. Father didn't seem to worry a bit as he trained me every day, as if he knew I had them inside like an egg, waiting to hatch.

I don't know what magic you wove into the crown. As soon as I put it on, light broke through my thick scalp and an O formed around my mouth. From my belly button came a long sigh—wuu-uuu. "You can't be a shaman unless you know how to let the sound come out from your guts," Father said. "It's the first step to connect us with gods, animals, and plants." Wuuuuuuuu—the sound of my family name and heritage as high priest, shaman, astrologist, mathematician, artist, seer. As I chanted, songs flew out of my mouth like birds, and my limbs moved with the rhythm of a crane. And quickly you joined in. We danced around the tomb, luscious with scented grass, till the bell broke its silence and rang on its own, and birds, hundreds of them, joined our chorus from the tree's canopy. And we knelt down to thank the earth, the sky, and our parents.

That day we became husband and wife. We were both sixteen, two wild monkeys in the hidden mountains of Wushan.

After the caviar was harvested with the hormone injection, the sturgeon queen was transported to Beijing for research and tour exhibitions. On the way to the north, she turned her giant body around to face the Long River, her home. The workers turned her around three times, and each time she turned to face the river. No one understood how she managed to turn the thousand-pound mass in the truck's narrow tank. In Beijing, thousands of people visited her daily, but the sturgeon refused to eat. She is on a hunger strike.

This is the second sturgeon on exhibition. The first one died after six months' hunger strike.

—Beijing Evening News

Pan Ge, my Hope Brother.

I've been in Beijing for six months, in a giant tank. Every day, a river of people flows to the show. They plunk down fifty yuan for a ticket—a big chunk of their earnings for many—to have a glimpse of "the living fossil of the sea," "the panda in the water," "the treasure of the Long River," as the loudspeaker blasts at the entrance. Poor suckers! All they see is a body emptied of seed, a body vanishing.

They gawk with their oily eyes and tap the glass with their fat fingers. They think they're my masters because they've paid good money for their tickets. They have no idea they're vanishing, too. We all come from the same origin. Our appearances are mere illusions.

In six hours when the Coffer Dam blows up and the water rises, everything along the river will go—the fields, the roads, the villages, the cities, the mountains, and our water fir. My Long River, artery of my home, how it's plagued by dams! Forty-eight thousand of them, all built in the past two decades. But nothing compares with this one—the Three Gorges Dam—the biggest on earth that will turn the mighty river into a placid lake. Once the white blood stops running, nothing will be the same again.

Pan Ge, you've often asked me where I came from, whether I was a dream, a passing cloud, an apparition of the Goddess Peak across the river. Well, I'm all and none of them at the same time. My family has been the keeper of the lost knowledge of transformation. We change from one form to another with the breath of the earth. Our lives renew before death comes. By not clinging to life, we become immortal.

I come from a family that knows no father. In the morning, I rise with the mist from the river to receive the first shaft of light on the peak. At dusk, after I see off the twilight, I come down as drizzle or thunderstorm. When night falls, I roam in and out of sleeping souls, adorning their dreams with love and sex. I fulfill young peoples' fantasies, lovers' prayers. I answer women's pleas for husbands and children. I balm injured animals and lead fish out of dangerous waters. I have many names—Goddess of the Twelve Peaks, Yao Ji, Fish Woman, Ugly Woman Cadaver, shaman, witch, whore.

For you, I have only one name—Shan Gui—mountain spirit. And for you only I kept my womanly form, though I had to pay a big price eighteen years later.

The night I crossed the water, Mama cried. "You'll go through many cycles of violent death and you'll know the pain of a broken heart—all because of your foolish attachment."

I hugged her with my dissolving arms. Who else knew more about the pain of passion and attachment? She gave up her own Mama for a fisherman who saved her from a speedboat. For a whole year, she stayed in the forest of Wushan and nursed his starving son till he grew teeth and uttered his first word. And the man didn't even know what she had sacrificed for his son. But she didn't care. She just wanted to be near him. Because of her foolish attachment, I had to share her breasts with a filthy boy who couldn't do anything except howl for milk. I couldn't stand him. I wanted her for myself. I wanted to be with my grandma, my aunts, and the rest of the clan. Then one day, he looked me straight in the eyes, and I was smitten. I belonged to him as he belonged to me. When she realized what was happening and took me away from the boy, it was too late.

Pan Ge, you're that filthy, toothless boy who took half of my mama's life, who changed my path as a mountain spirit. But no matter, you stole my soul with your green chert eyes and I am yours for this life and many lives after.

O soul, come back! Why should you go far away?
—The Great Summons

Shan Gui, my love, when you shed your tattered dress and placed your feet in my lap, the fog in my brain cleared. Suddenly I remembered you, my milk sister, daughter of our white-browed mother. You used to kick me with your lovely feet when your mama wasn't paying attention. You wanted her breasts to yourself, and I can't blame you. I was constantly hungry for her milk, pungent and sweet, almost as good as my own mother's, but more powerful. I'd probably have kicked you even harder if I had to share *my* mother.

Guess what I missed the most when your mama took off with you? Your feet, warm and smooth like jade, soft and firm like breasts, and more fragrant than flowers. I missed the kicking on my head and chest, mischievous and regular like my heartbeat. The moment you left, I uttered my first word—*jiao*—a waning moon that comes into my dream each night and fades upon my awakening, leaving no prints.

You vanished so fast, so completely. The only trace of your existence was my first word, first step, first bite of nuts. Even that became foggy soon after Father began my training. "We don't have time left, Son," he said. "You have a lot to learn, and my days in this world are numbered." I didn't know what he meant exactly, but I liked the idea that someday I'd be a Wu man like Father, a messenger between heaven, earth, and the underworld. Besides chanting and studying the stars and constellations, I also learned how to fish and hunt, tasted plants, flowers, animals, insects, fish, soil, and stones to know how they worked individually and combined as medicine. Some killed pains, some expelled gas and toxin, some helped women have babies, and some enhanced the pleasures of the body and mind.

I studied hard and grew up fast.

On my sixteenth birthday, Father woke me at dawn and took me deep into the ruins.

"There used to be a temple here for the Wushan Goddess." He pointed to a stone half buried in the red soil and roots. "When the King of Chu came here on a hunting trip, a beautiful woman visited him in his dream and offered to make love to him. When he woke up, the only thing he could remember was her fragrance and the promise she had whispered in his ear: 'I live on the sunny slope of Wushan. In the morning, I rise with the mist. At dusk, I come down with the rain. Whenever you want me, just look for me at the Sun Terrace.' The king built a temple with the hope that he'd meet the beautiful goddess one more time, but she never visited him again, in dreams or real. When he returned to his capital down the river, the King of Qin, his crafty rival from the north, sent him a dozen beauties and promised more girls if he would visit the Kingdom of Qin. His minister Qu Yuan begged the king not to go.

Over the years, Qin had trained the best swordsmen and generals. Their king's ambition was to wipe our all his neighbors and bring China under his thumb. He had succeeded in conquering all except for one—the Kingdom of Chu, his last and biggest conquest. The Kingdom of Chu had more land, more people, and more advanced civilization. Of all the resources in Chu's territory, the brine industry was the jewel on the crown. The King of Qin had been salivating over the brine pits for a long time, especially the ones in Wushan, the land of treasure and magic. Whoever controlled the pits would rule China.

No matter how much Qu Yuan pleaded the king to stay in his own land, the King of Chu would not listen, determined to find his goddess at any cost. He had no idea that Qu Yuan, his most loyal and upright minister, was a great shaman like us, apart from being a great poet. As a shaman, he would have known about the magic mushroom that could bring Goddess Yao Ji to the king, the very goddess who had made love to him in his dream. Who is this Yao Ji? She is the twenty-third daughter of the Sun God. She died a young virgin, yet the mushrooms on her grave can enhance sexual power and attraction. It also brings desperate lovers together in their dreams. Had the king trusted and consulted his shaman minister Qu Yuan, he would have fulfilled his dream, and the goddess would have helped him defeat Qin, and China might be a totally different country today. Instead, he exiled Qu Yuan and ventured into his enemy's territory. You can guess what happened. The love-crazed king was held hostage and died heartbroken in a strange, hostile land.

"Years later, the deceased king's son visited Wushan, accompanied by Master Qu Yuan's student Song Yu. When the young king saw a cloud floating on the mountain like a beckoning girl, he asked his poet what it was. Song Yu told him the love story between the old king and the goddess. That night, the young king dreamed of the goddess, dazzling and gentle like the sun and the moon. She was about to make love to the king, but stopped in mid-action, put her clothes back on, and left the room. Had she left without looking back, things wouldn't have been so bad. But she turned her head and gazed at our young king with sad eyes, leaving his Majesty prostrated on the floor, weeping as dawn broke. Like his father, he ignored his duties and searched among girls far and near for his dream goddess, and ended up losing his entire kingdom to the King of Qin.

"Love is a dark hole," Father said pensively, his face to the river. "Once you are in, you're done for." He looked me up and down as if checking for the hole in me. "But it can also lift you high like a rocket." He stopped, his hand on my head. "Wu Pan, my good son, you're a grown man now. You have never shown any interest in girls. I thought it was a good thing. I thought you needed all your energy to focus on your apprenticeship. You still need a few more years to complete the learning. But we're running out of time. *I* am running out of time."

I should have paid more attention to his last words, but my eyes were fixed on the stone half buried in the red soil. A carved face, broken but recognizable, was churning fog in my head. I had seen the face, somewhere, long ago. But my brain was a sieve in the river of memory. I clawed the air with my fingers. Who could help me? Who would help me?

Father grabbed my hand and brought me down on my knees. "Son, kowtow to the Goddess of Wushan. Today you're turning sixteen. It's time to taste the mushroom. It's time you know a few things about love."

The Sun God's daughter was called nu shi—*woman cadaver. When she died, her body turned into a plant. It has yellow flowers, and it bears fruit. Whoever eats it becomes beautiful and alluring.*
　—The Book of Mountains and Seas

Mama said:
"For your foolish attachment to a mortal being, you'll perform three impossible duties and die three painful deaths before you can redeem your place at home. First, you must find a new route

through the Gezhouba Dam so the green sturgeon pods can return to their birthplace in the Golden Sand River. Second, you must find another new route through the Three Gorges Dam so the green sturgeon can go home and spawn. If you can't find a new route for the royal fish, the flower of the river and sea, you must sacrifice your own life to show them that their origin is no longer there and they have to settle for a new home. You'll hurl yourself against the dam over and over, your flesh splashing over the concrete. You'll be shredded by the turbines, your blood dyeing the reservoir scarlet red. Your violent death may or may not be enough to shock them into finding a new home, but it's the only chance for those stubborn prehistoric creatures. They have seen the rise and fall of dinosaurs, the coming and going of the big ice and floods, the birth of mammals and humans. Will they survive this? We can only hope, before they disappear, before we all disappear.

"I don't know if they'll ever adopt a new home below the dam. For millions of years, they've been living like this: born in the Golden Sand River, swim to the sea, grow up in the ocean, then go back home to mate and spawn, no matter how many rocks and dams they have to jump over, how many fishhooks or nets await them. Once they return to the river, they stop eating or sleeping. The only thing on their mind is to swim upstream and produce their young at home. Their faith have moved all heavenly beings. We want to help them. Those ancient noble souls deserve to have a place on the planet.

"If your sacrifice can't stop them from the mass suicide," Mama continued after a long pause, "you'll have to offer your body as a breeding vessel. You'll be kept in a tank as eggs grow in your belly. You'll feel extremely agitated because your sturgeon instinct will urge you to swim to your place of origin at any cost. But you will be restricted in the tank until the ova are ready to be harvested, and you'll be injected with hormones to let go the caviar that will be hatched in a tank then released into the river. After you're emptied, you'll be shipped to the capital in the name of scientific research and displayed for money. You won't be able to eat because you'll be homesick. You'll hear the calling of your lover, but you won't be able to reach him. You'll wither in front of the crowd. Even in your dying, you'll not be left alone. You'll be prodded and cajoled to please the crowd. This will be your most painful death because you're away from your home air, soil, and water. Without them, you become nothing. Your organs will shut down one by one, till your heart stops pumping. Once that happens, your soul will plunge into the dark abyss from which nothing ever returns. I won't be able to pull you out, even with the help of your grandma, aunts, and sisters."

"Aren't you scared?" Mama asked in despair as I waded into the river, my insides boiling as my organs began dissolving and reshaping. "Once you cross the river, you may never come back."

A fisherman pulled up a large green fish with a white belly. He pulled it into his boat and covered it with straw. When he returned home, the fish was gone but under the straw lay a beautiful girl. She became his wife for three years. One day she told the fisherman she had to go home, and then vanished in the river.
—Wushan folklore

Father said:

"We're destined to live in between. It's written in our name: Wu— 巫 —two humans standing between sky and earth. And we're destined to be separated, be it from lovers, friends, or enemies. See the post in the middle, the post that holds the sky? It's a wall that supports us, but it also keeps us apart. All things are relative. All things change. So no need to laugh when you have your way; nor should you despair when everything goes against you."

In 223 B.C., the King of Qin finally defeated the King of Chu, unifying China for the first time. As soon as he was ordained as the first emperor, his most trusted minister came to Wushan, and paid a secret visit to Wu Fang, head of the Wu Clan at the time, known for his skill at healing the wounded

I don't have a choice, Mama, I wanted to tell her, but even my voice was transforming. The water had already been crossed when you gave your other breast to the boy. As we suckled your nipples, we entered each other's world through the river of your milk.

Mama, I know how much you wanted to cross the river, to throw yourself into the arms of your beloved shaman, to taste love's flesh and blood. But you lingered on the shore, hovering around him as a dream, an unfulfilled longing. You were afraid of losing your place on the Twelve Peaks, afraid of getting lost forever in the dark place. But we are all being sucked into that hole, yes, we the invisible force of dreams, spirits, and imaginations, they the formidable world of metal, rock, body, and logic. Two forces that used to be one and whole, but were severed when the first arrow was made to kill, the first compass to point directions, the first law to punish crimes, the first sage to set things in order.

I'm an anomaly, Mama. So are you. It's in our blood to love, to upset order of things. We can't help it, just as our ancestor, Yao Ji, the twenty-third daughter of the Sun and the Western Queen Mother, chose her exile to love a mortal being on earth. How she angered her celestial parents! They had assumed she would choose to stay with them in the palace where she could live forever without a single worry. But no, she chose Wu Peng instead, the humble messenger between heaven and earth. She chose to terminate her immortal status and die next to her beloved. Her parents wanted to recant the choices they gave her, but couldn't. Breaking their word would shake the kingdom's foundation. But allowing their daughter to die would also crack their heavenly superstructure. They were put on the spot by a sixteen-year-old girl, and they didn't like it one bit. So they banished her to Wushan where her lover performed rituals to please the gods for his tribal people. They turned their daughter and her eleven maids into pillars on the mountain peaks. There to this day, Yao Ji receives the first ray of the sun and sees off the last gleam of twilight. There she witnesses the ebb and flow of the water, the joys and sorrows of the people on the banks. During the day, she hovers near her lover as cloud, rain, bird, fish, or deer. At night, she enters his dreams with the help of the herb that grows on her tomb, and they love to their hearts' desire. If he wants her in blood and flesh, however, he must find her through *chou nu shi*—the Ugly Woman Cadaver—the sacred whore who sings, dances, makes love with priests in temples and teaches the youth how to love in mulberry woods during festivals. If she changes into the human form at any other time or place, she and her lover, his tribes included, will meet horrible deaths with unspeakable pain, and be condemned forever to the dark place where light is swallowed and nothing can be seen, heard, smelled, or touched.

This is her story, Mama, a story that each member of our female kingdom knows by heart, though we never speak of it. We don't need to. We follow her steps every day as we roam the mountains of the Three Gorges gathering herbs for lovers and mothers. We hear her wild calls as we guide fish and dolphins to safe places, help the young get away from boats and turbines. When we bathe in the sacred pond for regeneration, her spirit passes on through our bodies. We're all her clones.

You're an anomaly, too, Pan Ge, a mistake like the union of your parents. They were not even supposed to meet. Your father was about to marry his cousin from Fujian, with the mission to recover the secret knowledge of transformation. It had been lost since the

Wu Clan fled to escape the emperors' greed for the elixir. Their marriage would have pieced together many puzzles and increased their power a hundred fold. And your mother, the number one beauty of Chongqing City, had been engaged to a Flying Tiger pilot, son of the most powerful warlord from the north. Then she went to the mountains with her girlfriends one day and felt sick. She stopped eating or sleeping. At night, she became feverish, a maverick according to her mother and father, singing and dancing like a courtesan. Her father brought in Chinese and Western doctors from Chongqing, Chendu, Wuhan, and Shanghai, but no one could tell him what it was, let alone cure her. As a last resort, her mother took her to a humble looking young man in a dim alley. His store was lined with tall cabinets where hundreds of kinds of herbs were kept in small drawers. He brought out tea. As soon as her lips touched the amber colored liquid, she calmed down. When he put his fingers on her wrist to feel her pulse, she blushed, the first time since she fell ill.

Her mother was thrilled, thinking her daughter was cured. As soon as they got home, however, she broke her engagement with the Flying Tiger pilot. She was locked in her room while her parents prepared to rush the wedding, hoping the ceremony and her bridegroom would bring senses back to her. They were also anxious to wash their hands of her. Once married, she would no longer be their problem. A married daughter was dumped water. That very night, she climbed out the window to join her bright-eyed doctor. They went to his hometown in Wushan that very night and didn't return to the city until they learned that her family had run her obituary in the *Chongqing Daily*.

You're the son of a ghost, Pan Ge. You mama was willing to give up everything for love, and so was your father. When he dissolved his engagement with his distant cousin in Fujian, word spread throughout China where the branches of the Wu Clan lived. They all denounced him. To be denounced by the Wu Clan is worse than death. He became a motherless calf, a wild ghost, a maverick. No matter how much fortune and knowledge his father had passed to him, he would be alone forever. No one would lend him a hand when he was in danger. But they were happy. The moment your father and mother met each other, their souls exploded like fireworks, and their spirits joined as one. Nothing could break them apart, not even death.

You were not supposed to be born, Pan Ge. Babies are the results of souls pining for their counterparts. Since your parents already found each other, there was no need to have a third wheel. You were born to pay off the debt they left behind: their extreme happiness at the cost of other people's pain. Everything has a consequence, even love. Your fate is to shoulder the sorrow your parents escaped. That's why you couldn't eat, talk, or walk in your earlier life. You were not supposed to live beyond two, not supposed to do any of those things a normal person enjoys. When your mother disappeared in the river, you were supposed to follow, not to join her in the other world, but to linger along the bank as a wraith, forever hungry and homeless.

But your father saved my mama from the river. He pulled her out of the water after she was injured by a steamboat and nursed her back to life. When he released her, he had no idea that she would be following him, that she would save his son twelve years later.

Of the three gorges in Badong, the longest is the Gorge of Wu
Baboons' crying bring tears to travelers' sleeves
   —Wushan folksong

I was hanging on my last breath when she picked me up from the floor and held me to her chest. Mother, I thought, and opened my eyes wide. She had been gone for three days. Already, she had turned silver-gray everywhere: her hair, her eyebrows, her chest, even her hands. Her whole body was hazy like a cloud. The only color came from her blue eyes. I smelled the milk, and turned my head to latch on. Pungent liquid flowed into my mouth. Immediately I realized she was not my mother. My own mother's milk didn't taste as strong. I wanted to turn away but the milk kept coming and I swallowed as quickly as I could so as not to be drowned. Soon my curled fingers and toes opened up, and my body started to float in the white river. Out of habit, I reached for the other breast. A soft warm thing kicked my hand away. I opened my eyes and saw your foot, pink pearly toes wriggling and dancing on the sole of a crescent moon. I stared, forgot to suckle.

My father was lying motionless in the ash, next to the fire. He had chanted and spun himself into a trance to make me eat the porridge.

That was 1959. I was five years old.

Many things happened in Wushan that year. I guess many things had already happened in Wushan and all over China. The biggest thing, however, was the Land Reform. Peasants confiscated the land from the landlords and divided it evenly among the poor. Those who resisted giving up their properties or had made enemies in the past were executed. Before the killing wave reached the mountain city of Chongqing, my father voluntarily handed over everything he owned—hundreds of acres of orange groves along the riverbanks and a dozen teahouses in Chongqing, the center of business and industry of the Three Gorges. He moved to the quiet town of Wushan with his wife. When the ripple finally arrived in the deep belly of the Long River two years later, he had nothing under his name but an herbal store in his ancestor's stone house that nobody in town would want. He was awarded the title of "Enlightened Landlord" and the government wanted him to go to Chongqing and Beijing as a model of the Land Reform. He declined the invitation, citing his wife's health as an excuse. She was about to give birth and the fetus was a breach.

That fetus was me, ill-starred the moment I was born. My mother was in labor for three days. When I finally came out with the cord around my neck, I was not even breathing. Just as Father tried to revive me, Mother started hemorrhaging. Had he not been the best doctor in the region, neither of us would have survived. We had four peaceful years after that. Father practiced medicine with herbs and needles. When those didn't work, he would sing and dance to drive away bad spirits. For those who lost their fortunes, he sought oracles from *The Book of Mountains and Seas.* He never accepted money for his services, only small gifts like eggs, vegetables, rice, or homemade fabric. Born in a wealthy warlord's family, my mother had had everything done for her by maids before she eloped with my father. In Wushan, she wove, sewed, and cooked like everyone else, and she was happy. So was I, hanging on my mother's breasts like a monkey. I had been given rice, meat, fish, and vegetables. Mother chewed them up good and fed them to me mouth to mouth, but I spat them out, then shut my mouth tight. At five, I was still hairless and toothless. I had barely taken my first steps, had yet to utter anything that resembled a human word. People thought I was possessed by spirits. They wouldn't say out loud that I was retarded. They loved my father as they loved Buddha and Chairman Mao. Probably more. Buddha lived in the Western Paradise somewhere far away, and Chairman Mao was unreachable in Zhongnanhai and the Forbidden City. But my father lived with them. Anyone could holler and walk into his store whenever they needed him, day and night.

Finally they suggested that Father do something about me before it was too late. Father shook his head. My son will walk and speak when his time comes, he said.

Clinging to Mother's breasts, I listened and watched. I had no sound, but I had memory. My body stored everything around me in colors, shapes, and smells. Mother was white and round and soft and light. Father was black and square and firm and strong. She gave off the fragrance of milk, cloud, and river. He smelled of trees, rocks, and beasts. And the rest of the world was a vortex of white teeth hanging low in the sky.

In 1959, the sleepy town of Wushan was jolted awake by drums and gongs and people shouting "Big Leap Forward into Communist Paradise." Crowds gathered to cheer as they threw their woks into the homemade furnace to melt iron for the state-owned steel plants.

China was frog-leaping into the communist paradise where everyone would be equal and get whatever he needed. Why keep the pots
when one could eat bread and beef to his heart's desire from the
commune's canteen? And why keep the cows when the fields would
be ploughed by combines?

No one mentioned the big flood that drowned many people on
the banks that year. No one paid much attention to the drought that
followed the flood. They turned a blind eye to the withered crops in
the fields, and they cheered for the village leaders who reported to
Beijing the fake news of the biggest harvest ever in Wushan history.

Father's face became darker and darker. He paced the house and
stayed up late reading *The Book of Mountains and Seas*. He took
longer trips to the mountains and rivers but brought home almost
nothing. Mother finally asked him what was happening. He told her
in a hushed voice that he had smoked and stored his catch in secret
caves, along with bags of rice, flour, corn, dried fruit, and sugar.

We must be prepared, he said.

Soon, the bread from the commune's canteen became smaller till
it was replaced with porridge that became thinner until that stopped
too. People began to fight for the bark on the trees and the weeds
on the roadsides, then for the white soil that made their stomachs
bulge like drums. More and more bodies were found in beds, on the
streets, in the fields. People began to leave in large groups in search
of food in other parts of Sichuan, other provinces. This had never
happened to Wushan, the treasure bowl that had fed and sheltered
people and beasts alike since one could remember.

People visited Father at night. They wanted to know when this
would all end. Father sat in silence, head and palms raised to the
heavens. He had no heart to tell them that this was only the beginning. The drought would keep going for another two years. Over a
million people in the Three Gorges would die, and more would flee
down the river to search for food in Hubei Province. He couldn't
look further into the future, because it was just one dark wave after
another until the whole place went under.

Before dawn, when everyone was deep in their sleep, Father placed a strip of dry meat or fish and a small bag of grain at the doors where old people and children were dying. He went out every dawn until the young party secretary of Wushan caught him in action.

Our whole family was locked up in the cowshed. When night came, the secretary's military men took Father to our house, which had been turned into a makeshift interrogation room. They shouted and beat him with bamboo sticks. They wanted to know how he got the food and where he hid the rest. When they couldn't get a word out of him, they hung him by the ankles and beat him with a hot iron.

Then one night the Party Secretary came himself and took Mother away. I bit and kicked, but the secretary's military man hit me with the butt of his gun, pulled me off her breasts. I heard Mother scream throughout the night and I screamed with her. Father held me tight in his arms. Suddenly I heard her running past our shed toward the river, heavy footsteps and raucous laughter chasing after her. Then everything became quiet. At dawn, the secretary came and ordered us to get out of Wushan immediately.

"Listen carefully, Wu Luo," he shouted, his breath stank of white spirit. "Since you refuse to confess your crime, you can no longer live with the poor peasants and proletarians in Wushan. Considering you have a retarded child, the Party decided that you can stay in the Bell Tower for free. The only service is to watch forest fires, and to ring the bell every four hours for the workers in the brine pit. You must show gratitude to the Party. And don't forget to thank the old Man Wu. If he hadn't kicked the bucket a week ago, you and your son would be living on the streets. Leave now, and make sure you don't do anything clever up there."

"Where's the mother of the child?" Father spoke for the first time since we were locked into the cowshed.

"She ran to the river," the secretary said. "I tried to catch her, but she was slippery and fast. When I got to the bank, there was nothing but a fish in the river, long and slender and white like a beautiful woman, but I swear to God it was a fish with fins and tail. I'd have jumped in to pull her out if it was your wife, I swear to God."

Father nodded and walked into the mountain with me wrapped on his back in a bedsheet, a wok on his chest, an axe, a knife, and an old fishing net. He walked without stopping for water or food, and I finally fell asleep to the rhythm of his heartbeat. When I woke up in the hut, the sun was setting. A fire was burning in the pit in the middle of the room, licking the bottom of the wok. In front of me, a bowl of corn porridge was cooling. Did he get it from one of the caves where he stored food? Did he endure the torture to save this for me? Father picked me up and fed me with a spoonful of the yellow gruel. I turned my head. The smell made me sick.

Father cried. "Son, you must eat, for me, for your mother. She'll live as long as you are alive. She'll come to you someday, I promise."

I took a sip and threw up. My tongue, my throat, my stomach and my intestines had never been touched by anything other than milk. Father threw the bowl on the floor and howled. He howled with his head thrown to the sky, his chest heaving as if he were spitting out his lungs. He howled till he collapsed on the ground. I crawled to him. I wanted him to get up and watch me try the porridge again. Before I reached him, things went dark.

I woke up in your mother's arms. Her soft body was covered with white hair from head to toe. Her hands held me firm to her chest. She gave me her breast. She gave me you. Her milk saved my life, but you lit up my dim soul. When we finished nursing, we played among the stone hedges under the giant tree. You called it *shui shan*—fir from the water. You talked to me with your secret language that only I could hear, and you seemed to understand my gibberish perfectly. It was a hot summer that year. Small cones hung like partridge eggs among the green needles. One day your mother took us to the pagoda-shaped treetop and picked a bunch of cones. Inside there were seeds, tiny compared to the giant tree. She popped some in her mouth. So did you. Without thinking, I followed suit. The oily nuts tasted good. I grabbed more from your mother's palm.

She smiled as you laughed and applauded, pointing to my chewing mouth. I started laughing too just because you were laughing so deliciously. Suddenly I froze. I opened my mouth and dug out the half-chewed pine nuts. I was eating something other than milk!

Sometimes I wonder how we could have kept this big secret from Father for such a long time.

True, we hung out only when he fell asleep or went out hunting, fishing, working in the fields, or meditating on *The Book of Mountains and Seas* in the cave. As soon as he was gone, you two would appear out of nowhere, silent and fast and dazzling like two stars sailing through the sky toward the earth. And we would nurse and play to our hearts' content. How could he not know? People climbed high mountains and crossed dangerous rivers to seek his advice for everything: lost child, lost object, lost fortune, lost directions. They came with tears, and left with a big smile. Father knew everything. Saw everything. But how could he not know what was going on with his son? How could he not see *us*?

Once we were laughing so hard that we didn't hear him coming until he called out, "Son, is that you laughing?" I froze and shut my eyes tight. He came in, listened to the fading sounds of swinging trees and the echo of your laughter in the forest.

"That is the calling of a white gibbon," he muttered. "Strange. We haven't seen gibbons in the Three Gorges for hundreds of years. They all went to the South Sea when our virgin forest was cut down." He knelt and looked me in the eyes. "Was that you laughing?" he asked again. I cried *jiao* and got away. His feet smelled funny, not at all like your fragrant moons, and his burning heart terrified me.

"What did you say?" His eyes popped like twin bells. I looked up. Where were you and your mother? I wanted to go up to the treetop and crack more nuts. Father grabbed my arms and opened my mouth with his fingers. "Wu Pan, you got teeth," he said. He let go of me and called out in the direction of the river. "Pan's mother, did you hear him talk? Did you see his teeth? Our son is growing up. Soon, he'll become a man. Soon, I can come and join you."

Perhaps you were invisible, you and your mother? If so, was I also invisible around you? The moment I uttered my first word, ate the first bite of solid food with my own teeth, and took my first step into the world, I lost you. You vanished into the forest with your mother, who had also become my mother. I called out loud, but my sound no longer reached your ears. Only dark fog flowed through my heart. I clawed my throat, trying to take out my newly gained voice. Before I learned how to speak, we could hear each other perfectly. I tried to hold onto the memory of your smell and the sound of your laughter. Even that faded into a ripple, an echo, a twilight dream.

I grew up quickly as Father's apprentice.

There seems to be someone in the fold of the mountain, with eyes that hold laughter and a pearly smile.
—Nine Songs: Shan Gui

Pan Ge, love is anomaly, chaos, the overthrow of all orders. Without it, however, the world would never have come into being. In the beginning, when everything was in perfect order, when darkness and light balanced each other like a mirror image, nothing could live. Everything was a ball of heated light. Then something strayed away from the order, a maverick, an extra that tipped the balance, and *bang,* the universe was born.

You are that maverick, Pan Ge, with one foot in your world of folly and desire, the other in my world of dreams, cloud, and darkness. When my mama picked you up from the ashes and placed you next to me, you crossed the river. So did I.

The thunder rumbles as the rain darkens the sky. The monkeys chatter, and apes scream in the night. The wind sighs and trees rustle. I think of my woman, alone in sorrow.
—Nine Songs: Shan Gui

My love, we had eighteen years of pure joy.

The world around us was a chaos. Red Guards stopped coming to the bell tower after Father's death, but stories about their
terrible force continued. They destroyed temples, forced monks
and nuns to kiss and do things in public to entertain crowds. In the
Big Cold Mountains, they dragged Master Zhang out of the Soul
Mountain Temple. Master Zhang was a true sage and a great
Taoist. When he was alive, he helped thousands of people. When
he died, his body remained soft and supple as if he were just sleeping. His disciples put him in a gilded chair on the altar of the Soul
Mountain Temple. For hundreds of years, Master Zhang sat in the
hall as he watched a blind monk throw bones on the floor to predict the future. He was famous for the accuracy of his oracles. But
the rascals dragged the sacred relic through the town, then left it
on the street. The body rotted quickly. Everyone in town was
scared, but not those rascals. They thought they were immortal,
and nothing could touch them. But you know what? Everyone
involved died violently. None of them lived to their full age. That's
retribution. That's justice.

Apart from the Red Guards, there were factions among factory
workers. They stopped everything to make revolution, to guard
Chairman Mao and his party line. They armed themselves to the
teeth. Heaven knows where they found the weapons: rifles,
machine guns, grenades, daggers, clubs. They fought one another
to death, leaving cities filthy and paralyzed. Some of them came all
the way to Wushan trying to convert the peasants into revolution-
aries. But the peasants had learned a lesson from the Big Leap.
They had seen their entire families and villages and towns wiped
out by famine because of a few people's foolish ideas. They were
not going to repeat the same tragedy. So they allowed the workers
and Red Guards to paint bloody slogans on their walls and listened
to their slogan shouting. They let them sleep in their straw beds
and fed them with corn and sweet yams until their stomachs
bloated with gas and diarrhea, their bodies swollen with rashes

from flea bites. Then one morning, they fled quietly, leaving the peasants to tend their fields and row their boats into the river to feed their families.

Still the unsettling rumors from the capital darkened our valley from time to time. Old generals were dying off one by one, those old heroes who still had guts to stand up for people like us. Many were tortured to death. New faces popped on Tiananmen Square, then vanished. There was Lin Biao, who fled after trying to assassinate Chairman Mao, but his plane went down in the Mongolian Gobi. Beijing officials said it was an accident, though everyone knew it was hit by a missile. Everyone on it died: his wife, his son, and his generals. Why was he in such a hurry! Wasn't he supposed to be the next emperor? I guess he got impatient, or scared. Chairman Mao had fiery eyes that could see through everything. That pale scrawny man had a traitor's bone in the back of his head. He hid it under the green cap, but he couldn't fool my eyes. He couldn't fool Chairman Mao's eyes, either, I bet. That was why he had to flee to the desert.

But people suffered. There was not enough food to feed the country, not enough fabric to clothe the old and young. The markets were silent, only lines of green faces staring into space, hands clutching stacks of coupons for salt, sugar, soap, rice, tofu, meat, fish, cotton. My heart burned with pain—needles stabbing my body from all directions—strange pain that came to me when I learned walking and speaking.

But you soothed me and told me to be patient. You opened a garden near our hut, then an orange grove down the valley. Everything thrived under your green thumb. When we needed meat, you picked the date and time for me to hunt or fish, and I never returned with an empty hand. Our hut was always clean, our stomachs full with delicious food, our bodies warm with the clothes you wove and sewed. We gathered herbs and dried them in the sun, not to sell for money, but to give away, along with dried food and meat. People came to us secretly the way they had visited Father. You insisted that

I perform the ritual. "You're a real shaman, now," you said. "Just start singing and I'll join you." So I chanted and sang and danced, and you stepped in as you promised, your slender waist and strong legs swirling around my clumsy body. And soon I went into a trance, doing things I couldn't imagine when I was awake. The patients moaned and writhed with me until they felt better. They wanted to pay for the service with money. But we had no use for the printed paper. They brought eggs, chickens, ducks, cloth—things hard to find in stores, but we had more than we needed. So they went away, their sacs full of the herbs and food we gave them, their faces full of smile, their children laughing, and I no longer felt the pain.

They called me Master Wu Pan. They said I was better than my father, my grandfather, my great-grandfather.

But no one seemed to notice you. How could they not see your moon face, smell your fragrance or feel your jade skin?

Perhaps you were invisible to human eyes as we were invisible to my father? Perhaps the whole tangible world—you, me, our love, our mountains and rivers, the whole earth—was nothing but a dream.

But no matter. When night fell and visitors went home, when I held you tight in my arms, our breath intertwined, nothing was more real or precious. As days and weeks and years went by, that preciousness grew more urgent. I sensed something was up. More and more, you turned your gaze down the river at the end of the horizon, where the big dam was about to seal the river at Gezhouba. One day I caught you weeping under the tree, your body shaking with sorrow. Nothing could comfort you, not even my songs, my awkward dance, or my love. Then one day, you told me that the path to the natal place was going to be blocked forever.

"What are you talking about?" I shouted, though deep down, I knew exactly what you were referring to. "What natal place? This is our natal place, the most beautiful place on earth."

But you wouldn't look at me. "To save a few yuan," you said, eyes fixed on the distant mountain and river, "they scratched the original plan to build a narrow pathway for us! They are forcing us to find a new home behind the dam to spawn. There'll be a lot of deaths!" you shouted. "There'll be an annihilation!"

"What annihilation?" I asked in panic. "And who's they?"

You just wept and gazed at the blue mist down the river, and I knew your time with me was up. My heart tightened. There was no cure for the ache except for patience. You had to do what you needed to do, and eventually you'd find your way back. This is our home, this pagoda tree, this hut, this garden and grove, this mountain and river, this dream.

So one day, you fell in the orange grove and couldn't stand up again. Your bones had softened. They no longer supported your nimble body. Soon you couldn't lift your head, arms, legs. Your ribs and joints seemed to be melting into large chunks of soft plates. I gave you herbs, needles, massages. I chanted and danced and spun day and night. But you kept slipping away.

"Pan Ge," you called in a whisper one night. I froze. In the pitch darkness, your face glowed a pale luminescent green. I clutched your withered hand. It was time for you to go, I told myself, my heart split in two. I wished I could cry, but my eyes were burning dry. Now I understood why Father never shed tears over Mother's disappearance. Sorrow was a wildfire that scorched everything along its path.

"Pan Ge," you whispered. No sound came out of your lips, but I heard you loud and clear. "Get me ready for the journey."

I took out the crowns you had made on our wedding night. Eighteen years later, and they were still green and fragrant. I took out the tattered green dress you had on when I pulled you out of the Long River. Then I took out the snow lotus we had brought back from the Gold Sand River six months before.

I should have known what was happening when you said you wanted to go to the Gold Sand River. I was listening to the radio about the grand completion of Gezhouba Dam, the biggest dam on the Long River, when you came over and placed your hand on my shoulder. I wasn't paying attention, because the government was announcing the plan to build another dam in the Three Gorges, bigger than the Gezhouba, bigger than any other dam on earth. I was trembling when you squeezed my shoulder and said we must go to the Gold Sand River to pick snow lotus. I thought you were joking. The place was hundreds of miles away, hard to reach either by boat or the mountain road. Even if we got there, there was no guarantee that we'd find the flower. It grew only at the snow line among frozen rocks. Besides, how could we leave when they were planning to flood our home? Then I looked up and saw your eyes and I knew we had to go. We packed some bread and clean clothes and set off. For three months we walked along the ancient path that our ancestors had used for thousands of years to carry goods back and forth between Chongqing and the upper river. There were thousands of dams on the river, some small, some huge, some old, some new, and many still incomplete. You didn't say a word about it, but I knew you were weeping inside. I also knew our trip to the Gold Sand River had something to do with the two monster dams. The mountains became higher and colder, and the greenery thinned until there was nothing but rocks, rocks, and rocks. The air was freezing. The wind whipped our faces. Our food was long gone. You walked with such determination that I knew any plea to return home would fall on deaf ears. When we finally arrived, we saw a monk crawling out of a cave that was sealed with rocks. His beard, covered with icicles, ran all the way to his groin like a glacier. His eyes lit up when he saw you.

"What is real, what is illusion?" he asked, palms pressed to his chest.

"A flower is not a flower, a dream not a dream," you answered, bowing deeply.

The monk walked away laughing like a madman. You entered his cave and came out with a white gauze scarf. In the center was a furry white flower hugged by green leaves. Dark lines in the center swirled like a vortex. It looked frozen, but I knew it was very much alive.

You ran straight to the river and dipped the flower in the roaring white water, then wrapped it carefully in the monk's *hada*.

"We can go home now, Pan Ge," you said, looking straight into my eyes for the first time during our three months' trek, and all the ice in my heart melted away.

Slowly I dressed you in the green dress. It wrapped around your boneless body like a hammock. I started weeping when I remembered it had been eighteen years since I pulled you out of the water. For eighteen years, we had never been apart. We woke up together, ate together, worked together, and went to bed together. How was I going to keep living without you? Weeping, I put the crown on your head. You'd lost your bones, limbs, and voice. But your hair still shined with blue darkness, the deepest black I'd ever seen. I tied the *hada* around your neck. How you looked like the Goddess the Twelve Peaks! Finally I put the snow lotus between your parched lips. Then I lay down next to you as we had lain next to each other for eighteen years.

When dawn came, you were gone. Only the flower remained.

I picked it up. Its subtle fragrance filled my lungs, and the dark cloud in my heart cleared. In that moment of clarity, I saw you in a river path, alone and covered with blood. But the path also pointed your way home. I saw our home. Our home would be under the water, together with the souls and spirits, the animals and trees, the history and legends of the Three Gorges. And I'd be with you again, forever, in our origin. And I felt peace for the first time since our trip to the Gold Sand River.

There is a kingdom of yellow people. You Yin is the king. He is the son of Emperor Xun. He came to the mountains and established the kingdom of Wu. His people are called Wu, with Pan as their surname. They eat grains. They wear nice clothes even though they don't weave, and they have plenty to eat even though they don't farm. Phoenix gather here to sing and dance. They sing and dance at their own will. And beasts, big and small, live in harmony. It's a land where all treasures come together.

—The Book of Mountains and Seas

Wu Shan, my home where the sun rises and falls, the moon waxes and wanes. The mountains are steep, the gorges deep, and the river is long and fierce. There, morning mist dances around the mountains like a tender lover. At dusk, she changes her face and comes down as rain or thunderstorm, depending on the mood of a sixteen-year-old girl. There, the water nurtures many lives. There, the first gibbon came down from the tree and made the first arrowhead to hunt, the first hoe to plant grains, and that first gibbon became the first man who gathered herbs to cure, who drew and painted in caves and rocks, who counted the stars to predict the future.

"Guard the river," Mama said. "Guard it with your dream. It's our path from the land to the sea, from dark to light. If the river stops moving, we'll all be stuck forever."

We are foam in the sea. Things we see and touch and hear and smell—you, me, our ancestors, trees, rivers, mountains on the earth, sun, moon, and stars—are specks of dust in the universe. What is the universe compared to the dark matter invisible to our eyes, unreachable to our hands, and inaudible to our ears, incomprehensible to our minds? And what is that vast darkness compared to the love that holds time and space together?

Here I am, afloat in a tank of blue chemicals for a big show. They tap the thick glass to awaken me. They play this strange, vulgar noise called music. They give me shrimp, squid, and other live gourmet food. They send in divers to puddle around in the tank hoping to coax me into a dance. But I have shut down my body to save my heart. I'm saving my heart for the big wave. When it arrives, a path will open through the steel and glass and concrete. It will take me home, to Wu Shan, to my Brother of Hope.

Hope stands as long as the heart keeps going.

There is a fish called yu fu—*Fish Woman. Its withered body is half woman half fish. She comes alive when God Zhuanxu dies. As the northern wind blows, big water rises from mountain springs. This is the time when snakes turn into fish. Such a fish is called Fish Woman. She comes alive when God Zhuanxu dies.*

—The Book of Mountains and Seas

"Guard the tree, Wu Pan," Father shouted as the Red Guards took him away. I couldn't see him from the treetop. But the wind sent his voice, the secret language he had taught me. "Guard it with your name. We have hope as long as the tree stays alive. So do the mountains and rivers."

The tree is the ladder to flee the rising sea. It has been home for generations of Wu witches and wizards. They invented machines, jewelry, words, gun powder, weapons. They knew the past and future from grass, bones, turtle shells, and stars. They cured the sick and revived the dead with herbs. For thousands of years, they were believed to possess the ingredients of the Elixir that had been buried in twelve secret chambers. Every emperor wanted this formula. Every emperor wanted to live forever. The witches and wizards tried to explain to the emperors that there had never been a formula. Even if it had ever existed, it would have been broken and lost long ago, along with the clan that scattered all over the world. But no one believed them. They were chased relentlessly, bribed with power, land, gold, and other worldly things. They were punished when bribery failed, their families were killed, relatives exiled, and their women sold into brothels.

No matter what happened, one of us always stands by the tree, guarding. When we were exiled here, Father circled the tree twelve times thanking it for leading us home safe and sound. He spent many days and nights under its canopy, the only place he seemed to be truly relaxed and happy. He called it dawn red wood, because the trunk burned with scarlet red when touched by the morning light. I called it mother of the garden because I liked the way it talked to me in the middle of the night.

But you called it water fir. I laughed, I argued, I cajoled, but you stood your ground. You'll understand why when the time comes, you said.

The time has come, Shan Gui. In six minutes, the river will rise to the red mark on the trunk. With its roots in the water, your prophecy is fulfilled.

Around me and across the river, mountains are shaved clean. Forests have been taken down, along with the houses, buildings, factories, schools, hospitals. Garbage has been dug up and trucked away, filling the valley with a five-thousand-year-old stink. Graves were dug up too, ancient and new.

The government sent workers to cut down our dawn red wood, our water fir. They ordered me to remove the tombs, take the bones somewhere else. The reservoir must not be polluted.

"Who knows what sickness you father died of? T.B.? And how do you know your wife had never been infected with AIDS? Eh?" The young cop's beady eyes stared at me with lust. "I heard your wife was a beautiful creature who roamed the mountains at night. Is that right?"

I sprawled over the tombs. I must not look into his eyes. I must not kill him with my hatred. He raised his gun, but the peasants he hired for the digging pulled him away. They knew me. They had come to me for herbs and oracles. My great healing power was equaled by my curse, though I had never used it. But they knew.

Above the red mark of 175 meters, trees are dying mountain by mountain. They know what's coming. Every tree has a spirit, every blade of grass, every grain of sand. They choose to die with their brothers and sisters.

On the barren hills and abandoned beaches, teams of archaeologists dug like mad with shovels, spatulas, and toothbrushes. They were racing against time. They said the Three Gorges hosted the earliest humans and oldest cultural artifacts that traced as far back as three millions ago. There were tears in their eyes as they talked.

Yet who will cry for the tree that survived the ice age and is about to go under? And the green sturgeon that has been spawning in the Gold Sand River for millions of years but is blocked forever behind the dam? Who will cry for the one million people displaced from their homes and land? And you, Shan Gui, who will bring you back from the far north?

The river rumbles with impatience. It has six seconds to go. In six seconds, the river will no longer be.

But it will never die.

At your grave I wait. When the hot wind blows from the North Pole, the sea will rise like mountains, shattering every chain on the river's throat and limbs. And you, my mountain spirit, will come home in your original form, free, naked.

COLOPHON

The Lact Communist Virgin is set in Bembo.

FUNDER ACKNOWLEDGMENT

Coffee House Press is an independent nonprofit literary publisher. Our books are made possible through the generous support of grants and gifts from many foundations, corporate giving programs, individuals, and through state and federal support. This book received special project support from the National Endowment for the Arts, a federal agency. Coffee House Press also receives significant general operating support from the McKnight Foundation, from Target, and from the Minnesota State Arts Board, through an appropriation by the Minnesota State Legislature and from the National Endowment for the Arts. Coffee House also receives significant support from: an anonymous donor; the Elmer and Eleanor Andersen Foundation; the Buuck Family Foundation; the Patrick and Aimee Butler Family Foundation; Gary Fink; Sally French; Stephen and Isabel Keating; Seymour Kornblum and Gerri Lauter; the Lenfesty Family Foundation; Rebecca Rand; the law firm of Schwegman, Lundberg, Woessner & Kluth, P.A.; Charles Steffey and Suzannah Martin; the James R. Thorpe Foundation; the Archie D. and Bertha H. Walker Foundation; Thompson West; the Woessner Freeman Family Foundation; the Wood-Rill Foundation; and many other generous individual donors. To everyone supporting our program through the purchase of our books and through grants and donations, we extend our grateful thanks.

NATIONAL
ENDOWMENT
FOR THE ARTS

This activity is made possible in part by a grant from the Minnesota State Arts Board, through an appropriation by the Minnesota State Legislature and a grant from the National Endowment for the Arts.

MINNESOTA
STATE ARTS BOARD

TARGET.

To you and our many readers across the country,
we send our thanks for your continuing support.

Good books are brewing at coffeehousepress.org

Wang Ping was born in Shanghai and grew up on a small island in the East China Sea. After working in the fields of a mountain village commune, she attended Beijing University. In 1985 she left China to study in the United States, earning her Ph.D from New York University. She is the acclaimed author of the short story collection *American Visa,* the novel *Foreign Devil,* two poetry collections: *Of Flesh & Spirit* and *The Magic Whip,* and the cultural study *Aching for Beauty: Footbinding in China.* A frequent visitor to China, Wang now lives in Minnesota where she teaches at Macalester College.